THE
FIRST
GENERAL
ORDER

THE FIRST GENERAL ORDER

ROBERT STAVE

ABSOLUTELY AMAZING eBOOKS

ABSOLUTELY AMAZING eBOOKS

*This book is dedicated to my wife Pam,
son Bonner and our grandson Jack.*

"Ask not what your country can do for you,
Ask what you can do for your country."

- JFK

In the Vietnam War the U.S. Military fielded
the youngest Army since the Civil War.

THE
FIRST
GENERAL
ORDER

TABLE OF CONTENTS

PROLOGUE

I wrote *The First General Order* in some degree for myself in order to work through my own war experiences and feelings. I also wanted to tell the story of the teenage soldiers that fought beside me. Their bravery and selflessness in the face of overwhelming odds. They were members of the youngest Army fielded in a war since the Civil War.

Think of it ... teenagers, seventeen, eighteen and nineteen year olds humping through the jungle looking for a gun fight in a land that was unforgiving and totally foreign to them in every way. These young soldiers did not understand the language, customs or even why they were in Vietnam, fighting an enemy that was fighting for a cause. These young gun fighters pulled KP (kitchen police), were laborers and shit can burners when they were not humping the bush.

There are many misconceptions about our participation in the Vietnam War, propagated by both the media and folklore; more blacks and poor whites fought in Vietnam than middle or upper class whites. In truth, there were no more blacks, poor whites or Latinos per capita based on the demographics of the 1960's and 1970's serving in South Vietnam. On the Wall or on the rolls of West Point the class of 1965 holds the dubious distinction of the most KIA's in Vietnam than any preceeding graduating class. A Lt. (2nd Lieutenant, West Point or ROTC) had a life expectancy of about three weeks in the bush.

"If we are not marked to die.

i

We are now. To do our country less and if we live.
We are the fewer men."

- Henry V

In the end, one Airborne LRRP summed things up not as a pup-tent poet but as a trooper, Billy Walkabout of the 101st Airborne LRRP's: "I volunteered to serve, I saw a lot, men died, friends died. I got hurt, it was shit, and it was awesome. Yeah! I'd do it all over again."

It was not God or country these soldiers fought for; it was to stay alive for the next twelve months and for the soldier next to them. The twelve-month tour was a lifetime until DEROS arrived on the horizon and the soldier's status changed to "short timer". In a good outfit short timers did not have to go to the field or on patrol. The short timers stick was the symbol of their protective status. They had made it, going home to the world on the "freedom bird", a rice paddy one day and San Francisco the next.

That was the war in Vietnam, ten years, millions of one-year tours of duty and 5800 KIA. The war had no real goals other than NVA or Viet Cong body count.

The sorrow of the Vietnam War and the wars in Iraq and Afghanistan is that they are just repeating history. We have been in these two wars for ten years with the loss (not greater than Vietnam) of good young men and women...for what? That is the real sorrow – the fight in Iraq and Afghanistan does have a beginning but with no real end in sight.

- Bob Stave
Delray Beach,
Florida

CHAPTER ONE

"I LEFT MY HEART IN SAN FRANCISCO"
Above the blue and windy sea
When I come home to you, San Francisco
Your golden sun will shine for me"

SAN FRANCISCO, in all its beauty, lay across the bay. From where Specialist 4 James Green and Private Mark Morning stood waiting for the bus at the Oakland Army Terminal, they couldn't see it. That didn't matter because across that bay were very good times and they had the afternoon and most of the night. Green figured that they had until around four in the morning to get back before their group shipped out the next day for Nam. They didn't have a pass but no one would notice they were gone and even if they did, they wouldn't hold them at the terminal for being AWOL for a few hours before being shipped out.

So the two of them stood waiting for the bus knowing that Frisco would be a blast. They wanted to see Fisherman's Wharf, trolley cars, bars in the Tenderloin District, Chinatown, topless places and all kinds of people.

"Are we going to have a good time, Jim, or ARE WE GOING TO HAVE A GOOD TIME?!" Mark Morning took Jim by the arm, shaking him as he spoke. Morning jumped around looking for the bus. "Here bus, bus, here bus." Then he laughed.

Green smiled at Morning, then shook his head as

he stood quietly with his hands on his hips. He didn't answer Morning, but then there were a lot of times that he didn't answer him. Morning didn't seem to mind.

On the ride across the Bay Bridge, Green sat next to the window pointing out sights of interest to Morning. Was he his friend? Why, Green didn't know. He was obviously mad. They had been drafted together, which pleased Morning to no end. Both boys were nineteen, but Green looked older, in his mid-twenties.

"Morning, did you see that sign?" Green turned from the window.

"No, man. What sign?" Morning craned his neck to look out the window and Green pushed him back into his seat.

"The last cutoff was for Treasure Island. That's what I said -Treasure Island."

"B.S. ... Really?" Morning turned around to look out the back window of the bus. "You're B.S.ing me." Morning elbowed Green.

"No man ... really."

"Really! Goddamn, this place is something else. Too much ... just too much. Wish we had more time."

"Yeah ... like the rest of our lives." Green turned back to the window.

~ ~ ~

Green and Morning had joined the Army under the Buddy System and Airborne Unassigned. They had gone through Basic Training, AIT and Jump School together. They appeared on the same orders to Vietnam and their service numbers were just one digit different.

The first thing that they did after they got to the bus

station was to buy a set of civilian clothes; they got them real cheap, shoes and everything. Later that afternoon it started to get cold so Morning bought a jacket and Jim bought a sweater. After that they went back to the bus station and put their uniforms in a storage locker.

Then they felt free ... running down the streets, riding the trolleys, jumping off when the trolley started going up the hill, the two of them running beside the trolley. Then they would go into a bar and have a beer. Most of the bars were topless – that just killed Morning. At one bar there were topless waitresses and a topless shoeshine girl. Morning had bought a pair of white tennis shoes but he asked the girl for a shoeshine anyway. The girl smiled at him and said sure. Morning gave her five dollars and he tipped her two dollars. They walked out laughing at Mark's black tennis shoes.

They were both getting drunk; they'd look at each other and start to laugh. That was when they bought the flowers. Green bought red roses and Morning bought a dozen yellow mums. After that they walked along the street holding the flowers, pretending they were going out on a date. They stopped at a few more bars. When they got to the Stage Door bar, Morning wanted to stop.

"Maybe there'll be some Hollywood movie stars. You never know." They were standing outside the door on the street.

"Mark, we're not in Hollywood, this is San Francisco." Green rolled his eyes.

"Well, you never know. Come on, let's go in for a beer. You afraid you're going to be late for nowhere?"

"That's just it Mark. Nowhere. Might as well." They went in.

They had one beer and then another. There were no movie stars.

"Man, we got to get our shit together. This is our last night here ... Man, tomorrow Nam. We've got to get a couple of girls."

Morning grunted and ordered another beer.

"Look, why don't we ride the trolley car some more? Only every time we see a pretty girl – we'll give her a flower; maybe we'll meet someone that way." Morning got his beer and drank half of it.

Out on the street again it was dark; they walked toward the trolley car.

"Say, Jim?" Morning paused to get into step with Green. "What are we going to do once we get to Nam?"

"What do you mean, Morning?"

"Well, you know when we get into it, the shooting and everything. You know there's a good chance that we might get killed or something."

"What are we going to do?" Green paused, looking over at his friend. "We're going to do everything we can to stay alive, that's what we're going to do. What are you asking me a question like that for? Jesus Christ, Morning, we're coming back and that's all there is to it. Now quit talking about it, will you?" Green started walking faster.

"Yeah, okay. I just wanted your thoughts on the matter." Morning lengthened his stride to keep up with Green.

"Look, Morning, you got drafted. Whose fault is that?"

"I don't know, man, whose fault it that?" Morning

returned the question even though he knew the answer. It was a lousy deal but he'd never tried to place the blame on anyone. There wasn't anyone, really.

"Look my boy." Jim took the tone of a father talking to a small child as he often did with Morning.

"Go to hell with that boy stuff." It wasn't that Morning was stupid; it was just that he didn't think the way other people did. Green went on ignoring Morning's defense of his manhood. "This is the way it is. Some people have it made; we've talked about this before. You don't have to get drafted in this country. There are lots of things that you could have done. The most painless would have been to go to college after we got out of high school. Right?"

"Right." Morning nodded his head. "But I didn't want to go to college. Man, I didn't want to do anything. High school took a lot out of me."

Green laughed. "Now you know. You just can't do 'nothing' because when you do nothing, somebody always finds something for you to do." Green paused, catching his breath, grinning. "Besides, the Army's doing you a favor by letting you see the world. It's broadening your horizons. So shut up."

It was one more block remove to the trolley. Morning was walking along smelling his mums, one hand in his pocket.

"You know when we get back, I could really spend some time here before we go home. I bet we could have a lot of fun. It would sort of be a vacation after the terrible experience of war."

"Yeah, I could go for that, Morning." They heard the trolley car bell and they started running.

They ran the last block to the corner just in time to jump on the trolley. Morning was laughing; he almost fell off but Green held onto him. Morning put the mums in his back pocket so he could hold on with both hands. Several older people were smiling at them, Green noticed.

Morning saw the girl sitting by herself in the first car.

"Look man, our first girl." He pointed to her. "Who's going to go first?" Morning looked from the girl to Jim.

"You saw her first. So she's yours." Green looked at the girl. She was nice looking sitting by herself.

"Wait a minute, Green, that's no reason for me to go first. I've never done this before. You do it, you'd be better at it. Besides, I want to see how you do it."

"All right, shit head, I'll show you how it's done." Green moved inside the trolley car towards the girl. There was a seat open next to her. Green moved slowly and sat down. He looked at the girl again; he was holding the bouquet of flowers in front of him. He looked over at Morning who was nodding and laughing. Green looked back at the girl. She looked at him. He smiled.

"Hello," he said.

"Hello," she said.

Green looked at his roses. Holding the roses in one hand, he reached out with the other and pulled one rose from the bouquet.

"This is for you." Green held the rose out to the girl.

She looked at him for a long moment, and then she took the flower.

"Thank you, it's beautiful. Won't the girl that was

6

supposed to get it be unhappy if she knew that you gave one away?"

"Yeah, she would, but there is no girl. You see, my friend and I bought the flowers this afternoon just to give to pretty girls. My friend is over there." Green pointed at Morning. The yellow mums were sticking out of his back pocket.

"That's the craziest thing I've ever heard of." She stopped, looking at Jim Green. "No, it's not, it's the nicest thing. But why?"

"No reason really. Well, you see, Morning and I, Morning that's the other guy, well, we're going to Vietnam tomorrow and we just wanted to do it. We don't know anyone here and we thought that maybe we'd meet someone. It was Mark's idea." Green pointed again at Morning.

"What did you say his name was?"

"Mark Morning and mine is Jim Green."

She looked at the rose. "This is the first rose that anyone has ever given me."

"Then I'm glad that it was me."

"Thank you very much, Jim."

"You wouldn't want to do something tonight would you? Maybe you have a friend for Mark?"

The girl looked at Jim again. Jim smiled his sincere, disarming grin. "Well, maybe I do have a friend for Mark. I'm supposed to meet my girlfriend at a bar at the end of the trolley car tracks. It's called Buena Vista. She didn't move her eyes from Jim.

"That sounds great!" Green waved Morning over. "That's just great!" Morning had good ideas; he never thought this crazy idea would work, but it did. Green turned back to the girl. "I forgot to ask. What's your name?"

"Mary."

Green didn't ask her last name.

Morning came clumping down the aisle of the trolley car, holding onto the rail above his head, the flowers sticking out of his back pocket. Morning was a really funny guy, Jim thought, watching him coming.

"Mark, this is Mary, Mary this is Mark Morning."

"Hi," she said.

"What's going on?" Morning stood in front of them.

"The three of us are going to a bar called the Buena Vista. We're going to meet a friend of Mary's there."

"Really – no kidding? Mary's friend for me? I've got some flowers for her." Morning took the yellow mums from his back pocket and held them out for Mary to see. "They're a little beat up from carrying them in my pocket, but they smell pretty good for being hothouse flowers." Morning slipped the flowers back into his hip pocket.

"How do you know so much about flowers?" Green asked in a mocking tone.

"You'd be surprised what I know about. I just happened to have worked in a greenhouse before I joined up. I really liked it. Most people don't, but I did."

"Sorry, Mark." Jim turned to Mary. "You didn't realize you were going to meet a horticultural expert tonight."

"You'd be surprised who you meet in San Francisco," Mary said in an amazed tone.

Green and Mary stayed in the trolley car while it was turned around. Morning got out and helped, the mums in his back pocket. As he pushed he sang, "Old Man River" off key. Green and Mary could hear people outside laughing at him.

"Lift that barge, tote that bail, get a little drunk and you land in jail," came from the outside of the car. "Okay, Jim, the works over, you can come out now." The trolley had stopped.

Jim and Mary got up and walked to the end of the car. Mark was waiting for them on the street.

Morning stopped singing and began to cheer when he saw the two of them. "We're off to the Bon Voyage or whatever." He raised his hands over his head.

The three of them walked abreast across the street toward the Buena Vista.

"What's the name of this place?" Mary was between the two of them, Mark had his mums out in front of him again. "The Bon Voyage or something like that?"

"No, stupid. The Buena Vista," Green said.

The girl laughed at the two of them. "You two are the funniest two guys I've ever met." She laughed again.

"Hear that, Green, you're funny. I never thought about it before, but you are a scream."

"Go to hell, Morning."

They reached the bar, walked up the few steps and went inside. It was crowded. Along one side of the room stretched a bar with four bartenders behind it. The other wall was all windows overlooking Fisherman's Wharf. Next to the windows were a few small, round tables. The three of them went up to the bar where the bartender took their orders for beer. Morning lit a cigarette while Green and Mary talked and looked for her friend. Their beers came; Mark took a long drink.

"That's good," he said. He stood looking around. As he raised his hand with the cigarette in his mouth, the flowers were in the way so he put the beer on the bar and the flowers back into his pocket again.

Jim nudged Mary so that she could watch Morning. He was so busy looking at girls that he didn't notice the two of them watching him. Now that he had his hands free he held his beer in one hand and his cigarette in the other. He turned around, intent on watching people. Green could tell he was having a good time.

"Where's your friend?" Green was standing close to Mary because he wanted to.

"She'll be here, don't worry Jim. I can see that you and Mark are really good friends."

Jim smiled down at her. "Yeah, I guess we are." Jim looked over at Mark. "We really didn't have much choice since the Army. In a way we became brothers because of having to be in the same place in time, in the same geographical location, and in the same social condition."

An older lady came walking through the crowd. Jim noticed her stop and look at Mark Morning whose back was turned to her. The lady was in her sixties, white hair and very proper appearing to Jim. She stood looking at the flowers sticking out of Morning's back pocket. She moved closer to Morning, reached out and tapped him on the shoulder. Mark turned around looking a little surprised. Morning wasn't a particularly tall guy, but he still looked down at the woman.

"Excuse me, young man," she said, looking up at him.

Mark smiled down at her.

"I thought that I should tell you your mums are

showing." She pointed to the mums in his back pocket that were being crushed between him and the bar.

Morning began to laugh, his laughter of pure delight; it ranged from a snicker to wild happiness; all the time he moved his head up and down. It was a good joke, he and the old lady laughed together. Morning reached around taking the mums from his pocket.

"Here, they're for you. I was waiting to find someone to give them to." Morning pushed the mums almost into her face with his excitement.

She was pleased. Morning could tell by her expression.

"No, no, there's a young lady that you should give them to. I really won't take them, but thank you very much."

"No ma'am, really, I don't have anyone to give them to. I was just carrying them around. Please take them."

"No, you'll meet someone. But I'll take one."

This satisfied Morning and he took the biggest one and gave it to the old lady. "It's a little beat up, but..."

"No, it's not, it's beautiful. Thank you." She reached up and gave him a mother's kind of kiss on the cheek. Then she walked away.

Mark stood for a moment then he looked over at Green and Mary; he realized they'd watched it all. He went over to them.

"Did you see that?" Morning stood in front of them, happy with himself.

"Yes, we did Mark; you were so nice." Mary grabbed hold of Green's arm. Morning looked at the three of them; oh, they were very happy.

"Was that ever a cool lady...God, was she neat." Morning shook his head.

Green didn't answer.

"It was the nicest thing I've ever seen," Mary said.

"There she is." Mary let go of Jim's arm and went over to the door. She started talking to a blonde girl in a dark pantsuit. They talked together for a few minutes; the girl looked over at Mark Morning holding the rest of the flowers, his tan jacket, brown shirt, light tan pants and black tennis shoes.

Morning smiled at her. She looked back to her friend.

"Jim, I don't think she likes me." Morning kept looking at the girl. "Boy, she's really nice though."

"She'll like you all right; they just have to lay their plans before they come over." Green kept his eye on Mary. That stupid girl, she'd better like Mark; he was a little on the crazy side but the girls back home really liked him. Green glanced down at Morning's black tennis shoes. That was Mark Morning all over – black tennis shoes.

The two girls started walking toward them. At that moment Morning left. Green was aware of it. He wondered where that nut was going now as he vanished into the crowd. The girls came over.

"Jim, this is Pat."

"Hi," Jim said.

"Where's Mark?" Mary asked, looking around.

"I don't know – he was here a minute ago."

"I hope that I didn't scare him off."

"No, Mark's a brave soul – he'll be back in a minute."

"Green! Green! Over here." Morning was standing on a chair in the corner waving his yellow mums.

"Is he crazy? Pat asked. She was laughing.

"No – Mark's got a table." They made their way over to a small table with four chairs.

"Mark, this is Pat – Pat, Mark Morning, the table finder." Jim said.

"Hello, Mark," Pat said, sitting down across from him.

"Hi – here," Morning pushed the bouquet of mums over to Pat.

"They're for you."

"Thank you," Pat said.

"Oh, that's okay." Mark smiled, looking very proud of his self.

"What should we order?" Green put his hands together looking around.

"Let's get a bottle of wine," Mark said.

"What about you Pat, Mary – wine all right?" Green asked.

"Sure, that's fine," Pat said. Mary nodded her head.

"Great, I'll get it." Green made his way to the bar.

The three sat smiling and looking at one another.

"Pat, you live here in San Francisco?" Mark was making conversation.

"Yes, for the last four years."

"You work, I guess?"

"Yes, for Standard Oil Company."

"That must be nice." Morning lit up a cigarette. "I sort of work for the government."

"Oh really, what do you do?"

"He's in the Army." Green stood over them, holding a bottle of wine and four glasses.

"Well, that's working for the government," Morning

said, taking two of the glasses and moving over next to Pat.

"We're going to Vietnam tomorrow," Morning piped in while Jim poured a small amount of wine into his glass. "What are you doing?" Morning looked up at Green.

"Test it first."

Morning took the glass and drained it.

"How is it?" Green shook his head.

"Just fine."

"Glad you like it, sir." Green poured wine into the two girls' glasses, then Morning's again, then his own.

The four of them sat talking; they were on their second bottle of wine now. It was past one in the morning and the crowd began to thin out. Mark sat leaning over the table, both hands on top of his glass, his chin resting on his two hands.

"This is really a groovy place. I don't think I'll ever forget it. Will you, Jim?"

"No, I won't forget it." Jim turned his attention from Mary to answer. He took a drink of his wine. "Yes, this turned out to be one fine evening." Jim reached onto the table for a cigarette.

"Are you guys really going to Vietnam?" Pat seemed a little tight.

Morning turned his head just enough to look at her. He let out a long breath. "You tell her, Jim." Mark was looking straight ahead again staring off into space.

"Well, you see..." Green took a pull on his cigarette. "Mark and I are exactly what you see before you." Green pointed a finger at Mark. "Two stumble bums going out to fight the good fight."

Mark Morning, without moving, started to hum "The Star Spangled Banner."

14

Raising his voice so that he could be heard above Morning's rendition: "You see, Mark and I are going to fight against the yellow peril and the commies, and for the domino theory."

Mark moved from "The Star Spangled Banner" into "The Battle Hymn of the Republic."

"For God, country and Mom's apple pie we fight, for old and antique ideas we fight and, not to forget, we fight because we joined up to save some dominos or something."

Mark at this point ended "The Battle Hymn of the Republic" in a crescendo. Green held himself erect, his head held high, moving his feet as if marching.

"Both of you are really insane." Both girls were laughing. Morning grunted a reply. Green stopped marching and had some wine.

"Remember Frank Nelson?" Morning was laughing at the thought of their high school friend.

"Yeah, I do. Listen, I got to tell you about this guy, it's really funny." Green was talking to the two girls. "This guy, Frank, well he wasn't going to get drafted; he worked for the draft information center back home. His family was real liberal too. Anyway, Frank was always rapping about how, when his number came up, he was going to burn his draft card. Well, old Frank got his letter. His mother was making plans about visiting him in jail, you know, bringing him books and stuff. So what did Frank do? Did he burn his draft card?"

"No," Mark put in.

"Did he go to jail?"

"No," Mark said again.

"Did he take off for Canada?"

"No, he didn't do that either."

"You know what Frank did?"

"What did Frank do?" Morning half shouted.

"Frank took a blast of four. Four years in the United States Navy. He joined the god damn Navy." Green leaned back laughing. "Boy, were his parents disappointed. It had to be the funniest thing that I ever saw, old Frank getting his hair cut before he left for boot camp."

"It just kills me. There's Frank doing four years and all his big talk and here Jim and I are doing three. Sounds like a prison sentence, one to two and two to four." Morning laughed but no one joined him in his laughter.

"What are you trained to do in the Army?" Mary asked.

"We're ground pounders, Airborne Infantry. Airborne, gotta go, gotta go, all the way, gotta go Airborne, blood guts, over the hill, can't stop, gotta go, all the way Airborne." Morning was singing, tapping his foot and marking the beat.

"Airborne, Infantry, Ranger, all you idiots follow me, gotta go Airborne, two old ladies were laying in bed, one rolled over to the other and said, 'Gotta go Airborne'."

"Will you shut up, Morning?" Green reached across the table and playfully hit Morning on the side of the head.

"What was that all about?" Pat asked Mark.

"They teach us music appreciation in the Army, it builds morale. You see in jump school…"

"You mean that you guys jump out of airplanes?"

Mary asked.

"Not ships or trains or boats either, just air-o-planes," Morning intoned.

"You see in jump school we got to run everywhere because that gets us into shape and while we run, we sing that stuff. It really sounds neat when there's maybe thirty guys all running in step and singing stuff like that, what Mark was singing."

"Yes, but I really don't have my heart in it." Morning hadn't moved from his position over his glass for a long time.

"Mark, I don't know you very well, but I think you're a liar." Mark shot a glance over to Mary, then to Jim Green. "I think that you enjoy all of this, both of you. That's what really gets me, both of you really enjoy all of this."

"Mary, are you drunk?" Jim asked, turning to look at her.

"Maybe I am, but it's still the truth."

"What the hell do you know about it anyway? Me and Mark are just two guys caught in the system. We don't have a choice."

"I don't believe that, Jim."

Jim took another drink of wine, draining it. He took the bottle and poured what was left into his glass and drank that too.

"There," was his only word.

Morning hadn't moved. "Should we get another bottle?" Morning still didn't move.

Jim looked around the table, first at Morning, then Pat and then at Mary.

"Mary, can I take you home?" Jim looked at her.

"Yes," she said.

"Morning, do what you want. Mary, what's your address?"

"740 Turk Street, Apartment 40."

"You hear that, Morning, when you're done, come by and get me. We'll go to the bus station together."

Morning nodded as Jim and Mary got up from the table. "Nice to meet you Mary." The two of them walked to the door, Mary carrying the bouquet of roses.

Outside it was cold. Green put his arms around himself, hunching over, walking next to Mary. They walked in silence.

"Should we get a taxi?" Jim asked. "It's colder than hell."

"Let's walk a few more blocks first."

They walked in silence. Green looked over at the girl every few minutes. She walked looking at the windows, sometimes swinging her purse.

Morning still sat looking at the table not changing his position. Pat was rubbing his back now.

"Where do you live?" Morning asked, not looking at Pat.

"Not far from here."

"Good." Morning paused, enjoying her hand on his back. "You want to go over to your place and ball?"

Pat's hand stopped on his back. Morning turned to look at her.

"That's not nice or funny." She said.

"Forget it, I was just kidding." Morning's dark eyebrows went up.

"Well, we might as well go to my place so you don't go barging in on Mary and Jim right away. She really

18

likes him."

"Oh Christ, love at first sight. I'm all choked up." Morning got up, took his glass and drained it.

"That's no way to be, Mark. Life is something serious, you know. You're always making a joke out of everything."

They were both standing now.

"That, my dear, is about the only way I can take life. That is to laugh at it."

The two of them walked out of the Buena Vista, Morning with his hand around Pat's shoulder, Pat carrying the bouquet of mums.

"I'll have to remember this place. It's the Bon Voyage."

"No Mark, the Buena Vista, across from Fisherman's Wharf."

"Oh, thanks, I'll remember that." The door closed behind them.

"Is this it?" Green was puffing from climbing the four flights of stairs.

"Yes, this is it." She laughed at Green's being so out of breath. She opened the door and they walked in.

"I think I'm going to have a heart attack." Green staggered over to the couch that was just mattresses covered with red cloth and sat down.

"Would you like some coffee?"

"Well, do you have anything stronger?"

"Yes, I think that I've got some wine."

"Good, I'd love that," Green smiled.

Mary went to the kitchen. "I'm going to have some coffee. I've got to go to work in the morning. You want some toast?"

"No." Jim could hear her putting the water on to boil and other noises that sounded like toast being made and wine being taken out of the refrigerator. "This is really a nice place."

"Thank you," she called. She came walking back to the living room that was also the bedroom. "I'm going to get into something more comfortable."

"Fine," Green said not moving.

She turned and went to the hallway.

Green settled himself on the couch, he was almost lying down. Mary returned wearing a brightly colored kimono that went down to the floor. Green couldn't tell if she was wearing anything underneath it. He smiled to himself. Well, he would push it. If something happened, it happened. Mary went back to the kitchen. Green closed his eyes.

Mary came back with a plate of toast, a cup of coffee and a glass of wine.

"Here." Green half sat up, took the wine and plate and set them on the coffee table that had once been a dining room table; now the legs were cut off. Mary sat down putting her legs under herself. Jim passed her the plate with the toast on it.

"When do you think that you'll be leaving tomorrow?"

"I don't know, with the Army they get you up at five and then you stand in line till only God or some general knows when. Hell, I might not leave till tomorrow night." Jim sat up long enough to take a drink of his wine. He lay back down, looking at Mary. She was a really nice girl. Jim could tell that she was very particular about herself. He liked that.

"Do you think that you'll be here when I get back?"

"Yes, I've lived here now for two years."

"That's good, maybe I'll come by when I get back or maybe we can write while I'm over there. I really don't have a girl or anything."

"That would be nice, I'd like that."

Mary finished her toast. She took her coffee cup in both hands, taking small sips. Jim looked at her with half-closed eyes. He'd better sit up, he thought. He sat up, running his fingers through his short military haircut, then he took a cigarette from his shirt pocket and lit it.

"Morning and I were saying that we might spend some time here when we get back." He reached for his glass of wine.

"That's a good idea; the Bay area is really great. It's too bad that you two have to go to Vietnam."

"Why is that?" Jim took another sip of his wine.

"I don't know, it doesn't seem right somehow for people to fight and kill each other and then come back to San Francisco to have a good time. Anyway, it seems that more and more people are getting killed all the time.

"Well, what do you want me to do, go AWOL or something like that?"

"No."

"Well then, what do you think Morning and I should do?"

"Well, I don't know, I just don't know."

"You see, there isn't a god damn thing that can be done." Jim smoked his cigarette in silence. Mary sat next to him drinking her coffee. It was quiet in the room.

In the silence Green looked around the room at the bookshelves, the coffee table, the two director's chairs with the little stand between them, and the large pink paper flowers in a large urn in the corner. Green tried to think of what was ahead, a picture of hoards of Orientals coming down on him and Morning and the rest of their company. It would be bad, that he knew from his training. The hand-to-hand combat pit, the bayonet practice, always shouting the same words till his voice was gone, "kill or be killed." That's the bayonet fighter's creed, over and over again till the words now walked with him.

Morning thought it was all pretty funny and he would say the words in a high voice, like he was a queer, then real low like their platoon sergeant. Sergeant Mannley had more medals than anyone he'd ever seen. He once told them that if they ever were told to fix bayonets, to get ready to run like hell. This brought a big laugh from the guys in the platoon. "Kill or be killed," the words walked with him now, their weight becoming heavier and heavier. He looked at Mary sitting next to him and realized he didn't know how to tell her about this; she wouldn't understand, you had to live with it.

"I have to go, Mary. They've changed me in the last...it's almost a year now. I had to learn what we call the parachutist's creed. The second part is what I remember best. I realize that a parachutist is not merely a soldier who arrives by parachute to fight, but is an elite shock trooper and that whose country expects him to march farther and faster, to fight harder, to be more self-reliant than any other soldier. Parachutists of all Allied Armies belong to this brotherhood. In some way it makes me different from the rest. Morning and I have never been elite before now we have to pay the price."

"Jim, what a terrible thing they've done to you. It's the most terrible thing."

"No, it's not all that bad, or maybe it is that bad, I don't know anymore. When I get back, I'll have earned the right to belong to myself. It's a right I've never had before, something that no one can take away from me. I'll know that I put the whole thing on the line, the only thing that I really have - - my life. When I get back, I'll have earned the right to live." Jim took a long pull from his cigarette.

Mary reached over, putting her hand on Jim's knee. He looked at it for moment, then took her hand in his. "It's all right that you don't understand, it wouldn't be fair to ask it of you," he said. Mary put her cup down and they were kissing. Jim felt her breath, the softness of her face. He drew her to him, he could feel her against him, he pulled her down upon himself. He felt her weight on himself, her hands on his neck and face. They didn't speak, both of them let themselves go, neither hesitated. What they were doing was important to both of them.

~ ~ ~

Mark Morning sat on a couch looking at Pat sitting across from him in a Butterfly chair. She turned out to be a dud. He held the almost empty beer can in his hands.

"Well, I guess I'll be going." Mark turned the card in his hands. "You have to get up and all, I guess you're tired too."

"Yes, it is getting late."

Mark drained his beer. He then looked down at his black tennis shoes. "Well, if you can take a joke, Mark old boy, fuck it." Mark said under his breath, he said it just for himself.

"What did you say?" Pat looked over at him.

"Who me?" Mark looked around. He got her to laugh.

"Yes, there's no one else here, is there?"

"No, I guess not, I didn't say anything, just mumbling to myself. I do that a lot." Mark got up. "Well, thank you for having me over to dinner and to meet your Mom and Dad. I really liked your grandmother, but those four aunts of yours aren't too cool." Mark then went through the motions of saying goodbye, shaking hands and making polite bows to the ladies.

"Mark, you're too much." She was giggling at his act.

"Thank you," he said, walking to the door.

Pat got up to let him out. At the door he stopped, turned and looked at her. "Thanks really; I hope that you had a good time."

"I did Mark." She stood close to him, hesitated for a moment then kissed him on the cheek. Morning just stood there. She backed away, smiled and said "Mark, take care of yourself."

"Thanks Pat, I will. Well, I'd better get Green before he gets himself into trouble." Mark gave a little laugh. He opened the door and walked away. He didn't look back; he just kept walking.

The two of them lay, looking at the ceiling, a pink sheet pulled over them.

"You're really nice, Jim. You're a gentle man."

"Thank you. I'm glad that you think so." Jim turned his head to look at Mary. "I wish I could stay and find out what would happen between us."

Mary rolled over, putting her head on his chest. "Thank you for saying that. It makes it a lot better."

"Are you going to be in the fighting, do you think?"

"Yes, I'm Airborne Infantry, and they've taught me only one thing."

Mary seemed to be thinking this over

"It's really sort of funny, I mean when Morning and I were going through training we had to shout, 'Kill or be killed!' and 'It's the difference between the quick and the dead.' I don't know if I have that stuff in me. I guess I'll have to if I'm going to stay alive."

"It's not right for anyone to make you kill. It's just not right Jim," she said. Green could feel her hand and arm resting on his chest.

"You may be right. But when I signed on the dotted line, I gave up my right to make that decision. Tomorrow, I'm going to check my morality at the door and hope I can pick it up again in a year."

They were both silent.

"It's not fair," she protested.

"You're beginning to sound like a broken record. It's done, there's no way out. The whole thing is stupid." Jim took a drag from his cigarette.

They didn't speak for a long time. Green thought of tomorrow and the next day. As long as he kept control over his mind, his insides, then there was a good chance he'd make it.

"What time is it Jim?" Mary asked, half asleep.

"I don't know, it's late though." They both heard Morning at the door. "It's Morning. I'll tell him to wait in the hall." Jim got up, found his pants on the floor next to the bed. Morning knocked again. "Yeah, yeah, Morning," Jim said under his breath. He got his pants on, fumbled with the lock.

"What you doing, Jim?" It was Morning's voice through the door.

Jim opened the door. Morning stood, hands in his pockets. "Hi Jim, I didn't bother you, did I?" Morning's face broke into a smile.

"I'll be out in a minute, wait here."

Morning shrugged his shoulders. Jim closed the door. Morning looked at the door for a long minute, then he sat down in the hallway by sliding down the wall, never taking his hands from his pockets.

"Mark's here, I have to get going."

Mary didn't answer. Jim knew that she was watching him get dressed. "You got a paper and pencil?"

"On the table over there."

Jim went over, found them in the dark and came back over to the bed.

"Write your address on here. I'll write when I know mine."

Mary sat up in bed, keeping the sheet in front of her. She wrote her name and address and handed the paper to Jim. He sat on the side of the bed. They kissed. "See you in a year." He knew when he said it that it wasn't true.

Mary smiled and let go of his neck, falling back on the pillow. "See you too."

Jim got up slowly and walked to the door, opened it and walked out. Morning was asleep.

"Come on, shithead. We got to go fight a war."

"Whatever is customary." Morning got up, following Jim down the stairs to the street.

The bus station was empty at 3:30 in the morning except for a few G.I.'s. The station was lonely and cold. At the far end a man was mopping the floor. All of the vending stands were closed.

"Let's change into our uniforms, Mark." They walked to their locker.

"All right, I guess."

"Did you go to bed with her?" Jim took the key from his pocket and opened the locker.

"No, it was our first date."

Green opened the locker door, reached in and took out his uniform and boots. Morning took his turn.

"It's your last one too, most likely."

Morning shut the door of the locker very hard; the slam echoed throughout the bus station. He didn't answer Green.

They both stood looking around for the men's room.

"You see the can anywhere?" Morning started walking, then turned around so that he could see all of the bus station. "There it is." Morning pointed and they started walking.

Inside, the men's room was empty.

"What a shit hole." Morning said.

Green took off his sweater.

"Just once, I'd like to be in a bus station shitter that didn't smell like piss and something."

"Ammonia, that means it's clean piss."

"Wouldn't you know it? It's still piss."

"Get changed before we miss our bus."

Morning took off his jacket and hung it over the door of one of the stalls. After they'd gotten back into their uniforms, Mark spent a lot of time jumping up and down to keep his balance so that he wouldn't put his food on the floor before he got his boots on.

"Fuck, shit, piss, I hate this bus station." He put on his other boot.

Now they stood looking at each other.

Mark put his foot on one of the white sinks and finished lacing the boots and blousing his pant leg over the top. "What are we going to do with our civvies?"

Green looked at the clothes for a moment. He walked over and gathered them up. He looked at them again, walked over to the trashcan and dropped them in.

"What the hell are you doing?"

"Morning, where you're going - - where we're going, we won't need them."

"How do you know? You've never been there. Maybe we get Sundays off or something like that."

"Sure. And you just go put on your civvies and take a little walk through the jungle and tell the Viet Cong that you're on your day off."

Morning grunted.

"You might as well forget civilian life because now

it won't do you a bit of good."

Morning walked over to the trashcan and looked at his black tennis shoes on top of his clothes.

"Yeah, I guess you're right. Wish I'd gotten laid. Hell, let's get our tickets."

On the way to Oakland Army Terminal, Morning sat looking out the window. They were on the Bay Bridge again.

"I got the feeling we should have joined the Coast Guard." Morning turned to Green.

"Shut up, Morning." Green had his eyes closed.

"Green, I got the feeling we're going to a bad day at Black Rock."

"Morning, just shut your mouth for a while." Green opened his eyes. "What are those?"

Morning looked down at what he was holding. "They're my black tennis shoes. I thought I'd keep them as a souvenir of civilian life. When I'm over there, I can take them out and look at them and they'll remind me of civilian life and what a good time we had." Morning held his black tennis shoes together very tightly. Maybe they'd bring luck or at least it was something, at least something.

Green closed his eyes again. He wouldn't say anything about those black tennis shoes, no, not a thing.

Their plane left for Okinawa at 08:47 in the morning.

2 SEPTEMBER 1965: THE UNITED STATES ANNOUNCES THAT OVER 100 U.S. SERVICEMEN A DAY ARE VOLUNTEERING FOR DUTY IN VIETNAM, A SHARP INCREASE SINCE THE MARINES LANDED IN MARCH . . .

CHAPTER TWO

SEVEN SOLDIERS STOOD ON THE TARMAC IN THE LATE AFTERNOON SUN WAITING FOR THEIR HELICOPTER TO PICK THEM UP. THEY WORE FATIGUES AND FLOPPY HATS, THEIR FACES PAINTED BLACK AND GREEN. THEY WERE LRRP'S (LONG RANGE RECONNAISSANCE PLATOON), TEAM THREE:

Team Leader: Sergeant Winters, Senior NCO

Assistant Team Leader: Sergeant Swenson, Senior NCO

RTO: PFC Kolwosky

Point: PFC Green

Rear Security: PFC Morning

Team Member: PFC Billy C. Cook

KIT Carson Scout: Ca Way, Vietnamese Army

THE PROVISIONAL LRRP'S HAD BEEN DESIGNED TO OPERATE IN ENEMY TERRITORY IN SMALL TEAMS. IT WAS SAID THEY ARE THE BEST OF THE BEST.

LRRP TEAM THREE jumped from the chopper that was hovering in a clearing five feet from the top of the elephant grass. In the dimming jungle twilight each man hit the ground running, the elephant grass was whipping wildly from the downdraft of the chopper blade as it angled steeply away from the LRRP team. In moments it disappeared, long before the team reached the relative safety of the wood line. They were alone . . . except for the VC running directly towards them.

Sergeant Swenson was hit first, dead before he hit the ground, the force of his headlong fall flipping his body twice before he landed, arms and legs splayed at crazy angles. Two sets of hands reached down and picked up the Swede dragging him forward to the woodline. The remaining members of the team fired wildly to their front.

"Kolwosky, get on the horn – tell them to get us the fuck outta here! Shit, we're fucked!" screamed Sergeant Winters keeping low to the ground, firing his M-16 on full automatic. Behind him Kolwosky keyed the mike in his hand.

"Team Three, we are comp . . ." Kolwosky, the RTO, felt the rounds enter his chest, hot pokers tearing through him, coming to rest in the PRICK-25 radio strapped to his back. The 19-year-old RTO fell backward just as the others reached the woodline and cover.

"RTO's down!" Winters screamed over the firing. "Son of a bitch!" We are fucked, Sergeant Winters thought as he kneeled, changing out the magazine in his M-16.

"I got him, I got him. OH NO, SHIT!" yelled Green, firing his M-16 while he dragged the RTO over to Winters' position. "Sarge, Sarge, the PRICK-25 is dead and so is the RTO, what's his name?" Green reached down and found the dead boy's dog tag and pulled it, breaking the chain, stuffing the dog tag in his pocket. He then pulled a hand grenade from his web gear, pulled the pin; holding the spoon tightly, he placed the grenade on the ground, rolling the RTO over on it. *Sorry, you won't feel a thing but Charlie will get one surprise out of you,* Green thought as he booby trapped the RTO. "Sarge, we gotta get out of here. I'll recon the trail." Green left the radio on the ground. Winters nodded, and fired off another burst while Green, bent at the waist, moved past Winters in the falling darkness. Green had taken a few steps when he saw a trail. It seemed to be going away from the incoming rounds. "Sarge, TRAIL!" Winters nodded affirmative, fired off another short burst and started backing up. "COOK, MORNING, MOVE --- MOVE ON ME!"

Green didn't look back as he started down the trail in the darkness. The VC were still firing and shouting to each other. As Winters passed by the Swede, he pulled the dog tag and booby-trapped his old friend. It was difficult to see the three remaining team members in front of him as they moved quickly down the trail away from the VC. Green, Cook, The Kit Carson Scout, Winters was thinking, where in the hell is Morning, as greenish, lime colored tracers floated overhead.

After Green had gone what he thought was maybe four or five hundred yards, he stopped, motionless. The rest of the team stopped behind him, all vigilant, trying to get their breath back. The four men were silent, scared, frozen in place. The worse possible scenario had happened – an LRRP Team compromised at the LZ, no radio and two of the team already dead. Sergeant Swenson, known as the Swede, a senior NCO, one of the old nasty dudes on his second tour and the RTO Kolwosky were fresh meat. This had been Kolwosky first LRRP mission and his last.

Sergeant Winters thought about the two lost LRRPs. Who was left? Green and Cook, both good troops with experience, and still healthy. Then there was Ca Way, the Vietnamese Kit Carson Scout, he's the wild card, things got rough he might just turn us into the VC. Son of a bitch we might just get out of this alive.

The three VC soldiers that were moving down the trail stopped, surprised to see them crouched in the darkness. In that moment, seconds standing still, one of the VC raised his AK-47 and fired.

Green's scream began with the first rounds hitting the dirt to his left; he bolted forward, crashing onto one of the VC. At the same moment, Sergeant Winters fired, killing the other two with a short burst. Green could feel the smaller man beneath him writhing, fighting to just free himself. Green could smell the VC's sweat. He was hitting him in the face; he kept hitting him until the VC was still.

Cook hadn't moved; one of the AK-47 rounds had gone through his upper thigh. The Kit Carson Scout was next to him, face to the sky, his legs spread out, having taken two rounds in the chest. He rolled from side to side, groaning, softly, mortally wounded.

Sergeant Winters went over to Cook to look at his leg. The wound was ugly, torn and bleeding heavily. It made him sick to touch the leg. He took out the first aid packet, wrapping the wound tightly and gave Cook morphine. The Kit Carson Scout, Ca Way, threw up and died in his own vomit.

Green rolled the unconscious VC over. He was dressed in a regular NVA uniform. He tied his hands behind his back with a piece of parachute cord that he used as a rifle sling. When he completed the last knot, he slumped to the ground. He pulled the VC with him as he crawled towards Sergeant Winters and Cook.

"Green, clean up this mess the best you can. I'll take care of Cook." Green paused where he was looking at Sergeant Winters. "Where's Morning?"

"Don't know, Sarge." Green started pulling one of the VC bodies off the trail. He returned for the other one, then the three dragged and pulled themselves and the unconscious VC into the jungle, off the trail a few feet. They lay together, shielding Cook, waiting in the darkness. When the VC began to stir, Green thumped him. They held their breath while the VC continued searching around them.

The darkness was almost total, the jungle canopy shielding them from the stars. The moon hadn't risen yet and the jungle closed around them like a cave. They didn't move. Green relieved himself where he lay.

A hundred yards behind them Morning moved down the trail, half crawling, half walking, dragging the PRICK-25. He moved a few feet, then waited and moved again, with no real idea of where the others were or if they were still alive. He had heard the burst of M-

16 fire earlier. Morning kept moving forward. He stopped when he felt a hand on the back of his ankle.

He rolled over and crawled his way into the jungle next to Green. He had the radio. Green pulled Morning as close as he could, their faces almost touching.

"The radio is fucked, it got shot with the RTO," Green whispered in Morning's ear.

Morning shook his head back and forth. Green could not see him saying no, he felt him saying no. "It was the battery, man, it got shot, the radio is okay, I got the extra battery." Morning whispered back to Green.

Pure relief spread through Green's whole body. They had the radio. Green took the microphone and broke squelch twice, the sign that the team was in trouble. Whoever was monitoring back in TOC returned the signal; they understood. Green put his arm around Morning's back in the darkness while the VC moved away from their position down the trail. As the dense jungle night surrounded them in the thick choking heat, the VC were heard shooting in all directions. They didn't seem to know where the LRRP team was. They lay in a slight depression the undergrowth wrapped around them. They didn't move or speak. The jungle cave, black air and rotting undergrowth were their only safety. For hours the mosquitoes fed on their motionless bodies.

It had been quiet for some time when Sergeant Winters stood up silently, listening to every sound around him, alert to any kind of movement. He took one step, touched Green on the foot and motioned for him to get up. As he did so, Green rose stiffly to his feet. Winters motioned for Green to take point and for

Morning to take the rear with the prisoner. He would take the compass and carry Cook. Green hoisted his 60 lb. rucksack on his back and moved from their night cave to the trail. Winters in turn, slid into his rucksack, hoisted Cook over his shoulder and followed Green to the trail. He didn't like taking the trail but he had no choice with Cook. Going through the bush would be too difficult for him and Cook. Winters could barely make out Green a few feet in front of him.

Cook was high on the morphine and didn't care that he was upside down and that his leg hurt. His leg with the hole in it was next to Sergeant Winters' face and as he walked with Cook on his shoulder, the blood leaked from the bandage and ran down his cheek over his mouth. Winters didn't have a free hand so he shifted Cook the best he could and spit the blood out to the side. God damn, you're heavy Cook, you son of a bitch. What a cluster fuck this has turned into, damn, Winters thought as he labored down the trail. Maybe we can still get out of this, he thought.

Morning shouldered his rucksack with the radio safely inside, checked his M-16 to make sure it was on safe. He then tied another length of cord around the prisoner's neck. A slight jerk on his part and the prisoner followed without protest. Once on the trail, Morning stopped for a moment, listening and peering into the darkness. Another jerk on the cord and Morning was following Winters, fifteen paces to the rear.

In the darkness, the three men and the prisoner walked on. The trail kept them together, heavy undergrowth and bamboo surrounded them. Their progress was slow; each man putting his feet down slowly and carefully. Winters struggled forward under the dead weight of Cook, constantly off balance. Cook was beginning to smell. Winters hoped the wound wasn't becoming infected in the tropical heat.

They lost track of time. It seemed as if it had always been dark, a darkness that closed around them, sapping their strength. They had lost control of the situation and what was happening to them. It was the trail and training that kept them together. The heat was oppressive in the darkness. Even when it started to rain, it didn't cool down. The rain just added another misery, another obstacle in their journey to stay alive. Green wiped the water from his eyes so he could see better. At first the rain felt good, but as it intensified, it made everything more difficult. Green held up his hand, the others stopped where they were. It was raining harder.

The trail led them to a clearing, the black form of a hut outlined dimly on a small piece of high ground. Winters laid Cook down on the ground and lay down next to him, his chest heaving in almost total exhaustion. He watched the hut with glazed eyes.

Green and Morning made the Viet Cong lie face down on the ground; they took his sandals off and tied the man's feet with some nylon that Morning had in his pocket. They took part of the NVA's shirt and ripped it off, using it for a blindfold and gag. When they finished they sat down, bone tired, but they watched the hut for any movement that would indicate someone was there. Later, the moon would come out and improve their vision; until then they put off their approach.

The rain was coming down in sheets. What was left of the LRRP Team Three sat in silence. Rain clouds covered the moon and stars and darkness was total and complete. What a place to have a war, Green thought. If the NVA or the Cong didn't get you, the weather and the jungle would. An hour ago I was sweating hot and now I'm freezing my ass off. Green felt a hand on his shoulder. It was Sergeant Winters who had crawled over next to him. Winters pointed with two fingers to his eyes and then motioned with his hand in the direction of the hut. Green understood.

Slowly, Green rose and began to walk, bent at the waist, his rifle held out in front of him. As he got closer to the hut, he wanted to run, panic tore at his guts, but he didn't bolt. Every few yards he stopped and knelt to listen. He heard many things in the night but he wasn't sure what they were, so gradually he moved closer to the hut. It bothered him that he was doing this alone, without apparent support from Winters. Green stopped again and knelt down. What would he do if there was someone in the hut? The chances were pretty good that they would be Viet Cong. If there were more than one or two, he didn't know how he'd be able to kill them all. He checked the safety on his rifle, making sure the gun was on full automatic. No, that wasn't enough, thought Green. He took a hand grenade from his web-gear, bent the cotter pin straight, pulled it from the hole and held the spoon next to the grenade. The ring at the end of the cotter pin he put around his finger, he then rose very slowly and continued toward the hut.

He kept walking slowly, quietly, taking a great deal

of time, standing erect now. He reached the wall of the hut; he had his rifle in his left hand and the grenade with the pin out in his right. He moved along the wall and to a window. He wasn't sure what to do next. To look in might mean death, but he had no other choice. Green looked in the window but he could see nothing; he stood still and listened. All he heard was the raspy sound of his own breathing and the rain. He walked to the front of the building and stood at the corner, his back flat against the wall. He held the hand grenade up and close to his cheek; he hesitated just a moment, then stepped around the corner. There was nothing. He walked quickly to the door; without stopping, he entered the hut. It was empty. Now inside, it was clear that the one room hut was empty, empty.

Green leaned against the wall and put the cotter pin back into the hand grenade. He felt good, even powerful, yet somehow disappointed. He let his head fall back against the wall. His legs began to shake. He slid down to the hard packed dirt floor. "Oh God, oh God," he said out loud, then after a few moments, pushed himself back on his feet. Green left the hut and ran, bent low, back to Sergeant Winters. They looked at each other; Green nodded. Then he walked over to where the prisoner was lying and untied his ankles. He prodded him to his feet and began pushing him toward the hut with Sergeant Winters following, Cook on his shoulder. They made it to the hut and collapsed in exhaustion. In the hut they would feel safe until daylight, when they would call extraction with the PRICK-25. Green took up a guard position in the hut's doorway.

As morning came, the sky turned to a dull, hard gray in the east; to the west it remained dark. In the hut it was still dark; Green couldn't see any of the men sleeping inside. Across the clearing everything was wet from the rain, making things look shiny even in the gray light. There was always the smell of rotting vegetation surrounding him. At the front of the hut the land was flat and marshy with many stagnant pools of water. Most of the ground was covered with elephant grass; beyond this was scrub growth and then the jungle. In the distance there was a mountain; it was a long distance from where the hut stood in the clearing on the small hill. In the back of the hut was the jungle from which they had come last night; on two sides were banana trees with wide leaves. The trees were barren; the land had been farmed at one time, but the farmer had either left or been killed. Clearly no one had lived in the hut for some time; it would soon decay with the absence of the farmer.

Green was weary. He had been up for more than 24 hours. Pulling out his canteen, he took two hits of speed, fearing that he would go to sleep. The night before had been bad, and he didn't want to think about it; he only looked at the open area in front of him, watching. He held his rifle in one hand; the rest of his web gear was inside the hut. His worn, round, floppy bush hat was pushed down on his forehead, almost covering his eyes; they were half closed but saw everything that happened. He wore tiger-striped fatigues, black and gray in uneven stripes. The right knee was ripped so that his knee showed. With the light, Green went into his left shirt pocket and took out a cigarette; he hadn't had a cigarette all night.

Green liked the bush. Back home in Minnesota he'd done a lot of camping; he felt comfortable in the outdoors. When Green left to go to the Army, he'd packed his gear in boxes carefully, his pack board, mountain tent, fishing gear and maps. He liked his maps and he looked at all of them before he put them in the box. His favorite trip had been the one into Canada by canoe with two friends from school. Green wanted to see the Indian paintings on the rock cliffs above the water. The outfitter had told him about the paintings. They had been painted by the Sioux; it was a ceremonial place for them. When the Chippewa and the Sioux were at war for the land, the Chippewa had come on the paintings and shot arrows and thrown spears at them to disfigure what had been sacred to the Sioux. They had been at war for many years. The war ended when the Chippewa lost the land to the White men. It had all happened a long time ago.

When they got to Number Two Rapids it was difficult to see any of the paintings. Green tied a rope around his waist, swam out to the rock and then dove to the bottom several times to see if he could find arrowheads or spear heads. He found two arrowheads, but he had gotten tired in the swiftly running water and he had to quit.

Green stood now, smoking his cigarette, looking over the bush. Yes, he liked the land; he got along on it quite well.

The hut was small with a red slate roof. There were holes in the roof where the slate had broken and fallen to the floor. There was a fireplace with a window on each side; the NVA Regular lay in front of the fireplace. There were no windows on the back wall where Cook was. Two pillars split the hut in two; they held up the crossbeam. The white walls were cracked and soon would crumble. The floor was hard clay; it gave off a strong odor. Green spent most of the day outside the hut, watching the land, his rifle held loosely at his side.

Now off to the right he saw the line of men making their way along the woodline through the elephant grass. They were small, a long way away, dressed in black. They moved like a snake. Green stood in the open, watching, not moving himself. He was sure that they could not see him. He enjoyed watching the sight; he knew they were the Viet Cong but the distance made it possible to appreciate the sight. They would have to leave the hut now. He marked the place where the Viet Cong were so that he could find them again. They were advancing toward the clearing.

Green withdrew into the hut. "Sarge, Charlie's moving into our AO. We got to do something." It was the first time Green had spoken aloud since the previous day.

Sergeant Winters didn't move from where he sat in the corner with his feet drawn up to his chin. He didn't seem to be breathing; he was so still. He had sat there all day except for the three times he got up to help Cook.

Cook opened his eyes when Green spoke. He lay flat on his back along the wall of the hut. He was eighteen years old and high on morphine. He pushed himself up with his hands so that he leaned his back against the whitewashed wall. He looked down at his leg but didn't touch the bandage. Cook made a motion as if to speak, but said nothing.

Green went back outside. He looked out over the flat land. He no longer saw the Viet Cong, but he knew that they were there. He sensed they were coming to the hut the way an animal knows that it is being hunted. Green returned to the inside again.

"They're here, I saw them out in the open before. Sarge, they'll come up here, I know it. We gotta do something."

The Sergeant looked up at Green standing in the doorway, blocking out the last of the light. "Get out of the doorway!" ordered Sergeant Winters, then he slumped back down to his original posture. They made contact with TOC two different times during the day. The weather had grounded everything, including birds, it seemed. There had been no way the Old Man could get a chopper in to pick them up. Finally, Winters got up and went to the door and surveyed the scene before him in the last gray light day. "Let's saddle up, they won't find us in this shit any better than our own people could." Winters started to put on his web gear.

Cook opened his eyes. "Are we getting out of here?" Cook's face was pale; it looked very old and drawn. "Jesus, my leg. When are we getting out of here?"

"Right now." Winters said. "Morning you take rear security with this little shithead." He pointed at the prisoner. "Green, take the point and I'll walk the compass and carry Cook. Green, I want to go back into the woodline and follow the clearing around. Find a place we can logger in for the night and with any luck this weather will break tomorrow and we can get the fuck outta here."

"I hear that, Sarge." Morning said as he prodded his prisoner to his feet.

They went single file out of the door. Outside, Green stood watching the open area. He figured it would be at least an hour before the VA got to the hut. Green pointed toward the wood line and they started walking. The rain had relented to a degree. Until dark they would have to stay inside the wood line. At night they could walk along the edge where it would be easier. When the moon rose, the rain resumed. Winters motioned Green to keep moving on, away from the hut. The flat land was hard walking, the ground was soggy, the mud stuck to their boots in big clods, and sometimes it was open water. On higher ground the elephant grass was as high as they were, it ripped and tore at their legs as they walked. Without his sandals, the prisoner's feet became sore and bloody, which slowed them down, even though Morning dragged him forward.

It had turned cold in the early morning after the rain. They stopped just inside the wood line where they could see another open area and a good deal of sky. Green made a quick sweep of the area. There was room to get a chopper in and they had good cover for the rest of the time. He returned to Sergeant Winters' position next to Cook and whispered the information to him. Winters called in their situation report and the new landing zone on the radio. Morning hobbled the prisoner, while Sergeant Winters took care of Cook, giving him the last syringe of morphine. After that the four of them went to sleep curled up together in a dense thicket next to the open area.

Green opened his eyes at first light. His body was stiff and he was wet. He crawled over so that he could look at the open area. Then he heard the chopper, at first far away. It kept circling in wider and wider circles. Green dug into his pocket for his orange vinyl signal panel and mirror. He heard Sergeant Winters getting Cook and the prisoner ready to make the dash for the chopper. Green saw the chopper when it came low level along the tree line. He ran out into the elephant grass and laid one of the panels out. He then ran a distance from the panel and stood up, legs spread apart, holding the second signal panel between his hands, above his head. The chopper saw him and came straight for him. When Green was sure he had been sighted, he dropped the panel, signaling the chopper to land and he ran back to the others. Sergeant Winters was on his feet with Cook on his shoulder; Morning had the Viet Cong in front of him. The chopper was coming in, close to the ground. Green motioned for the Sergeant to go for the chopper.

"Go, Go!" He waved his arms.

Sergeant Winters, with Cook on his shoulder, started running for the chopper with Morning half dragging his prisoner behind him. Green was standing in the open, waving them on. From the chopper door two men jumped out, both with M-60 machine guns. Green looked again and saw it was Captain Moes, the CO, and their First Sergeant covering their race to the waiting chopper. The CO helped Winters and Cook into the chopper. A sniper started firing from somewhere in the wood line.

Green could hear the M-60's returning fire as he began his run for the chopper. He saw Morning push the prisoner into the chopper and jump in behind him, and then he felt the shock of a bullet as it hit his leg. He fell headlong into the elephant grass, his heavy pack carrying him forward. He rolled and got up and fell again when he tried to put weight on it. He felt hands pulling him up by his web gear and his arm went over Captain Moes' shoulder, who half carried, half dragged him the rest of the way to the chopper. Green felt the cold steel of the floor next to his cheek and the sound of the whirling blades muffled the sound of the door gunner's M-60. The chopper lifted off and pull-pitched toward the open sky.

Green looked down from the open door. The land looked quiet, emerald, soft and enticing. It's a lot different from up here, Green thought. He could feel someone putting a bandage on his leg, which had begun to throb painfully. His eyes closed.

18 June 1966: The JCS receive a new request from General Westmoreland, who states that he needs 542,588 troops for 1967 – an additional 111,588 men.

CHAPTER THREE

WAR ZONE D, 173rd AIRBORNE BDGE (SEP), COMPANY C, 503rd INF. THE HOME OF THE "HANGING IN THERE" TROOPS.

THE NIGHT SEEMED STRANGELY DARK BEFORE THE RISE OF THE MOON AS A SOFT BREEZE CAME THROUGH THE TOPS OF THE TREES. IT WAS EERILY QUIET. THE NVA WERE COMING BUT NO ONE IN THE COMPANY COULD SEE THEM.

AT FIRST LIGHT THEY COUNTED THE DEAD: FIRST PLATOON BROUGHT THEM BACK ON BAMBOO PILES, POLES BENT UNDER THE MASSIVE WEIGHT.

"SERGEANT JONES GOT IT," THE FIRST PLATOON SERGEANT SAID.

"YEAH, I KNOW." A BLACK SOLDIER ANSWERED LIGHTING A CIGARETTE. THE BLUE GRAY SMOKE HUNG IN THE AIR AROUND THE SOLDIER'S HEAD.

THE CALL CAME DOWN FROM THE C.O. TO SADDLE UP AND MOVE OUT.

THIRD PLATOON STAYED WITH THE DEAD UNTIL THE CHOPPER CAME. THE DEAD WERE ALREADY STARTING TO SMELL WHEN THE FIRST AND SECOND PLATOONS MOVED OUT WITHOUT A SOUND.

THE RAINY SEASON was almost over and the weather had turned hot and dry. Heat waves rose from the baked, hard ground in a shimmering wall. Specialist Four, James Green, shirtless leaned against the doorway of the Operations hooch or the Long Range Reconnaissance Platoon, looking down the platoon street. Nothing moved. Charlie, the platoon dog, lay in the shade of the lister bag, at the other end of the street.

"GREEN!" The young trooper turned in the doorway to face Sergeant Winters standing in front of the wall map of South Vietnam. He was looking at the map. "Did you hear about the Captain from the 101st who called in air strikes on his own position, and then they fought their way out?"

"Yeah, that was Captain Carpenter. They say he's going to get the CMH for that. If he gets the Medal of Honor, what do the troopers with him get?" Green left his position at the doorway and stood looking at the map with Sergeant Winters.

"It was his action that saved his company from the NVA. I'm sure everyone will get something," said Winters as he turned, dropping the red curtain over the map.

He walked over to the wooden desk, took a cigarette, thinking that he was smoking too much.

"You're smoking too much Sarge." Green said over his shoulder. He had taken up his position at the doorway again.

"Yeah, maybe you're right." He put the cigarette out. "I'm going to lay down for awhile. Why don't you go to the mess hall, get some iced tea and bring me some when you come back." Winters went into the other room that was his sleeping quarters. Green raised his hand in acknowledgement, otherwise not moving.

"Sure Sarge. Want anything in it?" Green called into the other room.

"Naw, just ice if there is any."

Green could hear Winters lying down. He remained at the door looking at the heat waves. In the nine months since that mission, he and Sergeant Winters had gotten pretty close. He was promoted to Speedy Four and when they were in base camp he had a job working with Winters in LRRP Operations. It was a good job and Green got to know everything before the rest of the platoon. It had taken almost a month for his leg wound to heal; a month of light duty, helping with the training schedule, going with Winters on aerial recons. Winters had taken Green under his wing. After that last mission, Captain Moes kept Winters back at Operations and the TOC. No one in the platoon minded. Winters was about to retire. He made it through World War II and Korea. Vietnam was going to be his last war. At home his second wife, Ruby, waited for him. Between two wives he had six children, four boys and two girls. They were grown up now and it would be just he and Ruby when he finished the tour.

Green shifted his weight, took his uniform shirt off the nail by the door and walked into the blazing afternoon sun. Each heat wave hit him in the face as he slowly walked up the platoon street past the sign that read 173rd, LRRP PLATOON, AUTHORIZED PERSONNEL ONLY, towards the mess hall. Green, tall and thin, had the conditioning of an athlete. Nine months humping the boonies had hardened every muscle, bleached his hair and put a deep tan on his face and arms. A farmer's tan as they called it back in Minnesota.

Inside the mess hall it was dark and cool. The Vietnamese kitchen girls chattered as they did their work. Green went over to the three foot high pot that held the iced tea, dipped some into a glass, walked over to a table and sat down, taking a drink of the tepid, brown water which had never been close to ice when it was made. The cooks were busy making the evening meal.

"Winters taking a nap?" The mess sergeant came over and sat down.

"Yeah, the weight of command, y'know. I'm watching things while he's sleep." Green took out a cigarette from the crusted pack in his pants pocket. "Got a light?"

The mess sergeant reached into his pocket for his lighter. "If you're watching things while Winters is sacked out, what the hell ya doing in my mess hall?" Green took a drink of the tea and made a face.

"Bull shit." The mess sergeant got up. He hated these kids they got in the Army now. Eighteen years in and now twelve months in this shit hole having to deal with these teenage assholes. He walked away.

There was the sound of a truck outside, the motor was being raced with the clutch in. "God damn it, Morning, knock that shit off." It was the voice of the mess sergeant. The truck was turned off. "Wow man, don't get so excited." The double doors at the other end of the mess hall flew open and in walked Private Mark Morning, silhouetted by the afternoon sun, sweat pouring from every pore, bootlaces dragging, shirt unbuttoned, needing a shave. "Okay girls, get your sweet little asses to work." The truck with the next day's rations, its tailgate down, stood almost inside of the mess hall. The girls started towards the truck reluctantly. "Let's go, let's go. I ain't got time to be fooling around here all day. I got things to do, people to meet," Morning yelled, sweating, clapping his hands. He saw Green sitting at the table, laughing. "We just can't get good help like we used to," he said, shaking his head, reaching into his pocket for a cigarette, where he knew there were none. Green took his pack from the table in front of him and tossed them to Morning.

"Thanks." One of the girls brought Morning a glass of iced tea. "Ya know, the Army's my life," he said, while he patted the girl's rear. "I am definitely leadership material."

"Shit." Green said, putting out his cigarette.

"Where's Sergeant Winters napping?" Morning drank all of the iced tea in his glass.

Green didn't bother to answer.

Morning leaned over the table, putting his shaggy face into Green's, speaking in a low, confidential voice. "When we going on a mission?"

"How the hell do I know?" Green leaned back. "When are you going to take a bath for Christ's sake, and maybe brush your teeth?" Green waved his hand in front of Morning's face.

"Next week, maybe. Come one, you've got to have heard something. You can tell me. I'm on your side, remember?" Morning was scratching his jungle rot, the scabbed sores on the right side of his cheek.

"Look, I don't know anything and if I did, I wouldn't tell you, that's for sure, asshole."

"I've got to go on a mission." Morning was looking off into the far beyond. "I can't take this mess hall too much longer." Morning turned his attention back to his jungle rot. "This damn country." He looked at Green. "I used to be a nice guy."

"That's what they all say." Green lit another cigarette.

Morning drained the last of his iced tea. "This stuff tastes like shit. You'd think that they would get the hang of making iced tea after awhile. Oh well, sixty days and a wake up. I'm so short, I've got to sleep in a matchbox. You'd think we would get more respect. Man, sixty days and wake up. Shit man." Morning played with his empty iced tea glass.

Green laughed. He looked at Morning, sitting across the table. He laughed again, he didn't know why. "Morning, you are never going to get any respect, period. You are an asshole."

"That may or may not be true. But I am alive. You keep that in mind, mother fucker." Morning hit the table with his open hand. At the sound, the Vietnamese girl brought more iced tea. "That is if this shit don't kill me." Morning took another drink.

"You ain't never goin' to die, Morning. You're too much of an asshole. Hell, I'm surprised they even let you stay in the country this long." Green took a drag off his cigarette and blew smoke in Morning's face.

"Yeah." Morning looked at Green across the table.

"I guess you think you should get a medal or something?" Green laughed.

"God damn right!" Morning looked down at the table again. I might be an asshole, he thought, but I'm still around and there are a lot of them that can't say that from inside a body bag. "How long, how long have we been in this country?" Morning pointed an accusing finger between Green's eyes.

"Ten months, right man, and you know what tomorrow is?" Morning didn't wait for Green to answer. "It's my birthday, asshole. And you know something else? I'll be eighteen years old. How many guys you know not even eighteen yet and been in this country ten fucking months with more years and more missions than I got? Nobody asshole. NO BODDDYYY." Morning was half standing, pointing his accusing finger at Green. "Man, I can't drink legal, I can't vote, and if I were home now, I could be picked up on a fucking curfew charge." Morning sat back down and withdrew his finger from Green's face.

"Yeah, but you're still an asshole and there ain't nobody going to give you a medal and you're not that short. A lot can happen in two months. So don't start any short time stuff with me and save your god damn war stories and body count for someone who just might give a shit." Green remembered their first day in this country. They were cherries; 1965 ... hell everybody was a cherry then. Maybe one, two NCO's out of the outfit had CIB and even the goddamn mail clerk got a CIB. Morning was right about one thing. He had outlived a lot of guys but he was still an asshole, some kind of unidentifiable clusterfuck. Ten months in Nam, over two years in the Army, most of that time spent on jump status, four months with Charlie Company of the 503rd Infantry and the rest of his time as a LRRP and he was still a Private doing shit work in the mess hall. Hell, nobody pulled mess hall duty anymore, except Mark Morning.

"Ya know, I hardly remember the States anymore. It's still there, ain't it? Maybe I left when I was too young. Do you think so?" Morning pondered his own question.

"Morning, you are a Section Eight, ya know that? Of course the States are still there. Man, I don't know why I even talk to you sometimes." Green looked around the mess hall; it had somehow lost the cool, quiet atmosphere it had before Morning sat down at his table. "Mark, I'll catch ya later after chow. We'll drink some beer, maybe go down to the movies." Green got up, heading for the door. He walked outside into the heat, took off his shirt, and headed back to the operations hooch.

He could hear the mess sergeant looking for Morning but Morning had already disappeared to the back of the mess hall, sitting on a garbage can, picking at his jungle rot, listening to the Beach Boys singing Surfing Safari, *"Come on baby, come with me, I'm taking you on a safari with me a surfin' safari."* Morning always said when he got out he was going stay in California. To Morning, it was the only place to be. He wanted to be a surfer just like the Beach Boys. He was always yelling "Surfs up," making everybody around him crazy with his "Surfs up." The totality of Morning's belief in "California Surfing" and that he would be there one day with the Beach Boys was also believed by the rest of the platoon. It was like a kind of amulet that kept Morning alive. Morning believed in the amulet of California, even though he hadn't been to California except to ship out almost a year before. Because of California, Morning felt he would never die and he said so.

It was common belief in the platoon that Morning was crazy. No one knew if he had gotten that way from Nam or if he came to Nam that way. Green wouldn't say one way or the other.

22 June 1967: A 130-man company of the 173rd Airborne Brigade is virtually wiped out by a NVA ambush near Dakto. Eighty men KIA and 34 WIA with 106 NVA killed.

CHAPTER 4

THE ENEMY CALLED THEM SKY SOLDIERS. THEY WERE PERHAPS THE YOUNGEST UNIT TO BE FIELDED IN A COMBAT SITUATIN, OTHER THAN IN THE CIVIL WAR, IN U.S. MILITARY HISTORY. THE AVERAGE AGE OF THE 173rd AIRBORNE BRIGADE WAS NINETEEN.

THE MAJORITY OF THE BRIGADE HAD NEVER VOTED, CONSUMED ALCOHOL, OWNED A CAR OR HELD A FULL TIME, CIVILIAN JOB. BUT BY THE END OF 1966, THEY ACCOUNTED FOR 656 KIA's (KILLED IN ACTION) AND 1007 WIA'S (WOUNDED IN ACTION) AGAINST AN ENEMY THAT WAS SUPERIOR IN NUMBER, POSSESSED AN INTIMATE KNOWLEDGE OF THE TERRAIN, CUSTOMS, LANGUAGE OF THE INDIGENOUS POPULATION AND THE WILL TO FIGHT FOR SOMETHING IN WHICH THEY BELIEVED.

THE 173RD AIRBORNE BRIGADE was made up of two infantry battalions, the first and second of the 503rd, E Troop of the 17th Calvary, an engineering company and headquarters, and support companies. Later a troop of Australian Calvary was added for their Armored Personnel Carriers.

The brigade had taken over part of the perimeter of the Bien Hoa Airbase, thirty or so miles north of Saigon. Each battalion took responsibility for a sector of the perimeter as well as did E Troop. Inside the perimeter were the C & C and support units and the LRRP unit, which was attached to the 17th Calvary for purposes of supply and support. The LRRP unit ate at the Cav mess hall and got their mail from the Cav mail clerk.

The LRRP never pulled perimeter guard because of the nature of their mission, nor did they run daily patrols outside the perimeter of the roads that led north, into War Zone D. One day the LRRP's would be at base camp for meals and the next some or all of them would be gone without a word to anyone at the Cav.

At the inception of the unit, they wore black berets and tiger-striped uniforms identical to those worn by Vietnamese Paratroopers and Pathfinders units. LRRP training had taken them to the Special Forces run parachute and pathfinder schools and to the Special Jungle Training School, also operated by the Special Forces. To be a LRRP, you had to have had combat experience and be a volunteer.

The unit's mission was to do long range reconnaissance. Their secondary mission, if compromised, was to turn killer and disrupt enemy activities where and when possible. The platoon was broken down into six six-man teams with a command and communications team. The T.O. and E. called for six active teams at any one time and for one member of each team to be Vietnamese. Because of the nature of the activities of the platoon and the heavy losses suffered during early missions, there were never more than four teams operational at one time and the use of Vietnamese was given up early in the platoon's development.

The LRRP's had four hooches that sat apart from the rest of the Cav. There was a small sign at the beginning of the rock-lined pathway that read "LRRP – NO DOGS ALLOWED." Past the LRRP hooches there was nothing but the perimeter and the guard in placements.

Mail call was held next to the Cav Orderly Room. This was done for two reasons, the first was so that if the First Sergeant, known as Banjo Belly, needed people for a detail, he didn't have far to go to find them. The second was that the mail clerk kept the mailroom and his sleeping area in the back of the orderly room since he was in tight with the First Sergeant. As Morning often pointed out they were of Mexican-American descent and were trying to start a Barrio of their own.

Morning and Green stood in the back of a crowd of 17th Cav troopers waiting for mail as it was called out.

"Morning! Morning!" yelled the mail clerk.

"He died, you want his toys?" yelled a trooper. Everyone laughed.

"Very funny, you guys really kill me." Morning

pushed his way through the crowd of soldiers. The mail clerk gave him a letter. Morning held it high over his head, "Eat your hearts out," in a tone of voice that led everyone to believe that it was a very special letter from a girlfriend perhaps.

Morning returned to where Green was standing, "Who's the letter from?" Green asked with interest.

"My mother, who knows." Morning stuffed the letter into his pants pocket without looking at the envelope.

"Aren't you going to open it?" Green asked.

"No, maybe later. You know, same old shit. Am I being a good boy, be good, come home safe, ya know, same old shit, your sister is pregnant." Morning stopped and looked at Green. "Did you hear that? My sister is pregnant, wow."

"Don't be an asshole. Christ, Morning. You don't even have a sister." Green cut him off.

"Yeah, yeah, right. Got a cigarette? Hey, any of you guys got a cigarette?" Morning was looking around the crowd of soldiers as they dispersed from the mail call formation. No one paid any attention to Morning as he was being towed by the shirt collar behind Green. Green pulled him along, stopping in front of their hooch.

Morning was in hysterics; he was laughing and stumbling around, bumping into the people around him. The platoon was gathered in front of the number one hooch, in a loose semi-circle, waiting for Sergeant Winters to arrive.

As Sergeant Winters walked to the front of the semi-circle, someone yelled "At ease! At ease!" While

Morning yelled "Surfs up!" Some of the troops around him laughed while others kept yelling "At ease!" to quiet the platoon down so Sergeant Winters would get the meeting/formation over with. It was starting to cut into their beer drinking time. Sergeant Winters would not say a word until everyone was quiet.

"Gentlemen, there will be a recon tomorrow at 0400 hours for Alpha Team, Delta Team will be back up and the C&C Team will have overall control. Team leaders will meet with the Old Man right after this meeting in the operations hooch for details. You people of Alpha and Delta Teams, get your gear squared away and be ready to move out at 0330 hours. Any questions?" There were none. "I would suggest that Alpha Team stay close and lay off the beer. That's it, DISMISSED!" Sergeant Winters turned on his heel and walked away toward the operations hooch. He made it a policy not to stand around with the teams or get too close to these people (as he referred to them both in public and in private). It was not that he didn't like them; they were separated by almost twenty years and they reminded him of his two sons still in high school. He would often write about these troopers to his wife much the same way they had talked about their sons when he was home.

"What the hell, Green? I asked you this afternoon and you said that you didn't know. What's going on man, that you can't tell me stuff? You getting to be big man hanging around the operations hooch and Sergeant Winters?" Morning said for those left to hear. "Man, that really hurts."

"Oh yeah."

"Come on, let's go get a case of beer before you say anything more that will show what a stupid jerk you are." Green walked away from Morning. "Jesus, you're dumb," he said over his shoulder. "Dumb, dumb," Green walked up to PFC Frank Battleford and Fat Turtle. Battleford was bobbing and weaving his head and shoulders. "Where you at, man?" Battleford said to Green.

"Nowhere, man, where you at Bat?" Green replied with the traditional greeting. Battleford fell into step with Green with Fat Turtle following. No one ever said much to Fat Turtle unless they were giving him a hard time.

"Fuck you Green, just fuck you." Morning yelled.

"You're such an asshole Morning, I can't believe it." Green responded.

"Will you knock it off? All the time you sound like two old ladies." Battleford looked back at Morning.

Morning took a few steps and started running, his bootlaces flapping as he ran. He got behind Green and pushed hard. Green, surprised, managed to keep his balance.

"One of these days, Morning, you're going to push too hard." Green turned but kept walking.

Morning started laughing again, his crazy hyena laugh. "Push too hard, that's funny." He repeated the words, turning to Fat Turtle, "Don't you get it? Turtle. Push too . . ."

Fat Turtle rolled his eyes. "That's not funny Morning, you're a cretin." Turtle had almost a year of college behind him when he had joined the Army on a drunken dare.

"What do you mean?" Morning asked.

"That means you're a low life." Battleford laughed.

"No shit." Green added.

"Wow, you're really going to regret this." Morning fell into step with him.

"Somehow, I can almost believe that," Green said.

They walked on up the main company street, the gravel making a crunching sound. On each side were wood and tin hooches that housed the Troop, all low and olive drab in color with spots of black. The sun was low on the horizon but there was no relief from the day's heat. The area had a smell and a forlorn look that Army camps have always had, no matter where they were. The smell of the cooking fire and food mixed with human sweat and waste mingled with the dampness and the mildew of clothing and equipment. Some dogs lay in the shade of the hooches, in the sand to cool their bellies after the heat of the day. The mess hall was just ahead of them. To the far left in back of the mess hall was the garbage of a hundred men on bivouac, and farther away in the open was the Rack, the place where the pots and pans and garbage cans were washed. Two men stood on the Rack, washing what was left of the grease and burned remains of the evening meal. They would be there another two or three hours before their job was finished.

It was common knowledge among the troops of the brigade that the General had said that not one "swing dick" was going out on pass to get laid in Bien Hoa. Not one. "Let them take their fucking sexual frustration out on Charlie and not on some slant eyed, noggy bitch in Bien Hoa." That's what he had said to his Battalion

Commanders and the Battalion Commanders had passed down the word to the Company Commanders and on down the line to the First Sergeants and they in turn had taken things a step further and had developed such tortures as working the Rack or burning shit cans or any number of other jobs they had devised over the past year.

They lounged on old ammo boxes in the darkness, next to the sandbag shelter with their case of Black Label beer that was not cold but lawful in the eyes of the Army.

"Man, did you hear what the movie was at Brigade tonight?"

"No, what?"

"Walt Disney, Walt Fucking Disney's *Cinderella*. That's right man, can you believe it. For Christ sake?"

Morning thought it was funny. Morning's favorites were episodes of *Gunsmoke* and *Combat*. He liked Vic Morrow, who was the platoon sergeant. He also liked the Army that he saw on the screen. It was much more comfortable, clean and orderly than his Army and his life. In his Army, he got laid at the garbage dump almost every day. He'd take the truck filled with garbage cans from the mess hall and go out to the dump. There were always Vietnamese out there, the women and children wearing black with covered heads and heavy leather gloves to protect their hands from the broken glass that was put into the discarded food. Morning said that they strained the food through screens, so they could eat it. He was always careful to keep the broken glass out of his garbage. Each day it was the same.

One time the mess sergeant had caught Morning separating the glass. "What the hell are you doing, Morning?" he said, red-faced, a veteran of Korea.

"None of your goddamn business, Mess Sergeant." Morning did not stop working.

"Do you know what you're doing? Feeding the god damn Cong, you shit head."

"So what, I'm doing the fighting. If you don't like it, get someone else to drive your fucking mess truck. Get someone else to do your dirty work." Morning hefted a garbage can on the back of the truck.

"You're hopeless, Morning, a good for nothing piece of shit. I hope one of them slopes that you're feeding pops a cap in your ass. It would serve you fucking right. Now get the hell out of here and don't let me catch you doing that again." He stalked angrily away.

"Fuck you, you non-combatant son of a bitch. Ain't never seen you out in the shit so it's no god damn concern of yours." Morning didn't say the words very loud so the mess sergeant didn't hear him. If he had, it would have been the Rack for fifteen days. But Morning didn't stop separating the glass from the food.

When Morning would go out to the dump, people knew him and they'd come running up to his truck because they knew that his garbage didn't have glass in it. They would unload his truck carefully, wash it and while they were doing this, Mark-san, as he was called by the kids, went into a hut a little way down the road and got laid by a young girl with a pocked, marked face and drank two or three Tiger beers.

"Mark-san, Mark-san, you number one. Me watch

your truck. It okay, no bomb."

"You better be right about that, you little son of a bitch." Mark-san would take his M-16 from his shoulder and walk around the truck.

31 December 1965: State of the War: U.S. Forces are reporting significant casualties; 1350 KIA, 5300 WIA, 150 MIA or captured during 1965. Direct operational cost of the war for the year was 460 billion dollars. It is estimated that 36,000 NVA troops came down the Ho Chi Minh Trail in the last year.

CHAPTER FIVE

"**M**OES KNOWS, man he knows everything. The CO ain't like other officers." Green pointed out to the rest. They sat around in a group, out in back of the platoon hutch on the bunker, Morning, Battleford, Green, Fat Turtle and the platoon dog, Tango. It was night, cooler only because the sun was not blasting down on them. It felt cooler, still Morning kept sweating, drinking warm beer, working himself into a frenzy on one of his favorite subjects, the officer corps.

"The whole trouble with the Army is the officers." Morning drank out of his beer can which was already mangled from his hand squeezing it. "They've got it too nice, too damn nice. Do we have an officers club and booze? Hell no!"

"Oh, shut up, Morning," Green said, draining his beer can and throwing it at Morning.

"You know I'm right," Morning said in his most righteous, hurt voice. "One time I had to drive the Old Man up to the club and there was music and they were dancing with the Donut Dollies and drinking, and it made me damn mad because you guys were sitting around this damn bunker drinking this hot piss and I had to drive him up there, and couldn't do anything."

"Yeah, I figured them Red Cross girls did more than hand out coffee and donuts." Turtle was being very profound.

"You're really on the god damn ball, Turtle," Battleford said with his New Orleans accent.

"Yeah, you're really on the ball," Morning repeated as did Green.

"Swim fish." Morning added, but Turtle was thinking about the Red Cross girls.

"Say what you want Morning, you instigatin' son of a bitch," Green said, opening another can of Black Label. "But, I'll never forget the sight of Captain Moes comin' outta that Slick with the M-60, layin' down covering fire till we get to the Chopper. Then he comes back and gets me when I'm hit. Shit, no sir, all officers are not alike." Morning shrugged his shoulders in the darkness while Green continued with the story they had all heard at least a dozen times. "And what about when you showed up for the formation in those black high-top tennis shoes and when he sees them not a sign, not a word, that he sees them and all the time Sergeant Winters is quietly going nuts; you march out in front of the formation to get your Bronze dangly thing, with the Bridge Commander standing right there. Jesus, and to top it all off, there are photographers taking pictures for Stars and Stripes. Morning, most CO's would have put you in the stockade for the rest of your life for what you did. But no, Captain Moes makes you permanent Mess Hall truck driver when you're not in the field." Green took a swallow of his beer and lit a cigarette. "Shit, and you think that Captain Moes don't know what you're doing out at the dump. Morning, Moes knows what you're doing out there. He knows, man."

Morning flicked his cigarette into the darkness. "I don't give a damn what the CO knows." Morning looked down at his black high-tops. They weren't so black any more. The one on the right foot was beginning to fray by the little toe and soon there would be a hole. The white laces were gone, they had broken too many times and now the laces were olive drab parachute cord. Morning couldn't help but smile at his high-tops; they were the best he owned. The rest of the guys Fat Turtle and Battleford, held them with the same reverence. They had heard the story of the high-tops a hundred times and they had become as important to them as to Morning.

The others pondered the all-knowing powers of Captain Tom Moes, West Point graduate, Airborne Ranger, Special Forces trained. He already had a total of three years overseas service in the Republic of South Vietnam, going back to 1961. He had taken on the provisional LRRP's at the request of the Bridge Commander – you don't turn down a general. He had created the LRRP's reaching back to Merrill's Marauders, Rangers and Recondo, all special operations units. He had combed the Bridge for a senior NCO who could bring special talent and experience to the Platoon. Most of all, he had a sense of Special Operations Military History. Captain Moes had something else, a sense of humor and a flair for the theatrical. Where this trait came from, even he wasn't sure. It didn't come from his upbringing in the Southwest, and it certainly hadn't been a part of the curriculum of West Point. It was Captain Moes who had authorized the black beret, the tiger stripes and the floppy hat. He had seen to it that all his people received special training with Special Forces, the Vietnamese Parachute and Pathfinder School, and the Delta School, all were cross-trained in communications, weapons, first-aid, ambush, escape and evacuation. As he said himself, they had the ability to operate in Indian Country, in Charlie's backyard, to remain there for days being undetected, raising hell with Charlie's ability to function. Even in a blown mission like the Winters Team, they had come through and had managed to snatch a NVA officer/advisor and brought him back with them. What they got out of him had been the basis for a major operation later.

Captain Moes had been brought up in New Mexico, his father was a rancher. His mother had died when he was five. Both his older brother and his younger sister had stayed on the ranch when he had been awarded an appointment to West Point. Growing up in New Mexico had been the kind of life that other boys only saw in westerns. The three brothers helped their father with ranching duties from the time he could remember. Their summers had been spent in the high country working cattle, sharing the same ground with Navajo and Mexican ranches. They hunted elk and deer in the fall and went to a small town high school during the winter. When it was noted that Tom Moes had ability not only for his studies but also for athletics, the entire Moes family got behind him, cheering him on no matter what sport he was playing. In his senior year when he got his SAT scores back, it was clear that he was probably the smartest kid in New Mexico. There wasn't money to send Tom Moes to college, but a neighbor of long standing suggested he try for West Point.

West Point on the Hudson was a long way from New Mexico. In the beginning, Tom Moes didn't have an easy time of it. Prior to his freshman year, his only contact with the military had been a few John Wayne movies. This was nothing like the "Sands of Iwo Jima". The classes were difficult and the physical expectations demanding; he disliked the hazing from upper classmen, a waste of his time and theirs, he thought. However, before his freshman year was over, he was already starting to make a name for himself. He could run farther and faster than most of his classmates. No matter what sport, he gave a hundred and ten percent with a sense of fair play inherited from generations of hard western life. He also took well to the discipline; he liked knowing who was who and what was what.

By the time he was a senior he had decided to be an Infantry Officer, "Infantry the Queen of Battle." After graduation he went home for part of the summer where he was welcomed like a hero. When it was time to leave once again, he was ready to get on with things. His orders had him reporting to Fort Benning, Georgia, and jump school. After three weeks of running, pushups, deep knee bends, PFF's and then "stand in the door," he found himself standing at the open door of a C-119, flying at 1200 feet, waiting for a jump master to tell him "go". After his first five jumps he was a second lieutenant and a Charlie jumper. Within a week he was on his way to Ranger School and the longest eight weeks of his life to date.

One of the most difficult positions to be in is that of a lieutenant cherry jumper but Tom Moes never notices. He had developed a way of going, a sense of command that most men don't possess in a lifetime. It carried him through one assignment after another and right to Southeast Asia with the 5th Special Forces and now with the 173rd Airborne Bridge and his LRRP's.

~ ~ ~

The conversion stopped and gave way to the sound of the 105th Howitzers firing down the road. The darkness around the bunker was complete, except for one candle flickering on a Black Label beer can sitting in the middle of them. The beer cans stood empty all around, Morning's cans were bent and wrinkled from his excitement. Each one of them were now thinking their own thoughts.

Fat Turtle was thinking of his mother, laughing at his jokes. She thought he was a supply clerk, safe, out of combat. He would have to write her another letter tomorrow complaining about the supply sergeant and how he would never give him any time off. She would write back and sympathize with him; he'd get the letter when he was out on the next operation, and it would make him laugh and feel better.

Green thought of the way it would be when he got out. Go back home with Morning and the two of them would turn home upside down. The girls that were back there, they would be real nice. People would know what he and Morning had done over here. They had done their part more than twice, and they could do what they wanted because they'd earned that right. He and Morning had done the right thing and people would know.

Morning thought of the stupid Army. But it was the best Army around, what did Morning care? Morning didn't care about anything, what was the good of it? "I don't care a damn about anything because when I do, something always happens to mess it up. Yes sir, my name is Mark Morning and I don't give a damn."

Battleford thought of his M-60 machine gun, he'd need to clean it tomorrow. That was the trouble with these guys; they didn't take care of their weapons and then they bitched when they didn't work. He knew he was there to kill gooks and that was it. When he got home he wouldn't have to touch another gun again. He used to like guns, but when he got home, no more. It would be over; he could do anything he wanted. He didn't know exactly what it was now, but there was time to figure it out.

Battleford was the first to get up and got into the tent. After him there was Fat Turtle, Green and Morning. It was dark and Morning couldn't find the candle, so they had to undress in the dark. It was difficult to undress in the dark and crawl under the mosquito-netting tent over the Army cots. Fat Turtle was already asleep and the two boys lay in the dark, listening to him snore.

"Jim?" Morning sat half up, leaning on his elbow.

"What do you want, Morning?"

"Good night Jim," Morning lay back on his back.

"Yeah. Go to sleep, Morning." Jim rolled over onto his side, away from Morning.

There was silence except for Fat Turtle's snoring. The 105's down the road at the New Zealand firing battery began their night fire. Somewhere between them and War Zone D the rounds were exploding on the unseen enemy. Morning tried to roll over onto his stomach but caught his foot in the mosquito netting. He cursed and untangled his feet.

"Hey, Jim?" It was Morning.

"What?" Green had been listening to Morning roll over.

"Do you think the operation tomorrow will be bad?"

Green grunted.

"Do you?" Morning persisted.

"You've been here as long as I have. They're all the same."

"Yeah, you're right." Morning was silent for a while. "How long do you think we'll be out this time?"

"I don't know maybe a month." Green sat up with a can of bug spray in his hand.

"Let's go over to Quartermaster laundry and take a bath."

"What for?" Green sprayed the mosquito netting with the bug spray.

"I don't know, for Christ sake. Let's just do it. Okay?"

"Find a light then. I'm not going to kill myself trying to get out of bed in the dark."

Morning got out of bed, getting his feet tangled up

in the mosquito netting again. He went down to the end bunk by the door and took Carlson's flashlight off the ammunition box and walked outside where the generator sat. After putting gas into it and two pulls on the rope, he got the generator started and the two naked light bulbs flickered on inside the tent. Morning came back into the light of the tent. He didn't have any clothes on.

"What's going on?" Battleford sat up in bed, looking around.

"Me and Jim are going to get a bath. Want to come?"

"Naw." Battleford rolled over onto his side away from the light bulb. "Unscrew one of the lights, will you?"

Morning grunted an answer, looking for his towel. Green got out of bed and wrapped his towel around his waist.

"You seen my damn towel?" Morning was standing in the middle of the aisle, scratching his head and looking around the tent. "Hey, Bat, did you use the towel?" Morning walked over in the direction of Battleford's cot.

"Will you turn off the fucking light then?"

"Yeah, I'm looking for my towel. If I had a towel I'd turn off the light."

"Well, take the god damn towel and get the hell out of here." Battleford sat up in bed to look at Morning standing in the aisle naked. "Oh, for Christ sake, will you take the towel and get out of here and don't forget the light."

"All right, already, I'm turning off the light. What

the hell are you getting so excited for?" Morning stepped up on one of the cots and unscrewed the light bulb. "There, you happy?"

"Yeah, I'm happy. I hope you drown, you son of a bitch."

Morning just laughed and wrapped the towel around his waist and he and Green walked outside into the darkness. They walked across the road past the orderly room and down to the creek, across the creek and up the other side. Both were being very quiet; they weren't supposed to be by the tubs of water. The Quartermaster laundry had been set up to do the sheets for the 120th surgical hospital down the road a few hundred yards. The tubs were high black rubber containers that were filled to do the next day's washing. They had been told a week before to stay away from the laundry or they'd get an Article 15. This had increased Morning's interest in using the newfound facility even though he had little use for baths or showers.

They walked quietly up to the big tub; Morning pulled back the tarp that was over the tub.

"This is like the movies when the good guys are sneaked up on by the bad guys." Morning was play-acting like in the movies, over-exaggerating his sneaking around the tub.

"Yeah." Green was laughing quietly to himself.

"And then the good guy is sneaking into the water and the shots ring out. Bang, bang, bang." Morning, playing as if he were shot, fell into the water.

"Then his buddy is trying to help him and some more shots were fired and his pal falls dead." Green fell into the water next to Morning and played as if he were dead, his body floating on top of the water.

"Yeah, and his buddy gets real mad and starts throwing hand grenades with his shot-up arm." Morning starts throwing hand grenades at the imagined enemy, until he is ripped apart by the pretend machine gun as he throws his last grenade and knocks out the enemy machine gun. Morning falls into the water as if dead. Green can't hold his breath any longer and comes up laughing. He and Morning stand in the water, waist deep, laughing at one another. "Would you really do that if I got killed? Would you, Green?"

"Yeah, I guess I would." They both started washing now with Green's soap.

After they finished washing they got out of the tub and put the tarp back onto the tub. They dried themselves off and went back the way they had come to the hutch. When they stepped inside, the one light was still on. Carlson sat on the edge of his bunk writing a letter; he looked up at Green and Morning as they came in and nodded.

Most of the hutch, looking shabby and bedraggled, was in darkness. Half the floor was wood; the other half was dirt; the supply of boards had run out when they were putting down the floor. Most of the cots were on the wooden side and crowded together. Each cot had a mosquito net over it supported by sticks so that each mosquito net went off in a different direction. Each cot stood for a man in the platoon and each cot had an ammunition box for a bedside table. Equipment hung from each bunk and an M-16 rifle, hanging from the cross bar, held up the netting. The overall effect was one of subsistence; poverty with its accompanying sweat, dampness and mildew filled the air. In the middle of the floor lay a beer can.

Green went to his bunk and lit a cigarette. Morning stood in the aisle.

"What you doin', Carlson?"

"Writing a letter to my wife." Carlson looked up.

"You're wasting your time. She's out fucking some guy right now."

"Shut your face, Morning." Carlson looked down at his letter.

"Make it a good letter because after tomorrow all she'll have is that letter and your insurance to share with the guy she's screwing tonight."

"Shut up, Morning, and get over here." Green spoke without getting up from his cot.

Carlson got up and walked toward Morning who stood his ground, a grin on his face.

"What you say, Morning?" Carlson was trying to give Morning a way out.

"You heard me."

The two looked at one another for a minute and Morning turned around. "Everybody wake up. Carlson feels froggy and he thinks he's going to jump on my chest." Morning was shouting loud enough to wake up Battleford, who sat up. Fat Turtle awoke, asking what all the noise was about. Green sat on his bunk, waiting for Carlson to do whatever he was going to do.

"I told you to shut your face, Morning." Carlson stood with his fists clenched by his side. He knew that he was new but he didn't have to take this and he didn't care how long Morning had been around. "Shut your god damn face, Morning." Carlson said again.

"You're going to get yourself killed tomorrow and your wife's going to get $10,000."

Carlson walked up to Morning, swinging wide; his fist hit Morning on the side of the face. Morning staggered but didn't fall; the punch wasn't strong enough.

Green stood and started for the aisle. "Carlson, that's enough. You gave Morning what he deserved."

By his own action Carlson had made himself madder. "Then you tell that son of a bitch to shut his mouth." He was pointing his finger at Morning whose grin had changed to a glare.

"I ain't gonna shut up. Your wife fucks for the troops."

Carlson lunged for Morning; at the same time Green stepped in front of him. "If you're going to fight, go outside. You hear me Morning?"

"Morning, put the knife away." It was Battleford at the other end of the tent.

Morning had taken a bayonet from the nearest bunk. Green turned around to look at Morning. "Carlson, go back to your bunk." Carlson saw the knife and did what he was told.

"Morning, put it down or I'll take it." Green looked at Morning. Almost at the same time he dove for the hand that held the knife. It happened too fast for Morning. Green already had the hand that held the knife and at the same time they both fell on the bunk behind Morning. The knife fell from Morning's hand; Green grabbed it and threw it in the direction of Battleford who was now standing. The knife stuck into the wood floor and Battleford grabbed it. Green could feel that the fight had gone out of the body of Morning when he lost the knife. He picked himself off Morning.

"Go out back, Morning."

Morning looked at Green, got up and walked down the aisle to the back door of the tent and went outside.

"Carlson, keep your mouth shut, it's forgotten."

"I didn't mean to hit him. But he shouldn't have said what he did."

"Just shut up, Carlson, and finish writing your letter." Green headed toward the back door.

"Don't take Morning so seriously." Fat Turtle said, looking over at Carlson.

"He shouldn't have said all that crap."

"He's always saying stuff like that. He doesn't mean it but he'd have killed you if Green hadn't stopped him."

"Go back to bed, Turtle," Battleford yelled. "You talk too much yourself." Battleford got back into bed. "Just forget it." Fat Turtle went back to his cot.

In the dark, Morning stood next to the bunker. He didn't question what he had just done. What he questioned was whether Green really was his friend after all. Hell, it had been Green and him against everything ever since they had got to Vietnam. Now he wasn't so sure. Green was really the only one he could trust; they had known each other a long time and now that they were over here he thought that Green had understood. But Green had taken Carlson's part; he couldn't believe it.

Green came out of the tent into the darkness. He stood at the door until his eyes got accustomed to the darkness.

"Morning?"

"What you want, Jim?"

"What did you do that for?" Green asked.

"No reason, I just did it."

"But why?" Green stood next to Morning now at the bunker.

Morning stood without answering Green. He couldn't. They listened to the sound of the 105's, looked into the darkness that was a rubber tree plantation, two outposts and several guard posts. It was late now, two o'clock in the morning. They would leave at four or five.

"Carlson didn't want to hit you," Green said.

Morning shrugged his shoulders, but didn't answer.

"We better go to bed," Green said.

Mark Morning turned towards the tent; in slow plodding steps he began to walk to the tent, his home, his bed; he would find his black tennis shoes and wear them tonight before the operation tomorrow.

Green stood watching him; Mark Morning, what has become of you? You would have killed Carlson. Oh Mark, I can't look out for you all the time. We've changed, you and I, and there's nothing to do for either of us, nothing. There's a part of us that's already dead, dead, dead. Green leaned against the bunker, the firing of the Howitzers down the road in his ears; he would only be aware of them again when they stopped firing. What's left for you? Was this what we were born to? Green shook his head, but Mark didn't know it and there was no way he could tell him. What could he tell Mark, that he was crazy? What would that mean? They were all crazy. Green smiled ruefully in the darkness. No, there was nothing he could tell Mark. Green heard the radio playing in the tent; it was late. He heard Morning singing to the music, his favorite song, "Hang On, Snoopy, Hang On," Green moved away from the bunker and headed for the door of the hutch; he felt tired, very tired.

Too soon, they were all in the truck. The men had kept their helmets on and taken their camouflaged shirts and rolled them up. Morning was sitting on his. "You think this fakes out Charlie" Morning was saying.

Fat Turtle at the other end of the truck yelled down, "It sure confuses the hell out of me."

"Who in the god damn hell was talking to you anyway, Turtle," Morning yelled back.

"At ease, god damn it, we're just about there," Sergeant Winters said.

The heavy five-ton cargo truck sped down the road behind the gun jeep. The men in the jeep and the driver of the truck were dressed alike: green camouflaged helmets with tinted green goggles, heavy green flack-jackets with a green T-shirt underneath. They appeared to be men without ages, going down the asphalt road, the reconnaissance platoon being taken to its jump off point.

The men in the recon platoon didn't pay any attention to the jeep or the driver of the truck. They seemed like part of the asphalt road, the open land between them and the rotting jungle foothills that lay 1000 meters from the road. They sat smoking in the back of the truck; they weren't allowed to smoke on patrol. They sat in the back of the truck shouting and talking since they could only speak in whispers on patrol. On patrol their eyes and their ears strained for sound, their nostrils and mouth filled with the smell of the rotting bamboo jungle, and their own sweat; the jungle chlorophyll made them sick to their stomachs. There they felt closed in, more closed in than if they were in a box. They would walk with the weight of the rucksacks on their backs, making their neck muscles strain and tighten until they were taut. Legs and feet became heavy and at the last minute would feel unwieldy, and the men would have trouble controlling them. They would look awkward and clumsy walking through the jungle that had bamboo, swamp, and underbrush so thick the patrol could only crawl under it. Some men told of walking fifteen feet above the jungle floor on woven vines that made up the underbrush, which was a barrier stronger than any cement wall.

The truck slowed down and turned off the road into a rubber tree plantation. "Let's go, everyone out." Sergeant Winters got off the truck and the rest of the men followed. They went into the trees. "Spread out, damn it." They reached the first dike. They were all busy putting on their face paint, green and black. Morning was making a design on his face. "Come on, let's go, let's go." Captain Moes was whispering, going up and down the dike. They put their helmets and shirts into the bag that was passed around; the driver of the truck would take it back with him.

"Green, take the point," Captain Moes, the CO, said. "Move out."

The men started walking through the dark, cool rubber tree plantation. They moved in silence. The platoon moved out of the rubber trees into scrub, a long line of camouflaged uniforms, hats and weapons. They moved swiftly and silently.

"This is just like a god damn movie I saw once. No kidding." Morning said, picking his way through the thick growth. "In the movie they all got killed though. I hope this isn't the same movie."

"Make sure they get your best profile. When in the hell are we going to take a break?" Battleford said. He was sinking into the soft ground. "Shit."

They kept moving. They moved out of the rubber tree plantation.

"I knew Green before he went into the Army," Morning said.

The column stopped and the men were bent forward at the waist, squatting or kneeling, waiting. The column started moving again.

"This is nothing but a bare fuck," Turtle said.

"Remember what happened to Sergeant Jones when he said that."

Turtle didn't say anything.

"Yeah, if people back home could see Green now they wouldn't believe it." Morning moved closer to Battleford. "I always figured he'd go to college and horse around. But he just joined up. Then he didn't become an officer or anything." Morning stumbled over a vine. "So now look at him up there on the point. That's one guy I don't understand."

The column kept moving with Green in front. It moved through the scrub and the land became swampy; the ground was half water. The going was hard, the column stopped again and the men waited. Word came back that they were going to cross a road.

Sergeant Winters went down the road to the south. Battleford went up the road to the north. The men were crossing, then moving along the road to the north.

The word was that the whole operation was called off. Everyone was going back to base camp. Morning was saying, "If we're going to fight, let's. Otherwise, let's all go home."

There was the sound of one shot. Everyone frozen where they were, waiting. There was another and another, and then the M-16 rifle went on automatic. "I thought the operation was called off ..." They went on down the road. "I just wish they would make up their mind," Morning said. He was running down the road.

Sergeant Winters crouched in the grass beside the road. "Stay off the god damn road."

"Where are they?" Morning asked, getting off the road. He let off a burst into the jungle along the side of the road.

"They went down the road, Green went after them." Sergeant Winters didn't move. More of the platoon was coming down the road.

"Oh, for Christ sake." Morning was off down the road after Green. He moved fast and stayed close to the ground. Green was standing in the middle of the road.

"What the hell are you doing?" Morning was fooling with the magazine in his M-16.

"Nothing. What are you doing?" Green stood there looking.

"I'm playing war ..."

Pop, pop, pop. Both boys jumped to the side of the road.

"You see where they came from?" Morning was

breathing hard.

"No." Green took the safety off his weapon. He opened up in the general direction he thought the shots came from. Morning took a hand grenade, pulled the pin, and threw it in the same direction. They waited for the explosion. It came. There was no return fire.

"Did Winters get one?" Morning asked. Green shrugged his shoulders. "We were going to meet his jeep at the end of that road."

The rest of the platoon had moved down the road on each side. Now they were waiting. Three gun jeeps came along the road now. They stopped in front of Morning and Green.

"They went that-a-way." Morning pointed down the road. The gun jeeps headed down the road. "The gun jeeps have run into some small arms fire..." A few minutes later they came back.

"We called an air strike."

The Yellow smoke was starting to rise now from a smoke grenade that had been thrown to pinpoint the position.

"Hop on, we're getting out of here," the car commander said. Green and Morning jumped on; a cavalry soldier held onto Green so that he would not fall off. Other men from the platoon were trying to get on too. The rest were running behind the gun jeeps.

The little plane flew very low, hovering over the yellow smoke. The plane was called FAC forward air control. The men liked watching the plane; they would point when she shot off one of the rockets to pinpoint a position for one of the jets that seemed far away. The FAC was close to the men on the ground and they understood it. The jets were far away, very fast, and the men didn't feel as close to them.

Morning was play-acting that he was a jet plane pilot holding the stick that controlled the jet and at the same time pressing the imaginary button that fired the 20-millimeter cannon. He swooped to the right, firing, then swooped to the left. Leaning to the left his dark eyes squinted right, almost closed, his whole body shaking as if under great stress from shooting the cannon as the plane screamed through the air.

"Rat-a-tat-tat...Man, I should have been a god damn jet pilot."

"Shut up, Morning, and get on the truck." Green sat on the bench that ran along the side of the truck. He held out his hand for Morning to take hold so that he could pull himself on.

"Oh man." Morning took hold of Green's hand and pulled himself up onto the truck. "Can't I have any fun? A guy starts to enjoy himself and they always tell him to get on a truck or something."

Green paid no attention to Morning as he went on about jet planes and "the problem with the ..." Green sank back onto the side railing of the truck with his rifle between his legs, the muzzle pointing upward. His eyes followed one of the jets as it made its bombing run. The rest of the men watched, except for Morning who was too busy flying his own mission from the seat of the truck.

"Boom! Boom! I just shot off some rockets." Morning was leaning to the right onto Green's shoulders, banking the jet.

Green looked at Morning scornfully.

Morning stopped in mid-bank. "Man, what's your pain?" Green shook his head, disgusted. "Maybe I want to get up in the world. You ever think of that, son of a bitch?"

"Cram it. You're more interested in getting to the airmen's club back at the base."

"That's a damn lie."

" You know damn well those jet pilots sleep between sheets every night and have a mama san polish their boots. They get up at five in the morning, stretch, and get to the mess hall to have some real bacon and eggs. They fly for a few hours, come back, and sip a few drinks by the pool as they get a tan."

Morning grunted and spit over the side of the truck.

"And what do we do? We sit in the mud up to our assholes and think they're real hot shots or something." Green took a cigarette out of his pocket. Most of the pack was wet from sweat.

"My ass. Those guys got to settle their nerves."

"Nerves, my ass," Battleford put in. This brought a laugh from Fat Turtle and some of the other men who had been listening to Green and Morning.

"Who asked you, Batman?" Morning returned. He had stopped altogether playing jet plane.

"Nobody Fish," Battleford said. This brought another laugh from Fat Turtle.

"Morning, you couldn't fly a broomstick, so shut your mouth for awhile." Green found a cigarette that wasn't wet and lit it.

Sergeant Winters climbed into the bed of the truck. Morning shoved over for him. "Where in the hell you guys think you are?" He stood up now. "All you do is talk, talk like old ladies. You're all so full of bullshit you got diarrhea of the mouth."

Morning made a noise with his mouth, made by running his fingers over his lips.

Sergeant Winters turned around. "Morning, straighten the fuck up." Morning shrugged his shoulders. "Listen boys, opinions are like assholes; everybody's got one and right now Morning you're overloading yours." The rest of the men in the truck laughed. "Now, all of you, stop screwing around and start looking on the flanks of this truck before Charlie pops a cap in all our asses."

The truck's engine started; the forward motion of the truck moved them down the asphalt road. The men turned and watched over the side, holding their rifles at the ready.

The driver drove for an hour; the road was deserted except for the truck and the jeep escort. The sun was high and hot; the wind from the fast-moving truck was no help; it was hot too. Most of the men had given up looking and were dozing to the rhythm of the truck moving along the road. The face paint they had put on that morning had nearly sweated off and now their faces looked dirty as they slept.

"Wake up, we're someplace," one of the men who had stayed awake to watch over the side called out. Each man woke the other next to him as they passed a roadblock with a machine gun and four American soldiers eating c-rations in the afternoon sun. The men waved at one another. Now they were going between open fields cluttered with poncho shelters and mortar positions, and on the far side armored personnel carriers. The men looked up at the passing truck with its camouflaged passengers, then resumed their eating, reading, cleaning and dozing. In the middle of the field there stood four helicopters.

The truck slowed down and turned off the road in a cloud of dust and headed for the helicopters. The truck geared down with a great deal of engine noises and shouting by the men from being bounced around, then it made a wide circle and stopped, the driver getting out and coming to the back to let the tailgate down. Sergeant Winters turned and told the men to be at ease; then he jumped to the ground.

"Follow me, men," Sergeant Winters yelled walking to the left side of the truck.

Each man climbed out of the truck, watched by the soldiers that were already there.

"Look at the Sneaky Petes." Laughter came from the crown.

"Take off you guys, got someplace to be," Sergeant Winters said. These men began to wander back to their shelter.

The platoon from the truck got into a loose formation, all talking to one another.

"At ease. Clear your weapons and take the magazines out." This was done. "Fall out and eat, but stay by the truck. You hear me, Morning and Green."

"Yes, Sergeant," they both called from the rear of the formation.

The men fell out and stood in the shade of the truck to eat.

"Man, I'm all itchy." Morning took off his

equipment, then his shirt and began to rub his back against the side of the truck, up and down, then sideways.

"Try taking a bath," someone muttered. This brought a muted laugh from the men around him.

"Anybody got water?" Turtle called out. "I'm out."

"Sergeant Winters said he was going to get some," a voice said. Turtle sat on the ground to wait for Sergeant Winters to bring water.

"Anybody want to trade for some ham and lima beans?" A man sat leaning against the front wheel of the truck, holding a green can.

"Yeah, I got some shit," Morning yelled back. The man didn't answer him. The platoon settled down to opening cans and cooking their c-rations over heat tablets that came from the bottom of someone's pack. Others were already lying on their backs asleep. Sergeant Winters came back with two cans of water. This caused a stir for a few minutes.

Captain Moes and Sergeant Winters sat in the front seat of a gun jeep. Captain Michelson had a canteen in his hand to wash down a piece of c-ration bread.

"Looks like we found something." Captain Moes had just come from a briefing with the Battalion Headquarters. "The old man wants us to go back into the area in front of the first battalion, keeping radio contact. When we find something, they'll be there to help us."

Sergeant Winters sat nodding to what the Captain was saying.

"We'll leave tomorrow morning at sunrise by chopper." Captain Moes took a map from the cargo pocket of his pants. The map was covered with acetate so that he could write on it with a grease pencil and be able to cross out the writing if he had to. He opened the map, put it on the steering wheel of the jeep, placing the open canteen of water on the hood of the jeep. "We'll land at LZ Bulldog." He pointed to a circle drawn on the map around the clearing. "The battalion will land here at LZ Hound Dog." He pointed to a landing zone in a clearing about a quarter of a mile away. "We'll both head north to here," said the Captain pointing to a green dot on the map that showed hill marking, "to Hill 69. By then we'll be together with the platoon in front."

Sergeant Winters nodded and made marks on his map. They sat talking as the sun started to go down. It was becoming cooler. "I guess we better talk to the platoon."

"Right, Sergeant Winters, call the men together."

Sergeant Winters got out of the jeep and headed for the truck where the men were lying around asleep. He counted to himself the number of days that he had left. One hundred and eighty one days before he would be back at the jump school at Fort Benning with his wife. Two of the instructors that he'd known were already dead; one had been killed last week. Well, it was only one hundred and eighty one days; he could make it through that; hell he was already short.

"Let's go. Everyone around the truck." The men that were by the front of the truck got up and wandered to the rear.

"Looks like we're going out." Green rolled over, waking up Morning.

"Thought the operation was called off. Who in the

94

hell started that rumor anyway?" Morning sat up on one elbow.

"You did, son of a bitch" Green replied, handing Morning a cigarette.

"Thanks." Morning took the cigarette.

Sergeant Winters was standing on the bed of the truck. "Make sure you've got your equipment together. We'll be moving out while it's still dark."

Morning puffed on his cigarette while Sergeant Winters explained the details of the operation.

"Anybody that needs ammunition or grenades, see me later at the jeep. Green, you'll be point in the morning. Captain Moes wants to talk to you, so come over to the jeep."

Morning nudged Green in the side. "You'll make sergeant before you know it."

"Don't hold your breath," Green sat up, making ready to see Captain Moes.

"Any questions?" Sergeant Winters called out. There were none; he got off the truck and walked towards the jeep joined by Specialist Four Green. They walked across the open space between the truck and the jeep; it was beginning to get dark.

"Hello sir." Green stood in front of Captain Moes.

"Green." The captain nodded his head in recognition. "We'll want you for the point tomorrow."

"Okay, sir." Green smiled, reaching in back of him and scratching, making his stomach protrude.

"No questions?"

"No, Sir." Green turned to go back to the truck.

"Green, wait a minute."

Green turned around and took the three steps back

to the jeep.

"I'm putting you in for sergeant stripes. You've done a fine job in the platoon. Sergeant Winters recommends you and I'm passing it along to you. You've done a fine job. Thank you. That's all. You go and get some sleep."

Green felt his face flush; he was glad that it had gotten too dark for the captain to see. "Thank you, Sir." Green turned and walked in the direction of the truck. He felt quiet, a good feeling that made him smile as he walked.

He got back to the truck and found Morning rolled up in his poncho.

"Hey, Morning." Green found his rucksack and took out his poncho, opened it, laid it on the ground and lay down on top of it on his back, looking up at the blue-black sky. The stars were the only light, the moon hadn't come up yet.

"What?" Morning had his head covered. He looked much like a mummy lying on the ground.

"I got put in for sergeant. The old man told me." Green got out his bug repellant, putting it on his face, neck, hand and arms.

"When you going to get the stripe?" Morning stayed covered, not moving from his mummy position.

"I don't know. Maybe when we get back."

Morning grunted.

"What's your pain?"

"You man. What you want to be sergeant for anyway?" Morning unwrapped himself from the poncho and sat up.

"That's getting over, being a buck sergeant and all.

That's why, son of a bitch." Green took a cigarette from his pocket. Rolling over on his stomach he lit the match, cupping it in his hands to keep down the light.

"Well, I'm really impressed, no kidding. Old Sergeant Green sits at the NCO table, goes to the NCO Club. Yes, you'll make a fine sergeant, you will." Morning reached over into Green's pocket, took his cigarettes, extracted one, and put the pack back. It was Morning's way of showing defiance to Green for his new rank.

"Are you going to take care of your pals?"

"Sure I am. What do you think?"

"I think them stripes will go to your head, that's what I think." Morning lay back down, smoking very quietly. Morning flipped his cigarette in the same direction as Green's.

"Naw, just different. Remember the water when we went swimming down at Vong Tow in the South China Sea? Even the water was more salty than at home."

Morning thought this over for a few minutes. "Yeah, I guess it was." Morning paused, they had gone as far on the subject of Vietnam being different as they could. "When you make sergeant, you can be my sugar daddy."

Green smiled. "I'll take care of you, Morning."

CHAPTER SIX

IT WAS DARK; any previous conversation had been suppressed by the overpowering darkness. Morning rolled up his poncho again, he looked like a mummy. It was hot inside the poncho and he began to sweat but he felt safer wrapped up. He closed his eyes and waited for sleep.

They had been pinned down all day. It was still early when the recon patrol met with the battalion at the foot of Hill 69. On this hill was a North Vietnamese regiment. Green hadn't seen the 50-caliber machine guns because they had been waiting in an ambush. No one realized the fields of fire as they passed through.

The dead numbered fifty or sixty; no one knew for sure yet and there was no way to get a body count. Green hadn't seen Morning all day. The battalion pulled back to the foot of the hill to organize for the assault. Captain Moes lay on the ground next to the company commander of "C" Company. "C" Company was in the middle on the left flank. "B" Company was spread out and pinned down, the company commander had been killed at the beginning of the day. "A" Company was on the right flank of "C", but they had started at half strength, leaving men back at base camp for guard. There only the platoon sergeant left from the First Platoon. The rest were dead or wounded. Headquarters Company hadn't come, their orders had been misread the day before. The Battalion

Commander was back at base camp.

Captain Moes knew that he had lost ten men in the early part of the day. The rest were either dead or had integrated with Troop E. There had been nothing they could do. They had called in air strikes and artillery on the Viet Cong. Still, they couldn't move. The Viet Cong had quad fifty-caliber machine guns; the bullets were like golf balls, red-hot golf balls that could tear off an arm, a leg, or tear the muscles from your chest.

Morning hadn't seen anybody all day; he sat behind an anthill. He just sat there with his back to the anthill and picked at his jungle rot. He had been there almost all day. He should really do something, he thought. Where were the others, Green, Battleford, Fat Turtle. They weren't dead, he knew that. Think of something besides the shooting and the killing, the ambush. Maybe he should think of home. A girl, that's what he'd think about, but Morning couldn't think of any girl worth thinking about. Besides, who could think of a woman at a time like this? "Damn it, Morning, do something, even if it's wrong," he said to himself. Nobody answered. So Private Mark Morning just sat there behind the four-foot anthill, not taking part in the battle going on around him.

Fat Turtle lay on his back eating a can of peaches. Oh, if they could see me now, Turtle thought. Turtle knew that they would try to get up on line again and take the hill. They had tried three times before that day, but it hadn't worked and a whole lot of guys had been zapped. He remembered the new guy that never said too much to anybody. The first time that they had tried to get on line, the kid had stood up and he had his thumb shot off and he fell down, and then got up again and he got shot again and he fell down again. Then he stood up again, but this time he just fell down with a real stupid expression on his face. He just lay there and the medic came and put a first aid dressing over his thumb and took off his shirt and fixed him up the best he could, and the new guy just lay there. Turtle asked if he was all right and the guy just held up his hand and said that his thumb was shot clean off. Fat Turtle couldn't get over it, how stupid the new guy was to keep getting up. Now, that's doing what you're told, Fat Turtle thought, throwing the empty can into the jungle.

Green lay flat on his stomach, his head propped up on his arm. He could feel the dampness from the ground seeping through his shirt. He felt tired, so tired that he could hardly keep his eyes open. Green smiled to himself, at least combat didn't affect his sleep. He remembered the time he and Morning were with the first battalion and they got pinned down with them in the middle of a rice paddy. A whole company was spread out along one dike and the NVA had them right by the ass. Green's eyes flickered shut; jerking his whole head he got them open again. It was a lot like today, only then they were out in the open and that was bad, real bad. All day they had stayed there behind the stupid dike, mostly in the water. When they started to get up, they'd get the shit shot out of them and they would fall behind the dike again. The only difference was that there were less of them alive, and then the wounded made a hell of a noise out in the hot sun. Green's eyes began to fall asleep again, and again he jerked his head up to reopen his eyes. He reached into the pocket that was sewn to the top part of his left sleeve and took out a small bottle. Inside were an assortment of pills – pills for colds, pills for malaria, pills for water, pills for everything, including staying awake, all Army issued! Cross tops that's what they were; he took two and a vitamin pill and reached back for his canteen. He washed them down with stagnant water he'd picked up in the morning. Green wondered what the cross tops were, they were either Benzedrine or Dexedrine, but he wasn't sure. Boy, did he get high on them. Getting high on the Army, Green smiled. He wondered where the rest of the guys were, that god damn Morning. What was the difference between our Army and the North Vietnamese Army? They get high on pot and we get high on dex, or something like that. Wild! Wild! Wild man!

Green waited for the drugs to take over; at least they kept him awake. Awake, awake, he really should stay awake. They had stayed behind that fucking dike all day. It was only fifty yards to the wood line where the NVA were, but they couldn't make that fucking fifty yards. Maybe it would be like that again here on this stupid hill. They'd waited till almost dark and then came the air strikes, napalm, and the whole ball of wax. Too much man, that's what Morning had said. They couldn't make it across that fifty yards because the water slowed them too much; too much time in the open and you're dead. Dead, man! Green hated the open areas; sometimes he knew that he was getting so paranoid that he could hardly walk. Green forgot what he was thinking about for a moment, and then it was back. Fifty yards, fifty yards, one-half of a football field and in that fifty yards, just about a whole company of men are dead. Over a hundred guys, fifty yards, that's what the gooks had on them most of the time. Right now it was fifty yards and they were pinned down and fucked up and he couldn't even find Morning, that son of a bitch. It was always the same, go out and look for the NVA and then when you found them, it was fifty yards. No one knew about the fifty yards, no one, only the dead and they weren't going to tell. I know, but then maybe this is the fifty yards that's going to get me. Green smiled to himself and looked at the fifty yards, but he didn't move from where he lay.

Then the air strikes came. He'd been sleeping and Morning woke him because he said it was neat to look at. The planes, like the ones in the old World War II movies, came in slow, real slow, and dropped the napalm. All of them that were still alive, could smell the smell of them burning over there in the wood line and a lot of guys said they could hear them screaming. The planes dropped a lot of it, and then the men moved out and they still got a lot of fire. There was close-up fighting in many places, but it was the smell that Green remembered, nothing else but the smell. Green looked up, he thought that he smelled the napalm and the burning flesh now, but it's probably the pills, he thought.

It was dark when they got to the wood line and they couldn't really see what they were doing, so it made no difference. Kill or be killed. Boy, they're right. States, Green thought, the goddamn fucking States. Man, he could read and see what they were saying, all the stuff they were saying about him and Morning, and that god damn Morning didn't know the difference, but that was all right. They didn't know what they were talking about but they pretended they did. They said a lot of things about the war being wrong and it was talk, just talk. I could kill any one of those son of a bitches and get a thousand years in jail. Kill or be killed, that's what he'd been told to do and so that's what he was doing. He'd seen pictures of those protesters carrying signs, calling him a murderer, a baby killer and stuff. Yeah --- they go to school and are told what to read and what to think by some punk professor, and then they go out and bad mouth us. Those damn fuckers.

He was fighting for them and all they did was bad mouth him and the rest of the slobs that were here waiting to move on that fifty yards; and the only thing those protesters know about fifty yards is that it's half of a football field. They don't know that fifty yards can kill you. If he wasn't doing what was right, then what was he doing? He didn't know. They were all talking back home and what did they know? Like Sergeant Winters says, opinions are like assholes, everybody's got one and that doesn't mean a thing. So, it doesn't make a difference what anyone says. Only he was the one that had to pay for that fifty yards and fuck them back home, that's all, fuck them all. School, all that irrelevant school talk. Pity, he thought, pity, alas poor Yorick. There's no way out, I'm lost. Green lay biting his hand because he knew when the word came down to move out, he would and would do it again and again, and he was lost and there was nothing that could be done.

There were so many wounded now. They were all

lying closing together, the dead and the wounded side by side. All around was the screaming sound of fighting, the rapid firing of automatic weapons, the pop of small arms fire from both sides, explosions of hand grenades, a radiomen trying to get contact. But from the wounded there was no sound. The chaplain sat next to his assistant who was dead. It was five o'clock and time for the rain and it fell on the dead, on the chaplain, and on the Viet Cong somewhere on the hill.

All the men that weren't wounded got up, very slowly and not standing but hunched over. They were all firing their weapons and it was still raining, and it was hard to see. Green got up with the rest, as did Battleford with his M-60 machine gun. They would fire and move, fire and move. Morning left his anthill now. He was next to Green, but neither of them paid any attention to the other. They moved together without realizing it. They fired and killed the unseen enemy. Now they stopped, hid themselves as best they could, waiting for the order. Morning looked at Green. He didn't look the same anymore; he'd never look the same. They waited for the next order and then they carried it out.

The men fell back around the wounded and the company command post. It was night and they wouldn't move until morning. The artillery was firing and would fire all night. It would keep the Viet Cong disorganized, and in the morning they would drive them off the hill and then leave, taking their dead and wounded with them back to base camp. The men that were alive would get drunk and talk about it then they'd feel better and it'd be time for another operation again.

Green, Morning and the rest of the company waited in the dark for the unseen enemy. The rain continued. From the humid, wet dark came the bugle and drum and symbol of the NVA, the night fighting had begun. Round after round was fired into the darkness and the enemy came, trying to encircle the company of the wounded, the dead and the men who were left to fight. Time and again they tried, shadows moving from tree to tree. Battleford was on one knee firing his machine gun, with the wounded around him. Each time he fired, death came. All through the night the Viet Cong tried to encircle the company, but Battleford, joined by Green and the other men kept firing their weapons. They called artillery in on their own position. In the morning the Viet Cong were gone.

All the dead couldn't be found so men were sent out to find them. Demolition men cleared a place for a helicopter to land. The first chopper brought in men that were fresh and clean with chain saw and axes. These men were clean-shaven and worked hard and fast. The men that had been fighting all night moved slowly, they were dirty, unshaven and their clothes were torn. The men wore the filth and their ragged uniforms as a badge. All had that 1000-yard stare in their eyes.

Battleford sat on a log, his M-60 machine gun on his knees, he was looking at the dead. Morning sat next to him eating chicken and noodles from a c-ration can. Green and Turtle came down the trail and joined them.

Morning dug into his pockets for a cigarette but they were all wet. He cursed silently, looking around. He saw one of the men who had come in on the first chopper, he was leaning on his ax, his job finished.

"Hey man, got a cigarette?" Morning got up stiffly from the log and walked over to the man.

"Sure." The soldier dug into his pockets, he was glad to give him the cigarette. The two of them looked at each other. "It got pretty bad." The man made the statement.

"Yeah, we got into the shit this time." Morning smoked the cigarette. A dust-off chopper came in and the air was filled with sound and wind and things blowing from the ground. Morning helped put the dead into the dust-off; they were wrapped in ponchos and heavy. The chopper left with its load and it was quiet again. The two men looked at each other. "See ya later," the soldier said. "Take it easy." Morning walked back to the log.

"Hey, Batman," Morning said. "Where are you at, man."

The Batman looked at Morning. "No, no, nowhere man. Nowhere." Battleford looked at his M-60. "It's jammed." He looked at his weapon again.

"When did that happen?" Morning looked at the weapon too.

"I d-d-don't know." Battleford was stuttering badly. "I can't m-make it work."

"Let me see." No move was made; they just sat there. The weapon was forgotten. Private Battleford didn't want to fix the M-60 machine gun, he just didn't want to.

The four of them were sitting on the log, Morning was picking at his jungle rot, but they were all looking straight ahead at the dead. A poncho blew off one of the dead and he lay there and Morning looked at the man but he wasn't a man, he was a boy. Morning shifted his head from one angle to another.

"Aw man," he said, getting up and going over to the boy. He got down on both knees. "His hand, it's all twisted." The boy's hand was in a grotesque position, torn, dried blood, dirty with the red mud of the land he was in. Morning tried to straighten his hand, but he couldn't.

"The guy's got some girl's high school ring on," Morning faced the others. "I'm going to remember his hand and his girl's high school ring on it. I'll never forget it."

Morning covered the dead man up.

The others got up slowly now. Green went over and helped the chaplain; his assistant was dead. The last rites were said over all the dead men. Battleford helped gather the equipment that was lying everywhere. Fat Turtle carried the dead to the choppers when they landed.

They had finished, the dead were gone now and the last chopper carried off the last of the equipment. The order was to saddle up. They were going to the Landing Zone they had come in on a day before. They moved slowly, stopping and moving again. Morning had a mental picture of the soldier's hand and his ring.

CHAPTER SEVEN

Two boys walked down the street, hands in their pockets, shoulders bent. It was Fall and the wind, bringing the promise of Winter, made their pants flap around their ankles.

"Where are you going to go?"

"I don't know."

"Well, what are you going to do if you do takeoff?"

"I don't know." The boy shrugged his shoulders making it part of his answer.

"Man, you haven't even finished high school yet."

The boy shrugged his shoulders again. They kept walking down the street.

"Does it really make a difference? Everything has gone to hell anyway." Jim Green pulled his coat collar around his neck against the wind.

Mark Morning didn't bother to answer.

"Got any cigarettes?"

"Yeah, but someone might report you to the Athletic Department if they see you smoking."

"So what! Gimme a cigarette."

Mark took cigarettes from his shirt pocket and gave them to Green.

"Who are you going to take to Homecoming?"

"If I'm still here. I don't know." They kept walking down the street till they got to Gray's Drug Store.

"HEY, GREEN," Morning called.
"What do you want, Morning?"

"Let me borrow your civilian pants? The platoon sergeant said I could go on pass to Saigon today."

Green turned and started walking down the company street; he still had his mess kit from breakfast.

Morning fell into step with him. "Sure, but don't wreck them like you did the last pair."

"I won't." They were walking past the first platoon's tent. Radio music filtered through the tent flaps.

"Yeah, well do me a favor and heave on your own damn pants Morning." Green put his arm on Mark Morning's shoulder.

"I'm not going to drink like that anyway. I got stuff to do this time. Let me borrow your shoes too."

"No. What are you going to do besides get drunk in those damn Saigon bars." Green was looking at Morning now.

"Well, for one thing, I'm going sightseeing. Saigon is a very cultural place you know."

"Bullshit." Green snorted.

"I am, no kidding." Morning persisted. "There's a lot of cultural stuff in an old city like Saigon."

"Where exactly are you going to go Morning?" Green was laughing now. A vision of Private Mark Morning with a camera and a guidebook in his hand was more than he could take.

Morning walking next to Green looked at the ground.

"First, I'm going to the U.S. Embassy."

"For Christ's sake, what are you going to do there?"

"I'm going to look at it. I've never seen a god damn embassy before and I was talking to the guy last night at the beer hall and he told me he went there and there were round-eyed American broads working there."

The two had reached their platoon hutch and they turned into the door. Morning took off his fatigues while Green lay down on his bunk. Green was laughing at him.

"Let me get this straight. You're going to the U.S. Embassy because there are women there?"

"Yeah. Maybe I'll go and say hello to the ambassador." Green went on laughing. Morning sat down to unlace his boots.

"You're going to . . . You've got to be kidding. Morning, you can't pick up women at the Embassy. Besides neither the women nor the god damn ambassador, whoever he may be, would give you the time of the day."

"Why not? – I'm fighting for the goddamn country, ain't I? I'm not going to pick up any women, I'm not that stupid. I know they're all spoken for by some officer. I'll just look at them." Deep inside, Morning realized that he thought it would be nice if it did happen. He had thought about it last night walking back to the tent from the beer hall and until he fell asleep. Maybe they would go out to lunch or something. Morning had thought about it. He remembered all the movies he had seen where the guy met some nice girl. Well, he hadn't seen anything but whores lately. A nice girl, not to do anything with, just to talk to one, that was all. He'd smiled to himself before he'd fallen asleep.

"Well, since you're going to have coffee with the ambassador, you'd better wear my shoes and new shirt too."

"Thanks a lot Jim. You're okay. A real pal." Morning came over to get the clothes...

"And take a bath, for Christ's sake."

"You know I will." Morning took his dirty white towel and walked out to the homemade shower, hoping there would be some soap left.

~ ~ ~

The day had been long, hot and uneventful. Specialist Four Green walked up the company street, shoulders stooped. The brim of the olive-drab, sweat-stained baseball cap was pulled down over his eyes to shade out the sun. His shirt wasn't buttoned. He put one foot in front of the other like a machine: an olive-drab army machine. He pursed his lips and put his hands on his hips at the idea.

"Green," a voice called out. Green stopped. He knew the voice; it was the First Sergeant standing in front of the orderly room. He was without a shirt, his fat stomach hanging out. Green turned to look back down the company street. "Come here Green." The First Sergeant waved his hand. Green walked toward the First Sergeant, not too fast, however, but not slow enough to antagonize the first pig.

"What you want, Top?" Green was standing in front of the first pig of the company.

"Come inside. It's too hot to stand outside." The first pig turned and walked back into the Orderly Room. Green followed, taking off his baseball cap.

"I want you to take my truck into Saigon and pick up the men on pass." The first pig sat down in the office swivel chair he had commandeered from some unknown place.

"Sure Top.' Green turned to leave.

"Hey, Green, don't wait around for any god damn body that don't show up. They're AWOL and if Morning's not there, I'll have his ass. You get me, Green?"

"Okay, First Sergeant," Green said.

"I want you back here before dark."

Green walked to his tent. When he got inside, he took his shirt off.

"Where you going?" A voice said from behind. It was Fat Turtle.

"Saigon." Jim opened his footlocker and took out a clean green t-shirt and put it on.

"What for?" Turtle asked.

"Get the guys that went on pass." Green took the tray out of the footlocker and picked out a black leather shoulder holster with a 32-caliber pistol in it and put it on.

"Is the strap straight?" Green asked, turning his back to Turtle. Turtle ran his finger along the black strap.

"It's okay. Can I go along?"

"No."

Turtle let out a breath. He never got to go along on anything good. He always caught the shit details.

Green took the pistol out of the shoulder holster and turned it over in his hand. He took two loaded magazines out of the footlocker, slid one up the grip of the pistol, pulled back the receiver and chambered a round with a little click. He returned the pistol back into the holster and the other magazine into his pocket, then put on his shirt and buttoned it. Turtle looked at the slight bulge under Green's shirt admiringly. He wished he had a pistol and shoulder holster.

"See you later, Turtle." Green left the tent.

"Yeah. Don't take any wooden piastas." Turtle flopped down on his cot.

Green went down to the motor pool, got the truck and drove out of the company area toward Perimeter Road. Getting through Bein Hoa was a trial on both brakes and driver. Thin narrow streets choked with small brown people, food vendors, bicycles, motor scooters, other Army vehicles of all types. Once on Highway One past the 93rd Evacuation Hospital it was a four-lane highway to Saigon. Still the road was packed with old World War I-looking trucks and motor scooters. The trip from Bein Hoa to Saigon takes fifty minutes if traffic isn't stopped by an accident. Green wove between the larger trucks across the bridge over the Saigon River with its barbed wire, concrete watchtowers, bunkers and guards.

At the outskirts of Saigon the traffic slowed to a crawl. For the first time Green thought of Mark and his plan to go to the U.S. Embassy. He smiled and shook his head at the idea. He'd know soon enough. He was close to the Ambassador Hotel parking lot where he was to pick up Mark and the other men on pass. It wasn't yet five o'clock when he pulled into the lot and parked the truck.

Morning sat on the steps of the Ambassador Hotel next to an MP standing guard at the doorway, legs spread out, shotgun resting on his hip. Morning's shirt was torn on the left sleeve, the pants were spotted with spilled liquor, his socks were missing.

"Where are your socks, Morning?" Green said, coming up the steps and sitting down next to Morning. "Did you lose them at the Embassy?"

Morning gave Green a stony drunken stare and looked down at his bare ankles.

"Naw, I lost them in a goddamn whore house down I Cholon somewhere."

"Is that where you went sightseeing?" Green asked.

Morning groaned. "Been trying to buy that shotgun off the MP, but he won't sell. Damn noncombatants."

Green looked at the MP but he didn't seem to be paying any attention to Morning. His black shiny boots and clean faded fatigues were a contrast to Morning, sitting there in his dirty sweat-stained civilian clothes.

"What do you want a shotgun for?"

"To shoot the gooks with. I remember when I was a kid and me and these other guys would go down to the lake and shoot frogs with shotguns to see them splatter. At first I didn't like it, but then it got to be fun. I'd like to see if a gook splatters like a frog." Morning put his head in his hands and looked out into the street crowded with Vietnamese and American soldiers.

"Forget the shotgun, Morning. I heard that a guy in one of the battalions was trying to sell one." Morning didn't seem to hear, he was looking out at the street. "Come on, Morning, time to go home." Green got up and started walking toward the street.

Morning stood up unsteadily. "You sure you don't want a hundred dollars for the shotgun?" he asked the MP

The MP didn't answer as Morning turned unsteadily in the direction of the street and followed Green out to the parking lot.

Green was sitting in the cab of the truck. Morning got in the other side, curled up into a corner and went to sleep. Green looked at his pants, thinking that he should have known better than to let Morning use them. The rest of the men were finding the truck now, some had souvenirs or clothes that they had had made. One guy had a bottle he'd bought at the P.X. and was passing it around. Green turned on the ignition and pushed the starter. The engine turned over, but wouldn't start. Green tried again but it still wouldn't start. He got out of the truck and walked around to the back.

"Any of you guys a mechanic?"

"No."

"Even if I was I wouldn't fix it."

"Do I get overtime if I fix the first pig's truck?"

There wasn't a sober man in the back of the truck.

Green got into the cab and tried it again. The truck still didn't start. There was a cheer from the back and the men passed the bottle around again. Green got out of the truck and walked back to the Ambassador Hotel.

A half hour later, when Green came walking back to the truck, a cheer went up.

"You want a drink, Green?" The bottle was shoved at him. Green took it, looked around, and took a drink.

"I just talked to the First Sergeant. He said that he's sending another truck down tomorrow morning and you guys should find some place to stay. The MP said there's a ten o'clock curfew and that you'd be picked up if you're out. So find a hotel and be back here by nine tomorrow morning." Before he was finished, the men were getting out of the truck, laughing with their newfound freedom for the night. Green stood looking at them as they went in all directions in twos and threes, slapping one another on the back. Green went around to the cab, Morning was asleep inside.

"Morning, wake up." Green shook Morning's shoulder.

"We back already?" Morning sat up, looking around.

"No, we haven't left yet. Come on, the truck won't run. We got to find some place to sleep."

"Naw, I'll stay here." Morning turned around to go back to sleep.

"Come on, Morning," Green insisted. He opened

the door and dragged Morning out of the cab. "We'll find a hotel and get something to eat." Green took Morning by the arm and led him to the street where he hailed a taxi.

"Number One hotel, where no MP go," Green told the driver. "Close by, you got me?"

"Number One hotel, yes." The Vietnamese driver nodded his head. "You want girl?" The driver was looking back, smiling.

"You go hotel," Morning said. The taxi weaved its way into traffic.

A few minutes later the taxi pulled up to the curb on To Do Street. The taxi driver got out and opened the door for Green.

"You wait here – I go see." He walked over to the plain green door and knocked. Green pulled the half sleeping Morning from the taxi and leaned him over the hood of the car. In a minute the driver was back. "You want one or two rooms?"

"Two rooms. How much?"

"Two rooms, he say 500 pia each."

"Too much," Green said indignantly.

"Too much! This very good hotel. No MP come. Have number one girls. He my brother. Very good hotel." The Vietnamese taxi driver acted very hurt.

"400 pia each room," Green said.

"No," the taxi driver said.

"Let's go then." Green turned to get Morning back into the cab.

"No, no, you wait." The taxi driver ran off to the door and knocked again. Green stood and waited while the man and his brother talked it all over. Green unbuttoned the first button of his fatigue shirt in case he needed his gun. The taxi driver came back.

"My brother say 500 pia each room. Give you beer and chop-chop, but girl cost extra."

"Okay," Green said. He picked up Morning who had passed out and carried him into the hotel on his back. After he went through the green door, he walked into a courtyard and the green door was quickly closed behind him.

"This my brother," the taxi driver said. "He good man, number one." The brother, dressed in undershirt and red shorts, nodded his head, smiling.

"How you do sir," he said, bobbing his head up and down.

"Nice to meet you," Green said, bobbing his head the best he could with Morning on his shoulders.

"Your friend drunk?" he said.

"Yes. Where room?"

"This way," the Vietnamese walked down a corridor. The walls were white plaster. After a few steps they came to a stairway, underneath it was a water trough. They went up the stairway to the second landing. At the far end of the hallway a hammock was strung with another Vietnamese asleep in it. The first door was open and they went in. The room was plain, square with the same white plaster walls. There was a wooden Vietnamese bed in the middle of the room and a sink, otherwise, nothing. Green put Morning down on the bed. He rolled over with a grunt and never woke. Green walked to the window, opened the shutters and looked out on To Do Street. There were bars and chicken-net screen on the window so a Viet Cong

Terrorist couldn't throw a hand grenade through it. Green closed the shutters, locked them and turned to the two Vietnamese brothers standing by the door.

They were both smiling and bobbing their heads. "Number one man no Viet Cong. Viet Cong number ten thousand." They both laughed like little boys telling a joke on one of their playmates.

Green walked toward them without smiling at their joke and motioned to see the other room. The three walked out, Green turned and shut the door. There was no lock so there was nothing he could do about Morning. As they walked down the hallway, two lizards ran along the wall. The one brother pointed to them. "Number One hotel." The door to the other room was open. It was the same as the other with a bed and washstand. Green went to the washstand and turned on the faucet. A few drops of rusty water fell from the faucet. Green looked at the two brothers.

"No water. Viet Cong." The brothers shook their heads in disgust, making hissing noises with their mouths.

"I'm dirty. Need water to wash...wash." Green motioned as if he were washing his face. The brothers smiled and pointed to the stairs. Green walked to the brothers, produced his wallet and counted out a thousand pias for the room and fifty pia for the taxi.

"Me go wash. Bring food and beer here." Green acted out what he wanted. The brothers nodded. Green walked over to the bed and made a point of taking off his fatigue shirt, showing the pistol under his armpit. The brothers saw it. The taxi driver pointed. "Number One – you kill Viet Cong."

They walked down the hallway and stairs together. As Green stopped at the water trough, the hotel brother's wife gave him a piece of dirty soap and a red and white checked rag that looked like an Italian tablecloth. She left and Green washed and went back to his room, checking on Morning who was passed out for the night. He'd never gotten to the Embassy. Green shut Morning's door and went in and sat down on his bed. Only three lizards were on the ceiling so it must be the best room in the house.

Green sat eating Vietnamese fried rice with six bottles of "33" beer sitting next to him on the wooden bed. The two brothers were watching him eat with chopsticks.

"You want girl for the night?" the taxi-driving brother said.

Green didn't answer or look up; he kept eating the rice and drinking the beer.

"Good girl, clean, number one," he said smiling. "Belong to other brother."

Green looked up at the man. "How many brothers you got?"

"Five." He put up five fingers.

"All in business? Make too much money."

"Yes, all in business," he laughed.

"How much? Girl."

"One thousand pias."

"Too much."

The tax driver looked at the pistol under Green's armpit and Green eating with the chopsticks.

"Seven hundred and fifty pias all night. "Number one girl."

"Bring her here. I look see," Green said.

The brothers left, closing the door, talking to each other.

The taxi-driving brother was explaining to the other brother the deal he had just made with Green.

Green sat on the edge of the bed until he finished the rice. He got up and took an empty beer bottle and the bowl and placed them next to the door. He then took the shoulder holster off and took the pistol out. It made him feel safer; he turned it over in his hand, checked to see if a bullet was chambered and shoved the gun into his belt, hanging the holster on the bedpost. He walked around the room feeling as if he were in a "B" movie. As he opened a window and looked out on To Do Street he heard laughter and the bells from a cathedral in the distance. The bells made him feel empty inside. "Am I in jail?" He wanted to think of home and how exciting all this would seem but he couldn't. He sat down on the edge of the bed, looking out at the street. He felt like crying but he couldn't; he wanted to laugh but he knew he didn't know how. He wanted to live but he was afraid and at the same time, he was afraid to die. He took his gun and aimed it at a young man and woman crossing the street. He could easily kill them if he wanted to, he thought; they were laughing, walking arm in arm. He slowly put the gun back into the holster.

Green ran his fingers through his hair, laid on the wooden bed and waited for the taxi driver to come.

He was almost asleep when he heard footsteps coming up the stairs. He got up, holding the pistol in his right hand and opened the door so that he was partly behind it. It was the taxi driver, a girl and another man. Green put the gun into his belt hidden from the view of the Vietnamese.

"I bring girl one brother," the taxi driver said.

Green nodded and stepped back. They came into the room, shutting the door behind them. The new brother looked around the room carefully: it passed inspection.

"She good girl. Seven hundred fifty pia please."

Green looked at the girl. She wasn't a raving beauty, that was clear. She had a flat nose and pockmarked face; her hair was black and dull-looking. She was plump and wore light green pajamas and rubber thongs. She at least had a figure and Green could see her breasts though the pajamas. He took out his wallet and counted out seven hundred fifty pias to the brother. The two backed out of the room. The girl sat down on the wooden bed. Green wanted to lock the door but there was no lock. He looked around the room for something to prop against the door. He walked over to the bed and took the end slat from the bed and propped it against the door. He pulled on the door; it wouldn't open. He turned toward the girl.

"You speak English?" he demanded.

She stared at him and at the slat on the door.

"You speak te te bit English?" Green demanded again; the girl didn't answer. "Parlez-vous Français?" Green tried. He didn't speak French anyway. She didn't answer. Green looked at her for a long time. "No speak." He pointed to her mouth.

She shook her head.

"Great. A night with a girl that can't speak a word

of English. You just come off the farm?"

She didn't move.

Green took out the pistol from his belt. The girl stiffened and cowered on the bed.

Green looked at the gun and looked at the girl. "No, no," he said in his nicest tone of voice. "Viet Cong me kill." He acted like he was shooting in another direction. "No you," he pointed at the girl and shook his head.

The girl understood and put her feet back on the floor.

Green put the gun into the shoulder holster and put it by the window. "You are about the ugliest..." Green shrugged his shoulders and got undressed. The girl took off her pajamas.

Green stood on the bed and turned out the light. He had forgotten the beer; he took one and offered one to the girl but she shook her head. Green lay on his back drinking the beer. The girl lay next to him, not moving, waiting. There was light coming in from the window.

Outside the room Green could hear footsteps. He put the beer down and took the pistol out and sat up. The girl looked from the gun back to the door and back to the gun. The footsteps passed; Green put the gun back.

"Some day Viet Cong kill me." Green made the motion of slitting his own throat. "Me" and he did the same motion.

The girl looked at Green and shook her head once and made a sharp hissing noise.

"Yes." Green nodded his head; he was enjoying himself. It was fun getting a rise out of the girl.

Green looked at the girl; big teardrops rolled from her brown eyes, down her cheeks.

"I'll be damned. You must be an Irish whore." Green lay back on the bed.

The girl put her head in the crook of Green's shoulder.

The girl shook Green; he opened his eyes. It was gray down on To Do Street. The street looked dirty and old in the morning light. The girl pointed to the light and got out of bed, dressed, removed the wooden slat and left without looking back at Green. Green watched out the window and saw her cross the street and go into an alley. He stared at the alley for a long time. Then he dressed slowly, putting on the shoulder holster last. He opened the door, carrying his shirt and went into Morning's room. Morning was just as Green has left him, snoring, his mouth open.

"Wake up." Green shook Morning. Morning cocked one eye and sat up.

"Am I AWOL?" He rubbed his head.

"No." Green sat on the edge of the bed.

"Where the hell am I then?"

"Hotel in Saigon. Come on, let's get something to eat."

"Wait a minute. How did we get here?" He was looking at himself now. "Kind of messed up your clothes."

"Ya, kinda." Green was resigned to the condition of his clothes.

"How did we get here?" Morning got up. They both went down the stairs and washed in the water in the trough at the bottom of the stairs.

"You sure we ain't in trouble?" Morning asked.

Green was putting on his shirt. "I'm sure."

They walked down the hallway through the green door and out into To Do Street. They walked toward the Ambassador Hotel.

"Did I missing anything?"

"Nope, you didn't miss a thing. How did you do at the Embassy?"

"You were right. That's no place for the like of me. Or you either."

They walked down To Do Street stoop-shouldered, hands in pockets, back to the truck. To Do Street was dirty and damp.

CHAPTER EIGHT

A black 1960 Ford convertible careened off the highway onto the gravel parking lot of the tree center stopping at an abrupt halt in front of the railroad tie that marked the beginning of the employee parking lot. The door opened and out came Mark Morning holding a thermos bottle in one hand. He was dressed in faded jeans, white tennis shoes, and an unbuttoned denim shirt.

"Good morning, Tree Center!" He called. He looked around while he walked toward the greenhouse and garden store, sometimes walking backwards.

It was July, but the morning was still cool; the sun was just beginning to come up. Mark was always the first one at work.

He had been working at the Tree Center since graduating from high school in June. He loved the greenhouse and he always got there early. The owner had given him a key after the first month so that he could let himself in.

The owner told his wife that Mark was the most hardworking kid that he'd ever hired. He had also given him a raise that same day.

Mark unlocked the door and walked in, leaving the door open. Sniffing the air, he said, "God, how I love the smell of this greenhouse." He poured himself a cup of coffee from his thermos and contentedly walked around the greenhouse looking at all the plants, as he did every morning.

PRIVATE MORNING was told that he had to go with the third squad second platoon to the outpost. He was delighted with the news. As he said, it was like getting away from it all. At four o'clock they were ready to leave. The platoon leader came out to wish them luck. He looked at Morning with disgust, and Morning returned the look with the same disgust while shaking his head.

"Good luck men. Remember, if you get into any trouble, we'll be here to get you out of it. Any questions?"

No one raised his hand.

Under his breath, Morning said, "at least I can sleep nights knowing that the young platoon leader will lead the bayonet charge up the hill to save my nasty ass. Ah yes, Lieutenant Mayson, the star and the hero, airborne, ranger, infantry, all you idiots can follow him."

The squad left quietly, each man ten to fifteen meters apart. After he got to the outpost, Morning made a little hut using native labor; the natives putting in the four corner poles and the sides halfway up to the roof that was made from ponchos. From the roof hung bunches of bananas, pineapples, beer and other goods that he had gotten from the Vietnamese.

During the day Vietnamese women came with tiger beer. They washed the men's clothes in the stream that ran next to the outpost. Morning had his clothes washed every day. He sat in the streambed naked, drinking tiger beer, and watching the women beat the clothes against the rocks.

"Yes sir, Sarge, we really got it made out in the outpost. I could stay here for the duration of the war." Morning took another drink of beer. Sergeant Smith wasn't much interested, and he left Morning alone.

Morning got along well with the Vietnamese people. He played their games, not winning all the time, but enough so they didn't think him a fool. His favorite game was the one where a 25-Dong piece was used. The game was best when there were six players. The object was to hit the other player's coin when it was lying in the dirt. Once hit, it belonged to the player that hit it. If it was missed, the other player got a chance.

During the long, hot afternoons Morning would sit

under a tree in a squat position with four or five young men around him; some in uniform, others with just a pair of trunks on. He looked and acted like a Greek philosopher, only he picked at his jungle rot and drank tiger beer. Morning would say, "War talk, man, war talk." He talked to them in half Vietnamese and half English, but they understood. He answered questions; he sometimes went into long dissertations on the Viet Cong and how when he found them, he would dismember their bodies so they wouldn't get to Buddha when they died. Morning impressed his following, and each day the number of pupils grew.

In late afternoon they would leave to return to their village, saying that they would be back tomorrow; all this with a great deal of chattering and bobbing of heads. Morning would walk down to his hut and sleep until dark. The squad knew that Morning was good man to have around: when he was there, the price of beer went down and the value of C-rations went up.

On the third night Sergeant Smith came to Morning's foxhole. The moon was up and they could see clearly the area in front of them.

"Why do you do it, Morning?" Smith sat on the edge of the foxhole.

"Do what, Sarge?" Morning lit a cigarette to the discomfort of Sergeant Smith. "Want one?"

"No thanks. You fool with those gooks so much, you look like you're holding classes for Christ's sake."

"Well, someone's got to tell them what it's all about without shoving a lot of charity at them. Besides, they act like girls, holding hands and carrying on the way they do. That's why they can't win this stupid war. They got no pride, that's why they think it's easier to beg around the GI's instead of working. So I don't let them beg. I trade with them, and I don't let myself get screwed on the deal. If they want something, they know how to get it. If more people treated them like men instead of stupid gooks, they'd quit acting like stupid gooks."

"Yeah, you might have something there. Too bad you're only a Private." Sergeant Smith sat on the edge of the foxhole.

Morning sat at the bottom, his legs sticking up against the dirt parapet in front. As he lit a cigarette he thought of an autumn scene. The leaves were turning brown at home, he mused and sometimes in the morning the ground would be white with frost. That's the way it was back home, but Morning wasn't there. It would have been good to be able to come home from a party drunk from keg beer. Somehow Morning knew he'd never see or do anything like that again. He wouldn't see the girl he'd liked in high school with the long brown hair and the steel blue eyes and the perfect teeth. She'd worn braces on those teeth through most of the five years he'd known her and he'd put up with them and now he'd never reap his reward.

Morning moved easily in his hole and blew heavily through his nose, short breaths, the kind taken after a long run. There'd be no end to this. He didn't want to think about Vietnam, about the short Italian kid with the long black matted dirty hair in the water up to his chest, unable to go any further, weighed down by a heavy rucksack. A silver crucifix hung out of his shirt. The 50-calibre machine gun ripped the water. The

Italian kid couldn't make the safety of the shore and he
stood there and cried, the tears coming down his dirty
cheeks as he pleaded to God for help, and all the time
the 50-caliber machine gun bullets ripped the water
around him but not hitting him. Morning could almost
see the one bullet that hit the Italian kid in the head.
His head exploded and the muddy brown water turned
red, and there was nothing after that. Morning made
himself think of the chalked-up sidewalks back home,
the hopscotch games drawn and the kids playing.

"Morning, Morning, there's something out there."
It was Sergeant Smith next to him in the darkness.
Morning was back in his hole again and there was
nothing in front of him, nothing he looked at changed.
He kept his eyes moving all the time, as he had been
taught in basic training, but his eyes always started to
hurt when he did that, so he quit.

"Where?" Morning moved slowly for his M-16 rifle.

"There, out there, I heard them." Sergeant Smith's
voice was a harsh whisper in the darkness. The moon
was behind a cloud and it was very dark now, a good
time for Charlie.

"For Christ's sake, don't you know anything more
than "there, out there?" Damn Sarge. I don't see a
damn thing, nothing."

"Look Morning, there, out there, I heard them."
The moon was still behind the clouds. They could be
there; it was very dark. Morning was scared, the
sergeant was scared, and if there was anyone out there,
he was scared too. Morning peered into the blackness
until the rocks and trees started to move around.

"Morning, Morning." The sergeant's voice was

urgent. "I know there's somebody out there."

Morning stood up in his foxhole. "There's one way to find out, shit." With his rifle in his hand, he walked around to the front of the parapet, sat down and lit a cigarette. The light from the match lit up the area, making Morning a light in the blackness.

"You're crazy, Morning."

There was no answer. Morning got up and walked around the parapet, still smoking the cigarette. Sergeant Smith followed the glowing light of Morning with his eyes, waiting for the shot or the explosion. It didn't come, the night stayed the same.

"There ain't any damn body out there and I'm going to bed." Morning flicked the lit cigarette up into the air in a high arc, it landed about four feet in front of the foxhole and glowed for a minute and went out.

"Morning, you know what?" Morning was talking to himself. "What? You always get stuck with the dirty work. Yeah, I know."

It was the first light of dawn, the ground was wet from the heavy dew, ants were just coming out for their day's work. The men of the squad were asleep, rolled up in their ponchos, weapons lying by them, equipment at the ready. Morning was squatting, trying to get his fire started. He blew on the small flame softly, making it grow and envelope the small piece of wood and paper that he had kept in his pocket during the night so they wouldn't get wet. After the fire was going and the number ten can filled with water was over the fire heating, Morning poured the coffee into it very carefully. This was the best time of the day for Morning. He liked making the coffee and toasting the c-rations, brewed over the fire and eating it with c-ration jam and having some fruit cocktail. He looked over at the squad asleep; there was no snoring, they didn't move in their sleep. To Morning, this was the best time of the day.

The coffee was almost ready now. Morning went over to Sergeant Smith all curled up in his poncho, not looking like a sergeant at all, just another lump under a wet poncho. Morning kicked the lump, not too hard, but hard enough so it made him feel better than he did before.

"Come on, Sarge, wake up." There was an urgency in Morning's voice that made the sergeant sit up.

"What, what?" Sergeant Smith was looking for trouble.

"Didn't you hear that loud noise out there?" Morning pointed to their front.

"No." The Sergeant twisted around to look.

"The sound of dawn breaking over Nam." Morning went into howls of laughter, bending at the waist, going down on his knees, laughing so hard that tears came to his eyes.

"God damn it, Morning, you're going to go too far one of these times, just one time." Sergeant Smith was really mad, he was standing up pointing a finger at Morning now on the ground laughing.

"Look Sarge, if you can't take a simple joke." Morning jumped up to stand in front of Sergeant Smith. The two looked at each other for a brief moment, both tense.

"You're a sorry son of a bitch." The sergeant walked over to the coffee.

The noise and the commotion woke the rest of the

squad. The men got up from the ground and staggered over to Morning's coffee pot. One of them muttered to himself, "Good morning, Vietnam." This sent Morning into another howl of laughter. The squad was around the fire, the coffee was ready now and each man was putting some into his cup. Some were heating bread.

"Morning, what in the hell were you doing last night with that cigarette?" Carlson asked. He was the M-60 machine gunner.

"I was just seeing if Charlie was really out there." Morning was putting on more water for coffee.

"You're out of your mind," another squad member said.

"Well, I wasn't going to play horse-around all night." Morning looked at the man.

"I wouldn't miss this one for nothing knowing that you're in it, Morning. The only thing I hope is that you get it before me, because when you get it, it will be worth a million to see." Sergeant Smith said.

"Yeah, Sarge you keep wishing that. Just remember, when I'm gone, who'll steal the coffee for you? You guys got it made and you don't even know it, I should be charging you for a cup of this stuff." Morning pointed at the can he was using for a coffee pot now with the new water in it.

They all looked at Private Morning sitting on a log, needing a shave, dirty, one side of his face scabbed over with jungle rot, his clothes the dirtiest of the squad, and he didn't even have his boots on. He sat there with his burnt-over canteen cup of coffee, a smile on his face.

"Morning, you are definitely a morale factor in the third squad," Sergeant Smith said.

"Flattery will get you nowhere, Sarge." Morning took a drink of his coffee. "My name's Mark Morning and I don't give a damn for nothing."

Morning heard the sound of a jeep coming up the road. It geared down and turned off the road to come to their position. It was the platoon sergeant and platoon leader. What did they want this early, Morning thought. It was trouble and that was a sure thing. The jeep stopped; two men got out and started toward the position. Morning could always tell the difference between the Platoon Sergeant and the Platoon leader. One had a big belly and the other was slim. Morning kept an eye on his coffee. They went over to Sergeant Smith.

"Sergeant Smith, everything go all right last night?" the platoon leader asked.

"Yes sir, fine, no trouble."

"We need one man for KP, how about Morning for the day? You won't miss him too much, will you?"

"No sir. Morning, come here."

"Don't bother to tell me. I got ears Sergeant. What's wrong with the rest of the platoon back at the strip? They working so hard that you had to come out here, Sir? Or were they massacred last night and we're the only ones left for the KP roster?"

"At east, at ease, Morning," the platoon sergeant said.

Morning went over and kicked the coffee on the ground, put out the fire, got his weapon and web gear. He then got into the jeep without saying another word. The men watched him in silence.

"He'll be back tonight before dark," the lieutenant said, getting into the jeep.

Nothing was said on the way to the airstrip. Morning wasn't talking and the lieutenant had nothing to say. The platoon sergeant had a sick expression on his face.

Morning spent the day doing as little as possible in the mess area. Every chance he got he went off to sleep and the cooks would find him and put him back to work. It was the last meal of the day and Morning was lying on the ground eating his third helping so that he wouldn't have to work.

"I should have told the lieutenant to shove the KP up his ass," Morning said to Green and Battleford. "Nothing like going out of your way to get a KP."

"Damn, Morning, don't get so hot and bothered over it. Go back tonight and go to sleep. I got a letter from home. Nothing new."

"Come on, no gossip to report, no one getting married or anything." Morning didn't have a chance to finish. The Mess Sergeant was standing over him.

"Morning, knock off the bullshit and get to work. We want to get done sometime tonight," the Mess Sergeant said.

"Don't bother me none when we get done. I've got about one month left. Remember Sarge, you can work me long but not hard." Morning got up and disappeared into the mess tent.

The work got done about eight that night. Morning was hot and sweaty and dirty, and there was no ride for him back to the outpost.

"Hey, Mess Sergeant, how about giving me a ride to the outpost?"

"Not on your life, Morning, we're not all crazy like

you. Nobody said anything about you going back out to the outpost, and I ain't goin' out there if I don't have to."

"You non-combatant son of a bitch, the lieutenant said I was going back out there tonight."

"Go see the lieutenant with your problems then." The Mess Sergeant walked off.

"Stupid ass," Morning said, picking up his rifle and web-gear. He put it on and started walking to the outpost. There were about five minutes of daylight left, he thought. I'll show these asses that are afraid of the damn dark, he thought. He slung his rifle over his shoulder and picked up the password so he could get out of the company perimeter before darkness came.

Ten minutes after Morning left the mess tent Sergeant Smith called the CP to find out where Morning was. The question went on down the chain of command; no Morning could be found. The Mess Sergeant told the platoon leader that Morning had been looking for a ride to the outpost the last time he'd seen him. He was most likely off some place goofing off and he'd show up soon. This wasn't good enough for the lieutenant, so a search for Morning was made and he wasn't in the company area.

"Come on Sergeant, we're going out to the outpost. That god damn Morning must have walked out there," the lieutenant said, getting into the jeep. The platoon sergeant got another man to ride shotgun and they left the company area on the way to the outpost. This in itself was a dangerous thing to do. Not only were they in danger of attack from the Viet Cong that roamed the area at night, but also in danger of getting shot by a nervous guard on the perimeter. This fed the fire of the lieutenant's anger, but he had to account for Morning before something happened. That damn private had him over a barrel and he knew it, and he was going to get even with him for this stunt. The jeep sped down the black deserted road that during the day was full to overflowing with Vietnamese. Now it was empty and it looked like some road that he'd never seen before. He wasn't even sure where to turn to the outpost.

He heard the outpost before he could see it. This made him smile, some of these guys had no class, he could take the outpost by himself if he were Charlie.

For Christ's sake, don't shoot. It's Morning coming into the outpost," he yelled at the top of his lungs. He waited for the shot to ring out or would the bullet hit him first, he couldn't remember. There was no sound from the outpost. "It's me, Morning, walking your way," he called out again.

"All right, Morning, we know it's you. Knock it off and get in here before someone gets killed." It was the voice of Sergeant Smith.

Muffled laughter came from the rest of the squad and someone said, "That crazy son of a bitch." Morning went back in the outpost trying to find his gear in the dark.

"Morning, what the hell you trying to pull," Sergeant Smith said. "You trying to get yourself killed? The lieutenant's out looking for you now. You better hope that nothing happens to them."

"Right, Sergeant. I was just trying to get back to my squad like I was told to do this morning. You heard the lieutenant, ain't my fault no one wanted to give a poor private a ride. They was afraid of the dark." Morning found his poncho and started out to his foxhole.

The jeep with the lieutenant came from off the road.

"Morning's here with us," a voice informed the lieutenant.

"Morning, get over here." It was the lieutenant. Morning changed his direction and headed for the jeep. The outpost was a scene of mass confusion, people all over the place, talking and making noise.

"Yes sir," Morning said, lighting up a cigarette.

"God damn it, Morning, put that out. I don't have time to talk to you tonight. First thing tomorrow morning you better be at my tent. You got that." The lieutenant couldn't even see Morning in the darkness. "Sergeant Smith, you better make sure he finds his way up to the company in the morning."

"Yes sir," Sergeant Smith couldn't see the lieutenant or Morning. The lieutenant got in to the jeep and it tore off back to the company area.

"You heard the man, Morning. Now get with Carlson on the machine gun." Morning turned and headed for the machine gun emplacement. He had a big smile on his face that no one could see for the darkness. He lived to see second lieutenants jump through their asses, it was well worth the effort. Morning climbed into the hole with Carlson, leaving his poncho at the edge.

"Good evening, Mr. Carlson," Morning said. "What's new with the rocks and bushes tonight?"

"Everything's quiet except when you're around. You're going to catch hell tomorrow," Carlson said with a touch of awe in his voice.

"For what, Carlson, old pal. I was just going to my post like I was told to do. I got a lieutenant by the ass. I'm going to get some sleep. Wake me if you see anything." Morning got out of the hole and rolled up in his poncho at the back of the hole.

"Okay Morning," Carlson said, but Morning was already asleep.

Morning's experience woke him up, the moon had already gone down, there was something wrong.

"What's going on?" Morning said, sliding down into the hole headfirst, coming back up and looking out over the parapet.

"There's someone out there, they got candles or something, see the lights," Carlson said from behind his machine gun. He wanted to start shooting, but Morning stopped him with his hand over the sights of the gun.

"Yeah." Morning reached for his rifle. "Just wait a minute, let's see what they're up to."

They watched the lights out in front of them. Their breathing became labored under the strain.

Rat-ta-tat—Rat-ta-tat of a machine gun, white tracers coming at them.

"They're setting up a machine gun, oh man." Morning returned the fire. "Now shoot the god damn machine gun, that's what you got it for."

"It'll give our position away," Carlson whispered.

"They already know where the hell we are, now shoot for Christ's sake."

The M-60 machine gun returned red tracers for the white ones. Every fifth bullet was a tracer and Carlson didn't let up on the trigger and it was almost a red line going out of the darkness. Morning was really excited; he watched the tracers ricochet off the ground and head up into the blackness of the sky. The incoming white tracers came in high over their heads; sometimes they would hit the dirt around the foxhole. Morning used up one magazine after another. Sergeant Smith was on the radio reporting the action to the platoon leader back at the airstrip. Then as fast as it started, it stopped. Morning fired the last shots.

It was so quiet, Morning could hear Sergeant Smith on the radio. He kept looking out over the parapet and reloading his expended magazines. "Get some sleep while you can, they'll be back later," Morning said to Carlson. Carlson got out of the hole and rolled up in Morning's poncho. Morning leaned over the parapet, waiting. He waited for a half hour and the white tracers started coming in again. Now there was a lot of small arms fire too. There were both red and white tracers coming in on Morning and the rest of the squad. Morning and the squad were returning the fire, Carlson was still in the poncho. Morning turned to him.

"Let's go boy!" Carlson didn't move. Morning heard whimpering from Carlson. It seemed loud in comparison to the firing going on. Morning turned to the firefight that was going on pell-mell between the squad and the Viet Cong. Morning yelled over to Sergeant Smith to call in artillery flares so they could see what the hell was going on. He didn't know if Sergeant Smith heard him. He turned back to Carlson. For Christ's sake, all I need is to have you go chicken on me, he thought. "Carlson, let's go, time to play, come on kid." Morning was close to the boy's face now, there was something wrong. "You hit?"

"No, something bit me on the mouth." Carlson was barely whispering. Morning reached out and felt his face. The area around his mouth and the lips was swollen three times its size. Morning rolled Carlson over on his back. The firing was still going on. Morning turned his attention to the front again and fired off a magazine of ammunition.

"What did it?" But Carlson was in shock. His only answer was whimpering. It seemed louder than the shooting. Morning knew that he had to do something or Carlson might die. Morning was getting mad because of the rotten luck of having something happen to Carlson. He turned to the front again, looked out at the firing and the tracers. He reloaded his weapon and fired off a few shots. He stood there looking out over the area, it was so damn dark he thought. He put a magazine in his pocket, took off his helmet and put it very carefully on the parapet. The incoming fire from out in front seemed to be slacking off some although the squad fire hadn't. Morning took his rifle, got out of the hole, picked up Carlson and started for Sergeant Smith's hole. In daylight it seemed close, but now it seemed really far away. The medic should be at Sergeant Smith's hole. White tracers kicked up dirt around Morning's feet. He stumbled and the two of them fell to the ground. The artillery flares that were called for came now and the area was flooded with a white eerie light. Morning got out from under Carlson, stood up, cursing the artillery, and picked him up again. He kept going, staggering and weaving with

Carlson's weight. He was waiting for a red-hot tracer to hit him. He stumbled into Sergeant Smith's hole, falling over again.

"What's wrong with him, hit?" Sergeant Smith asked.

"No, something bit him and he went into shock. I didn't know what to do with him so I'm giving him to you and that sorry medic." Morning was so out of breath he could hardly talk. The light from the flares showed Sergeant Smith, the medic and Carlson, who was foaming at the mouth, and Morning's dirty unshaven face, beads of sweat dripping off. Morning got up and headed for the machine gun.

"I'll send someone over to help you," Sergeant Smith called after him. There were only a few incoming rounds now. The light from the flares went out and the blackness closed in around Morning as he made his way back, bent over at the waist.

Another man came to take Carlson's place, bringing news that Carlson was going to be all right, it was just a scorpion sting. The Viet Cong pulled out for the night and Morning went to sleep.

The next day Morning made coffee again. To Private Morning it was just another stinking day and there would be nothing to make it better.

Still, it was the best time of the day, his name was Private Mark Morning and he didn't give a damn.

Morning was waiting for the jeep to come out to pick up Carlson and he thought he'd save himself a walk by riding with them. Carlson was much better; the swelling had gone down and he was no longer in shock. In fact, he made Morning uncomfortable by thanking him at least fifty times in the space of an hour. Morning sat with his back to a log drinking his coffee slowly and smoking a cigarette.

The jeep came and Morning helped Carlson into it. He got in, riding half on the outside and half on the inside of the jeep. The road looked the same to Morning as it had done the night before. He kept his eyes open for any sign of change, anything that meant danger, a landmine or any vehicle of death that would somehow change the landscape, the surface of the road, the ditch.

They pulled into the Company CP, Morning jumping off the jeep before it stopped and heading for the lieutenant's tent. On the way he met Green and Battleford; they were waiting for him.

"You really got yourself into a mess for last night," Green said, lighting a cigarette and handing the pack to Morning.

"Yeah, you're a crazy son of a bitch, but the lieutenant isn't going to let you get away with it. He can't. You made a monkey out of him and now he's got to save face by hanging your ass," Battleford said. Battleford was right, the lieutenant not only didn't like Morning, but now he was out to get him. Morning was too much of an individual in the platoon for the platoon's own good.

"Hide and watch, men, that damn lieutenant isn't going to get anybody this time. If he don't know it now, he will or he'll be a bigger fool than I think he is now." Morning was truly enjoying himself this morning. To Morning, this was good triumphing over evil.

"I'll be back in a minute. Wait here." Morning headed to the lieutenant's tent. He met the platoon sergeant outside the tent and the two men looked at each other. The platoon sergeant jerked his head at the doorway. Morning went inside.

"Sir, Private Morning reporting as ordered sir." Morning saluted.

The lieutenant returned the salute and got up and stood in front of Morning for effect. The lieutenant was clean-shaven and neat. Morning was unshaven, dirty, his uniform full of mud from the night in the foxhole.

"Morning, you fucked me up last night and almost got me killed." The lieutenant looked right in Morning's face, for he was only two inches away. The lieutenant walked over to the desk and picked up a red book. "You know your rights under Article 31, Uniform Code of Military Justice."

"Yes sir," Morning said.

"I'm charging you with an Article 15 and you'll be going before the Old Man the first chance, which will be in a half hour. Do you have anything to say?" The lieutenant sat down.

"Yes sir," Morning said.

"At ease. Let's hear it."

Morning relaxed, putting his hands behind his back. "Sir, first I'm not going to take the Article 15. I'd take a court martial first. If it gets that far, I'll get the best lawyer I can and I'll make this the biggest thing since the court martial of Billy Mitchel. I'll make myself look like a war hero for going back to my post after you ordered me to and didn't make sure I had a way to get there. It will look real good in the papers and they'll eat this up. That's about it, sir. I got nothing to lose." Morning stood there waiting for the next step. His heart was pounding, he was so excited, he couldn't lose.

The lieutenant looked at Morning for a long minute as he sized him up. He had his career to think about and he didn't want to blow it over a bum like Private Mark Morning. "That's all, Morning. Stay in the area."

Morning came to the position of attention and saluted, turned on his heel and walked out of the tent. He stood in the shade of a tree. The platoon sergeant went into the tent and in a few minutes came out and walked over to Morning.

"Morning, I don't know what you told the lieutenant in there, but you better keep it to yourself. He's dropping all charges. I been in the Army twenty-two years and I know what's going on. You lucked out this time, don't push your luck." The platoon sergeant stood there, hands on hips.

"Sure, Sarge. Even in the Army when you're right you win two times out of three," Morning said, turning to go.

The platoon sergeant reached out his hand and grabbed Morning by the shirt, putting him up against a tree. "Morning, I ain't telling you again to keep your damn opinions to yourself. Understand?"

"That's right, Sergeant, I understand." Morning freed himself from the grip of the platoon sergeant.

"Walk the straight line for a while. He'll be looking for a chance," the platoon sergeant warned, walking away from Morning.

Morning didn't mind the platoon sergeant at all, he was a straight guy. Maybe the lieutenant might learn something from him, if he didn't get killed first, but he didn't think so. Anyway, now he could go back to the outpost.

31 December 1965: State of the War: U.S. Forces are reporting significant casualties; 1350 KIA, 5300 WIA, 150 MIA or captured during 1965. Direct operational cost of the war for the year was 460 billion dollars. It is estimated that 36,000 NVA troops came down the Ho Chi Minh Trail in the last year.

CHAPTER NINE

CAPTAIN MOES KNOWS NEW MEXICO. CAPTAIN MOES WAS FROM THE WEST, BUT EDUCATED IN THE EAST, WEST POINT. HE BROUGHT THE WEST WITH HIM TO VIETNAM. HE DID NOT HAVE MEN UNDER HIS COMMAND...BOYS. HE HAD NOT EXPECTED THAT IN A FIGHT, HE AND HIS BOYS COULD WIN.

THE PLATOON was sitting around Captain Moes in a "U" shape formation. He was standing, legs spread apart, hands on hips, waiting for the men quiet down. Morning was telling one of the new men a bald-faced lie and the new man was eating it up. Green came out of the hutch. Morning saw him and frantically waved him over.

"We're going out, what's the job?" Morning said.

"All right men, at ease, at ease," Captain Michelson yelled out.

There was an echo of "at ease, at ease, damn it," from the group. The loudest of them was Morning.

"Everybody here? Sergeant Winter?" The Captain took a notebook from his pocket.

"Yes sir," Sergeant Winters returned.

"Well, we've got a mission for one team, just two days and a night out. Brigade wants us to find a crossing place on the Song Dong Ni River. They have two possible locations and we're going to take a look at both of them. It's a short job; get in and get out. Sergeant Turner's team will handle the relay, so Sergeant Turner, check with the commo sergeant. Sergeant Winter's team is going to do the mission. There'll be a briefing at 1930 hours tonight for the relay team and for the operating team of Sergeant Winters. That's about it for the mission.

"There's going to be a Company party on Sunday so we'll try to get you men back in time for the beer. That's it. Sergeant Winters, if you don't have anything to put out, the men can fall back into the hutches to get ready." Captain Moes turned on his heel and headed for the jeep that he always drove himself. He was going up to Brigade headquarters for his briefing and maps and would find out all he could.

When the Captain left, Sergeant Winters got up and took charge of the platoon. "There will be a laundry pickup tonight at 1800 hours, so if you got anything you want washed put it in the back of that truck." He pointed at the three-quarter ton truck standing by his hutch. All heads turned to see the truck as they did every time the announcement was made. "The Captain didn't say anything but the rest of you bums are on standby while the team is operational, so nobody goes anywhere. We're going to have one hour block of instruction to keep up with the training program we're on while in base camp." Sergeant Winters spread his legs to steady himself to the response that he knew was going to come, it always did.

From the platoon there was rumbling of assorted swear words, boos and hisses.

"I hope it's not the Code of Conduct. Man, I'm not going to give up and I know that we're fighting for the free world," said one voice from the platoon.

"Maybe we'll have a first-aid class on mouth to mouth resuscitation."

"Shut up, Morning."

"Let's have a class on how to put on rubbers." Everyone laughed.

"You're so dumb you wouldn't know how. What a damn shit." Everyone laughed again.

Sergeant Winters stood waiting for them to get the wise cracks out of their system before he continued.

"Let's have a class in cutting off Charlie's head, it's been so long since I've had the chance." More laughter.

"You son of a bitch, you never cut off anyone's head."

"That's a damn lie."

Someone was yelling from the back of the platoon. "War atrocity, war atrocity."

Sergeant Winters turned from the platoon, shaking his head. What a bunch of mad men he had there. Keeping control of them was like taking care of a box of dynamite. At any time they could explode, what they could do ... Sergeant Winters closed his eyes to the thought.

"KILL, KILL, KILL!" someone was chanting.

"All right, knock it off!" Sergeant Winters had turned around again. "Knock it off. Save it for the bush. Talk, talk, talk, talk, talk. Don't you maniacs ever get tired of working your jaws? Now shut up or you'll all be out filling sandbags for the rest of the time you're here."

There was a chorus of, "At ease, at ease!" Then quiet.

"Now to continue. Battleford's going to give a class on the "Standing Orders of Rogers Rangers', you ready?"

"Yes, Sergeant," came Battleford's voice, its nasal quality more pronounced in his effort to seem off-handed at the idea of giving a class to his friends.

"Then get up here, unless you all want to sit in the hot sun all afternoon."

"Hey Battle Bat Battleford, hey, hey," Morning yelled out.

"Morning, one more word from you and your ass is mine." Sergeant Winters walked over to where Morning sat on the ground. He stood over Morning bent at the waist and looking down at him, his neck muscles tight, making his face red. "You got that!" It was not a question for Morning to answer.

Morning looked up at Sergeant Winters, a hurt expression on his face. He debated with himself whether to answer, but he decided to remain quiet this time.

Sergeant Winters straightened up again and

walked to the back of the platoon satisfied that he had made his point with Morning. He liked Morning all right, but a little Morning went a long way, he thought to himself.

Battleford walked to the front of the platoon. He stood in front waiting for the class to settle down before he started. He'd done this before, it was part of being in the platoon. He and Green gave a lot of the classes.

"Sergeant Winters? Is it all right if people take off their shirts and smoke during the class?"

Sergeant Winters nodded his head in agreement.

"All right, take off your shirts and smoke if ya'll got 'em." Battleford was imitating a drill instructor.

The platoon laughed. Most of the men took off their shirts and there was some commotion about who had cigarettes and matches.

"Everyone is going to get a copy of Roger Rangers Standing Orders some time today. First, I'm going to start off by telling ya'll about Major Roger Rangers and his ranger outfit. They fought in the French and Indian War on the side of the British. The Rangers fought Indians mostly. These were the General Orders for his outfit that was a lot like the LRRP that we're in now. They did a lot of long range reconnaissance behind the English lines and had to be pretty good because the Indians were good fighters in the bush." Battleford paused, trying to judge if he had enough to talk about for an hour.

"Indians, is he kidding me or what," Morning said out loud, forgetting what Sergeant Winters had said. The rest of the platoon laughed. Sergeant Winters let it go.

"Anyway, he had these 19 orders made up and they're still good today, if ya'll don't get hung up on the wordage." The hot sun beat down on the small group, all sweating freely in the heat. A few of the men had fallen asleep sitting up, their heads nodding. "The first order is: Don't forget nothing." Battleford stopped for emphasis.

"Nothin', don't forget nothing, boy that's getting to the point, that's getting to the point, nothing – Wow!" Morning slapped his leg.

Green laughed, Battleford looked up from the card that he held with a smile on his face.

"Them Rogers Raiders didn't mess around." Morning laughed.

"Shut up, Morning," someone yelled.

Morning put his hand up giving the unknown voice the finger.

"It's Rangers not Raiders, you're really dumb."

Morning's hand stayed up in the air.

"Order number two: Have your musket clean as a whistle, hatchet scoured, sixty rounds of powder and ball, and be ready to march at a minute's notice. For us that means having your shit together and clean your ammo magazines and make sure they're loaded."

"Man, my musket is clean as a whistle." Morning pointed down between his legs. Then he elbowed Green, laughing.

Sergeant Winters broke into a smile. If it didn't get out of hand, he'd let Morning go.

Battleford smiled. "Order number three: When you're on the march, act the way you would if you were sneaking up on a deer, see the enemy first. That means knock off the bullshit when you're out on patrol." Battleford looked up to see what the reaction was.

"Fat Turtle! That means you, you club footed, route stepping…"

"Order number four: you'll like this one. Tell the truth about what you do. There is an Army depending on us for correct information. You can lie all you please when you tell other folks about the rangers, but never lie to a Ranger or officers. That means you, Morning, knock off the war stories."

Everyone laughed again. Green pushed Morning. "It must have been your great grandfather in Rogers Rangers for him to have to write that."

"You guys are really insulting, you know that." Morning sat up again.

"Order number five, Don't never take a chance you don't have to. If you want to stay alive, that is."

"Don't never? You sure that stuff wasn't written by some private someplace. Don't never! That's the Army for you." Green shook his head.

"Order number six," Battleford wiped the sweat from his forehead. "When on the march we march single file, far enough apart so one shot can't go through two men." Battleford paused, scratched the back of his head, then looked out over the platoon. "What it means is stay far enough apart so that it's hard to get two of you at once."

"This isn't for real, is it Sergeant Winters?" a voice called out. There was no answer.

"Order number seven: If we strike swamps, or soft ground, we spread out abreast, so it's hard to track us. Now this is something that we don't do."

"You bet your life we don't do it. Fat Turtle would get lost every time." Morning howled out his laughter.

"Up yours, Morning." Fat Turtle called back.

"Will you two guys shut up for Christ's sake?"

"How long is this going to go on?"

"What are you worried about, you got a lifetime here as it is."

"Shit man, shit."

"Order number eight: When we march, we keep moving till dark, so as to give the enemy the least possible chance at us."

"Order number nine…"

The sun was reaching the top of the sky, beating down on the platoon.

"I didn't know they were fighting the NVA back then."

"They weren't, stupid shit. It was the Indians that they were fighting."

"Who won anyway?"

"The Indians."

"Who's a stupid shit?"

"Well, you know who's going to win here."

"The NVA."

"What in the hell are you guys talking about?"

"They don't know. Will you guys shut up so we can get out of here?"

"Order number nine: When we camp, half the party stays awake while the other half sleeps. This is something that we should remember." Battleford wished that it was all over, he was tired, the sun was too hot.

"Hey Green, let's go to Cambodia. I think that we

would be a lot better off there."

"You may have a point there."

"Order number ten: If we take prisoners..."

"Kill the son-of-a-bitches."

Everyone laughed; the sun kept getting hotter and hotter all the time.

"... we keep 'em separate till we have had time to examine them, so they can't cook up a story between 'em..."

"Then we kill them."

"Man, you can't kill prisoners."

"Says who..."

"The god damn Geneva Convention, that's who."

"Bullshit. The NVA don't even belong to the Geneva Convention, and you know what the hell they'd do to us."

"What? You ever been captured?"

"I don't have to be to know. We've all seen GI's that have been captured by Charlie, and they've been messed up bad."

"Well, we're still a member of the Geneva Convention and it says that you can't kill prisoners."

"That Geneva Convention is full of shit. I ain't never seen no Genevas out in the bush yet."

"I'm for war atrocities."

"Shut up, nobody asked you."

"You guys are crazy."

"Order number eleven: Don't ever march the same way home. Take a different route so you won't be ambushed. We do that."

"You sure we're not fighting the Indians? It sure sounds like it to me."

"It would."

"Scalp 'em, that's what we should do. Scalp 'em."

"That's a good idea. That would really freak out Charlie."

"Battleford, will ya keep going. It's almost time for chow."

"Order number twelve: No matter if we travel in big parties or little ones, each party had to keep a scout 20 yards ahead, 20 yard on each flank and 20 yards in the rear, so the main body can't be surprised and wiped out."

"We're already wiped out."

Everyone laughed.

"Order number thirteen: Every night you'll be told where to meet if surrounded by a superior force."

"We should meet in San Francisco."

"I left my heart in San Francisco." Someone starting singing.

"That's where you left your brains."

Everyone laughed.

"Order number fourteen: Don't sit to eat without posting sentries."

"Order number fifteen: Don't sleep beyond dawn. Dawn's when the English and Indians like to attack." Battleford wiped the sweat from his forehead again.

"I told you we were fighting the Indians. How come no one said anything about the English?"

"Because we're not, that's why."

"Are you sure?"

No answer.

"Order number sixteen: Don't cross a river by a regular ford."

"Damn it, it's hot."

"I wish I was crossing a river right now, into Cambodia," Morning said under his breath.

"Order number seventeen: If someone is trailing you, make a circle, come back onto your own tracks and ambush the folks that aim to ambush you."

"Oh brother! Folks, this had to be a joke."

"No, I don't think it is."

"Then it should be."

"Order number eighteen: Don't stand up when the enemy's coming against you, kneel, lay down, hide behind a tree."

"How about run like hell?"

Everyone laughed.

"Order number nineteen. The last one."

"Thank God."

"Let the enemy come till he's almost close enough to touch. Then let him have it and jump out and finish him with your hatchet."

"Anybody got a hatchet?"

"No man, no one's got a hatchet."

"This is stupid."

"I wonder if the NVA have stupid classes like this."

"If they don't, they should have."

"Remember, we're the best trained Army in the world."

"Who said?"

"I read it in the "Army Times"."

"You would read the "Army Times, LIFER!""

"That's the end of the class. You'll all get a copy of Rogers Rangers Standing Orders to have as your very own."

"I'd rather have a discharge."

Everyone laughed.

"Sergeant Winters, should I dismiss the platoon?"

Sergeant Winters nodded his head.

"Dismissed!"

"Is this for real?"

Sergeant Winters turned and headed to the Mess Hall.

"Hey, Battleford!" Morning called.

"What?"

"That was some strange stuff."

"You're telling me." Battleford walked over to Morning, Green and Fat Turtle.

"My mother would freak out if she saw this stuff, Christ."

"Yeah, she'd think you were fighting Indians."

"Will you knock off that Indian stuff," Battleford punched Morning in the arm.

"What's that for?"

"You make me nervous, that's why."

Morning started doing his interpretation of a war dance, dancing circles around the other three.

"He's hopeless." Green pointed at Morning dancing.

"I'm going to the Mess Hall." Fat Turtle headed in that direction.

"Anybody coming?"

"Yeah, I'm coming too." Battleford pushed Morning out of his way.

"Freak."

"You coming Green?" Turtle asked.

"No, you guys go ahead."

"Wait, I'm going with you guys." Morning stopped dancing and ran to catch up with Battleford and Turtle.

Jim Green walked slowly to the low black and green painted hutch, stopped, and looked down the uniform column of the low black and green camouflaged hutches, the sandbag "Z" shaped bunkers in between each one. They weren't much but they were better than what was there before. The jungle and ponchos were made into lean-to's stretched across foxholes; it had been during the rainy season and they had always been wet, and there had been little difference between base camp and being out on an operation. They lived like hobos, eating out of tin cans; that's what it had been, a hobo jungle. Everything was grown over and there had been firefights almost every night. The patrols that went out usually brought back wounded and dead; there were always choppers flying to Evac Hospital down the road, and they'd spend a lot of time just counting the number until one day they had stopped at fifty, and they never counted again. Then they had gotten the GP tents, and there had been the trips down to Saigon to the ships that had come up the Saigon River to the harbor. With lumber from the ships, they made floors for each of the tents. There had been long sheets of tin for the hutches.

After completing an operation at Pla Coa, they spent time painting the sheets green and black camouflage. Over the months the jungle had given way to the Brigade. Underneath the hutches had been sand and without the jungle, the ground had begun to shift. There used to be two feet of sand under each hutch now, some of the hutches had less than a foot. The sandy ground, the walkway, lined with sandbags on each side, the latrines spaced the proper distance, the hand-to-hand combat pit, and the black dog ambling up the walkway, sniffing each sandbag individually and giving some extra attention...all in a day's work.

Tango had been four months old when he and Morning had gotten him at a hamlet outside of Bien Cat. He had grown and gotten big and strong on mess hall leftovers; he was a good dog to have around. There were a lot of dogs in the Brigade area but Tango was one of the better ones. My time here can be almost measured by the size of Tango, Green thought. The day that he got Tango they'd gone up by Bien Cat to make a parachute jump. That was before they changed the regulation about having to jump once every three months in order to get jump pay. Now, if they were in a combat zone, they didn't have to make a jump. Well, they were still jumping then. It was sort of crazy, but they did and it was accepted as part of the routing.

They had gotten up at four in the morning and were loaded into cattle cars, great long semi-trucks, and they had gone out to perimeter road and waited for three hours. Later, some infantry came and they all waited until the two-rigger trucks came with the parachutes. Then the MPs came giving them an escort with their gun jeeps, and everybody made fun of them because they were MPs and not grunts.

"Tango, come here." The dog looked up from his sandbag. "Front and center, damn it," Green called. He clapped his hands together. The big dog broke into a run, leaping, striding, pink tongue hanging out. He still showed some of his puppyness, just a little awkward, but not as awkward as last week or the month before. Jim liked to watch Tango run, he was a good runner.

"Come on Tango." Jim turned, knowing that the dog would follow him as he walked.

It wasn't a long ride to Bien Cat, maybe two hours. Just about everyone had gone to sleep on the way up, even though the way to Bien Cat was bad country and Bien Cat was no safe area by a long shot. They got to the open area where they were going to jump; it was just a big open field with a hamlet at the far end. The truck pulled around in a circle in a cloud of dust. The only movement was from the men getting out of the trucks; they were the only thing that broke the stillness of the hot day.

"Tango, where in the hell have you been all day?" Jim didn't turn to the dog that was following at his heel; the dog nudged his hand with his nose, which was his only answer.

~ ~ ~

He and Morning stood off by themselves. That was when they were still pretty new and some of the other soldiers were talking about hearing rifle shots on the way up.

They waited till the choppers came. Once the jumping began, while half of the men jumped, the other half kept guard on the perimeter of trucks. They couldn't jump with their weapons. That would have been a combat jump by Army regulations. Jim was glad that he had a pistol under his shirt. He and Morning were going to jump in the second group, so they had been assigned a place by some buck sergeant, and they sat there not really watching but just talking. Fat Turtle and Battleford had joined them; they had been together for a long time. Jim realized that it was almost a year ago. No one had really watched the front; there were three guys down a couple trucks that were blowing grass. A lot of the guys around them were talking about pulling a slip and going to the hamlet when it was their turn to jump, and that seemed like a good idea. When the jumpmaster talked to them later, he told them that under no circumstances were they to land over at the hamlet since it wasn't secured. That didn't make any difference to anyone though. A lot of guys said that they couldn't help it if the wind blew them over to the hamlet. That wouldn't be their fault. It was really a hot day and a tiger beer would have been perfect, but when the choppers came and the jumping started, no one pulled any slip to the hamlet and it had just been talk. That was when Morning looked at Jim with his funny smile and they knew that when their turn to jump came, they were going to the hamlet. They both had smiled and when it came their turn and they chuted up and were ready for the next chopper, they were in the same stick.

Morning had said, "Meet you in the hamlet over there." That was all, he said it under his breath and Jim had winked back.

They stood crouched over, the parachutes being heavy and uncomfortable even without the heat. The chopper came in and the dust rose; someone was there helping them in. It was difficult moving inside the HU-1B chopper but they got turned around. The other three guys they didn't know. They had just straightened around and the chopper started rising. It was always a scary feeling to have the chopper rock back and forth just a few feet off ground and then start to move vertically, rising very fast. They got the get-ready sign from the pilot and the chopper stopped in mid-air; it felt strange to just hang there. Then the chopper started to move fast, making the pass at the drop zone.

Green and Morning were the first ones in, so they were the last two out of the chopper. It didn't take long for the other three to get out. Jim waited a few moments before he jumped so that he could be as close to the hamlet as possible. He remembered the pilot motioning him to go, that he was waiting too long in the door, but he didn't pay any attention to him as long as he flew closer and closer to the hamlet. All this was just a few seconds, but seemed longer. Then Green kicked off from the chopper, fell free for fifteen feet, and then his static line pulled open the parachute. He looked around for Morning, and he was to the left rear; Morning waved hanging in the harness, then pulled himself up on his left riser pulling the canopy of the chute down so that he drifted in the direction of the hamlet. Green did the same thing, pulling himself up on the riser. It was quiet after the noise of the carpet. The descent wouldn't be more than two minutes before it'd be over, and he would be crashing down on the earth again. He realized that he hadn't checked his canopy as he had been taught to do in jump school. He looked up and it was fine, and then he was hitting the ground and it was all over now. He performed the PLF and was standing again. He saw Morning coming down. Morning was pulling on both risers now and just before he hit the ground, he popped his chute and made a stand-up landing that was really beautiful to see. As soon as he hit the ground, he began to run and the chute settled down behind him, and he gave out with his crazy laugh of pure enjoyment.

They gathered up their chutes, figure-eighting them over their arms and then stuffing them into their parachute kit bags. Both were sweating from the work of putting away their chutes. Now they stopped and looked at each other, sweat running down their faces and dust caked to Jim's face and clothes from doing the PLF, and both of them laughed at the prank that they were playing by landing at the hamlet; it was a good joke.

"Man, we may be new dudes but we got balls," Morning had said and laughed and laughed.

Green nodded, feeling pleased with himself about the whole thing too.

"You got your pistol, don't you?"

"Yeah." Green patted his underarm where the pistol rested in its shoulder holster.

They both laughed again, and Morning jumped up and down as he reached over and patted the place where the pistol was.

"Let's see what we got ourselves into." Green picked up his kit bag and headed for the main street of the hamlet with Morning running after him to catch up.

"Let's get a beer first."

"Right." They walked over to the main street where children and a few old men gathered to look at the two who had come from the sky.

Morning dropped his kit bag, put his arms out. "Tien Bing, Tien Bing. Me Tien Bing." He pointed to himself and to Green. "He Tien Bing, Tien Bing ... Sky Soldier, Tien Bing ... Sky Soldier."

The Vietnamese he was talking to motioned that they didn't understand, none of them moved from where they stood.

"We're all right." Morning picked up his kit bag again. "They don't understand Chinese."

"Well, neither do you."

"What do you mean? I just got through talking to them in Chinese."

"Big deal, two words, sky soldier. If any of them could speak Chinese, they would really be impressed. What would you have done if one of them had started talking to you in Chinese? You wouldn't have understood a word."

"Yeah, but I would have run like hell. This is South Vietnam, you know. No one is supposed to speak Chinese. That's what I was doing, seeing if we were safe or not."

"Oh brother!"

"Come on, let's go, I'm thirsty." Moring started off again to find where the Tiger beer was sold.

The main street wasn't much, a few huts that looked like a store, a barbershop, and there it was a small bar or sidewalk café, if there had been a sidewalk. As they walked along the street a small boy came up to them.

"You American ... DINKY DOW, DINKY DOW." Then he made the motion of shooting the two of them.

"Dity Mo, Dity Mo, you little Cong son-of-a-bitch." Morning turned and pointed a finger at the little boy. "You DINKY DOW ..." The boy showed no sign of fear and kept on shooting them with his pretend gun.

"I'm really glad that the local people like us." Green walked over to one of the tables and sat down, putting his parachute kit bag down close so it wouldn't be stolen.

Morning sat down across from Green, but sitting sideways, feet on his kit bag using it as a hassock. "Do you think they'll send somewhere after us?"

"Yes, we better drink down a couple and get the hell back."

"Yeah, you're right."

An old man who seemed to run the restaurant, came over smiling, and then bowed a little without saying a word.

"Two Tiger beer." Morning put up two fingers.

The man motioned that he didn't understand what Morning had said to him.

"Two." Morning raised his two fingers again and pointed at them with his other hand. Then he pointed at a bottle of Tiger beer that was sitting behind the counter in the café. "Tiger beers."

The old man understood and nodded his head, speaking the words in Vietnamese for himself, not for either of them. He went off to get the beer.

"You notice something around here?"

"What?" Green was looking around the street and the café. There was a group of kids and old men watching them from the other side of the street. They were sitting down Vietnamese style in the dust.

"Have you seen any young men in this place since we got here?"

"No."

"Me neither."

"Yeah, but maybe they're out in the fields or something like that."

"Or maybe they're playing Viet Cong."

"Maybe."

The old man brought the beer, two quart bottles and two glasses with ice cubes in them. He set them down and then showed Morning a slip of paper with the price written down on it.

"He wants two hundred pias," Morning looked up at Green.

"Pay him."

"Hell, that's too damn much, Vietnamese don't pay a third of that."

"Pay him, it's good for the economy."

"It's guys like you that raise the price of everything." Morning dug into his pockets and took out 2500 piasters. He counted out two hundred and gave it to the old man, who smiled and thanked Morning, backing away.

"Come on, come on." Morning nodded his head. "That means thank you. I'm getting to speak this stuff pretty good already."

Green didn't answer but started pouring his beer over the ice cubes.

Morning followed suit. "Do you think they ever wash the glasses in this place?" Morning held up his glass to the light. "Look at this, it's filthy."

"This isn't exactly the Hotel Hilton, for Christ's sake."

"Thanks for telling me."

The two of them sat drinking their beer in silence.

"Boy, if they could only see us now, wouldn't it be something."

"Who do you mean, they?"

"The guys back home, THEY!"

"Yeah, it would be something else."

Morning smiled and drank more of his beer.

"This place isn't all that bad," Morning said, after taking a large gulp of beer.

"I'll wait a while before I say anything."

"Look, that kid over there!" Morning pointed in the opposite direction from where Green was looking.

Green spun around in his chair, reaching inside of his shirt for the pistol. "What?"

"The kid with the puppy on the rope."

"Yeah."

"Well, god damn it, that's a black Labrador retriever if I ever saw one."

"A black Lab?"

"Yeah. How in the hell does a kid in Vietnam get a black Lab?"

"Got me."

"That's a black lab."

"Are you sure?"

"Yes, I'm sure, I know a black Lab when I see one."

Green turned around again, back to his beer. "That would be a neat dog to have, you know that. Maybe the kid will trade or sell him."

"Maybe. I'll get him over here and see what he wants for him. Hey kid, Boy son, Boy son," Morning yelled out and waved at the boy with the dog, pointing and then waving. The boy stood in his tracks, not moving. Morning got up and walked across the street and knelt down and patted the black Lab. The three of them came walking back across the street in a moment. "The kid can speak some English. He said that he got the dog at a special forces camp before his old man got killed. I think that he was in the army or something like that."

The boy stood not speaking, looking at Green. Green reached over and petted the dog. He might very well be a black lab. The boy couldn't have been more than 10 or 11, Green thought, he looked pretty healthy.

"He willing to trade him or what?"

"Now take your time, for Christ's sake. The more he sees we want that dog, the more he's going to cost us. I haven't even asked him yet."

"All right, just see if we can get that dog, Morning."

"I will." Morning turned to the boy with a smile on his face.

"He," Morning pointed to Green, "thinks your dog is number one." Morning spoke in halting Vietnamese but the boy seemed to understand. "But the dog is very sickly and not too good, but he still would like to acquire it from you." Morning talked slowing, searching for the Vietnamese words that weren't familiar to him.

"Chow yoy, he's good dog, not sick. He be good to eat," the boy said in Vietnamese to Morning.

"He says it will make good eating."

Green put his hands up in the air in disbelief.

"Boy-san, he give you three hundred pia and…" Morning stopped in mid-sentence.

"Hey, you got any "C's" on you?" Morning started digging into his own pockets bringing out the "C" rations that he had not eaten for lunch that day.

"Yeah."

"Get them out and we'll have that dog in no time flat."

Green dug out the "C's" in his pockets, putting them on the table.

"Look, you see this, good chop chop, chop chop five cans." Morning held up five fingers. He took out two hundred pias from his pocket and put them on top of the cans.

"All for dog. Too much, too much."

The boy looked at the pile of cans and the two hundred pias.

"Chow-yoy." He put the rope leash in Morning's hand and took the cans and money. He stood holding the things in his arms, smiled, bowed twice, and turned and ran down the street.

"There's your dog. You owe me lunch and two hundred pias."

"Thanks, Morning, you are really getting good." Green reached out for the puppy and pulled him over to him. The dog looked after the boy running down the street but never made a move to follow.

"Good boy," Green rubbed the dog's ears.

"What are you going to name the dog, Blackie?"

"No, I'll think of something."

~ ~ ~

The radio blared.

"Long –haired hippies again attempted to stop troop movements in the Oakland and Presidio area of San Francisco today. Police and military policemen removed the demonstrators without incident." The radio went on: "Units of the 1st Air Calvary began a sweep of the Asaw Valley encountering little resistance." The news continued. Green made no sign that he had heard it but he did, all of it. "Next we'll have the best of country music. Climbing on the country western charts is "A Letter for Vietnam.""

Tango sat in the middle of the aisle between the two bunks, tongue hanging out, gray-green eyes watching each movement of his master, waiting.

"Good boy, Tango."

The song ended on the radio.

The dog sat, waiting, his excitement growing, his hindquarters moving in his excitement, his rattail stirring up a dust storm behind him. Tango made noises in his throat that grew to the full roar of his bark; he pointed his head skyward and sounded out his reply.

"Now Barry Saddler and the 'Ballad of the Green Berets'" 'Jumpin' soldier from the sky, born to jump and die, for they knew just what they are' The radio went on...

"War atrocities, man! War atrocities, man!" the words suddenly flashed through Green's mind and were gone in an instant.

"Okay, it's okay, Tango." Jim put his hand out to the dog, rubbing his big square head and ears; the dog was silent, panting happily.

"Kill 'em! Kill 'em, that's what it's all about!" The fleeting thought was gone again. But I don't give a shit...I can't give a shit.

"But my wings on my chest tell the world I did my best..." The radio went on ...

Battleford, Turtle and Morning came slouching

into the hutch; Morning flopping on his bunk with a loud groan, making Tango turn his head. Battleford sat in Turtle's lawn chair and Turtle followed Morning's example, making his bunk groan under his weight; no one spoke, they looked straight ahead.

There was no answer.

Green lay back on his cot. "Morning, what do you think of the war now?"

"It's a piece of shit." Morning continued looking straight up.

"Man, do you always describe everything in terms of shit?"

"If that's what it is, I do."

Fat Turtle sat up on one elbow. "You know what I think about this war?"

"No one cares what you think about anything." Morning said.

"Shut up Morning," Green said. "What do you think about the war?"

"Well," Turtle paused because someone was listening.

"That's a deep subject," Morning laughed his hyena laugh.

"I don't think it's right that we're here at all."

Morning grunted.

"What are you guys worrying about anyway? You're here and that's a fact and no matter how you look at it, there's no changing it." Battleford closed his eyes again.

Turtle thoughtfully mused. "Well, I can't see how anything that these people do over here can bother people in the world."

"Well, it's sure affecting us." Battleford didn't bother to open his eyes.

"What about the domino theory?" Green asked.

"I been here a long time and I've not seen one god damn domino," Morning said just for the hell of it.

"What about the people here?"

"What about them? All they want is full rice bowls."

Battleford opened his eyes. "Will you guys talk about something else? Broads, home, anything, but just stay off this god damn war. I'm trying to sleep. All we're doing over here is spinning our wheels, we're not getting anywhere. Listen to the music on the radio."

Green was aware of the oppressive heat in the hutch.

"Come here, Tango, my mangy mutt." Morning slapped his chest. Green took his hand from the dog's head and the dog stood up, backed out of the aisle and walked slowly, tail wagging, tongue hanging out, to Morning. He put his head on Morning's chest. Morning dropped his hand on the dog's neck.

Green lifted his rifle off the two nails that were pounded into the two-by-fours, he pulled the bolt back, looked into the chamber, then let the bolt fly forward making a metallic click. No one paid any attention except Tango, who pricked his ears. Green sat with the rifle on his lap, looking at it.

Norton, the sergeant's runner came into the hutch. "Hey Green, Winters wants you right now." Private First Class Norton stood in the doorway.

"God damn it, Green, you heard the man, Sergeant Winters wants you. Let's go, let's jump through our ass," Morning jeered, not moving from his position on his cot.

"Blow it out your ass," Green returned, getting up and putting on his baseball cap.

"Come on Tango, I don't want you hanging around bad company, let's go and play on the old team. Come on boy, let's play the game." Tango lifted his head, then went to Jim's side. They left together.

"You guys never do nothing," Norton said, sitting down on Green's cot.

"What you mean?" Morning sat up. "We're getting ready for an operation."

"Yeah, on your back. You're getting ready for nothing," Norton replied. He got a cigarette from his pocket and lit it.

"What do you know about it, you noncombatant son-of-a-bitch," Morning said. "I'm thinking."

"You're right Morning, you couldn't think your way out of a paper bag."

"Look private, when you've been in the Army as long as I have, then you can shoot off your mouth." Morning lay back down on his bunk.

"Who you callin' private. You can't even make private first class, dud," Morton returned.

"Look, it ain't my fault that certain members of this command don't appreciate the fine work I do." Morning sat up. Battleford and Turtle were looking at each other, laughing.

"Name one thing you ever did right and I'll kiss your..."

Morning cut him off. "How about the time I killed forty-seven gooks without firing a shot. You guys remember that don't yah?" He looked at Bat and Turtle.

"Hell yes," they both said.

"Okay, I'll bite. How?" Norton threw his hands in the air.

"I told them you were coming over on the next plane and they all died of fright." Morning went into peals of laughter. "Now don't bother me. I got to get some rest, I'm a growing boy." Morning lay down, laughing. Norton shook his head, and walked out of the hutch still shaking his head. They were all crazy, he thought, and Morning was the craziest guy in the Army.

"He's a pretty good guy," Morning said to the others. "He should come into the platoon and quit kissing the first sergeant's ass."

"He never will. He's got it too good where he is," Battleford said.

"Hey, you guys got your stuff ready?" Morning said. "I'm always ready."

"You better get straight Turtle," Battleford said. He was tired. He walked over to his cot and lay down and went to sleep. Morning lay staring at the ceiling, listening to the radio. Turtle went to work cleaning and getting his equipment ready. He had cleaned it the day before.

~ ~ ~

Green ambled into the operations hutch and threw his shirt over the Wicker chair. "Sergeant Winters, hey, Sergeant Winters." No one answered. "Where in the hell are you?" Jim looked under the typewriter cover as he walked around the room. He went over to the table that served as his desk, opened the box of Marsh Wheeling cigars, took one out, bit off the end and lit it, sat down and put his feet up on the typewriter.

A few minutes later Sergeant Winters came through the door, followed by a second lieutenant that Jim had never seen before. Jim didn't move from his place in the wicker chair.

"Green, this is Lieutenant Donnally."

"Sir," Jim said, getting up from his chair.

The lieutenant nodded his head stiffly. Green took a closer look at him. He wasn't much older than he was. He had just come from the states, his skin was pale and his uniform was still a very dark green. It would be three months before he looked a part of the Brigade. He would have to live through being a new guy.

"Call me Green, Sir." Green sat back down on his char. "What did you want me for, Sarge?"

"I didn't want you. The lieutenant wants you." Sergeant Winters looked at the lieutenant, almost saying, here he is, it's out of my hands. Green looked at the lieutenant waiting.

"Well, thank you Sergeant Winters for your help. Let's go Green, up to the Brigade."

The two men left, walked down to the troop parking lot where the jeep and the driver were waiting. The driver and Green eyed each other; nothing was said. The driver started up the jeep; Jim got into the back and the lieutenant walked around and got in. Jim was wondering what was going on; he kept trying to think of the different crimes he'd committed with Morning. However, nothing was serious enough to warrant this attention. Yet, the Army didn't send lieutenants down to pick up SP/4's for no reason. Jim sat in the back of the jeep, wracking his brain for the reason.

"Okay sir, what the hell's going on? You got me, I give up," Jim said, hoping to get an answer. The lieutenant looked at Jim Green without saying a word. They were almost at Brigade headquarters now. Jim shrugged his shoulders and sat back in the jeep.

The jeep turned off the dusty road at the heliport onto the little used road leading to the area where the officers' hutches were. They passed the helicopters parked on their pads, went on down the road past the general's living quarters, to a small newly built hutch almost at the end of the road. Jim didn't remember the building and he didn't know who lived there. The lieutenant got out of the jeep and headed for the door. Jim got out, stopped and looked at the driver. "Who lives here?"

The jeep driver smiled. "That's the house of Colonel Woodworth, the most gung-ho man in ... Good luck."

Jim looked at the house and then back at the jeep driver; he touched the brim of his baseball cap, stuck the cigar into his mouth and walked up to the door. The lieutenant had already gone inside, so Specialist Four Jim Green followed him in.

"Who in the hell asked you to come in?"

Jim was looking at an older man sitting on top of the desk. He turned on his heel and walked out into the hot sunlight. The jeep driver, who had heard the colonel, was sitting in his jeep laughing.

Jim found some shade in the overhang of the roof and waited for what was to come next. The lieutenant came out, looked at Jim Green. Green shrugged his shoulders and stood with his weight on both feet. The lieutenant motioned him to go in. Jim took the cigar and threw it over his shoulder and walked in before the lieutenant could say a word.

Green was standing before the same older man with salt-and-pepper hair, steel blue eyes set in a hard face, not yet gone soft from age. Colonel Glen Woodworth sat straight as a stick in his swivel chair.

"Sir, Specialist Green, reporting as ordered." Green held his salute, standing at the position of attention, not moving, looking straight over the head of the colonel. Colonel Woodworth returned the salute.

"At ease," he said, looking over the man standing in front of him. Green stood waiting for the colonel; he would have to make the next move, it was up to him. At the moment he was looking Jim over as if he were a personal piece of property, something the colonel was deciding whether he should keep or let go.

"I've heard a lot about you, Green, you're a real tiger," he said, leaning forward on his desk. Jim said nothing. "That's what they tell me, a real tiger."

Jim still waited, it wasn't his turn yet.

"Tell me, Green, how long have you been in country?"

"A little over ten months, sir," Jim replied.

"You've got two months left. Is that when your discharge is too?"

"Yes sir,"

"What are you going to do after you get out? I take it you are getting out."

"Yes sir. I don't know. Maybe go to college or something. Haven't given it much thought."

The colonel nodded. "I've got a job for you Green.

It will last about two weeks. Think you'll want it?'

"I don't know. What's the job?"

"Guarding me." The colonel leaned back in his chair.

"You say it's just for two weeks?"

"Two weeks, maybe less. I already have it cleared through Captain Moes."

"Okay, sir. When do I start?"

"Good. In a few days there's going to be a little operation. Sit down." The colonel motioned to a deck chair that sat in a corner of the small office. Green went over to the chair and pulled it in front of the desk.

"Thank you, sir." Jim sat down.

"Smoke if you like. We'll be living together for awhile."

Green brought out a pack of cigarettes, lit one, and put the pack back into his pocket. He felt uncomfortable sitting in the presence of the older man. It was partly rank and partly the man himself. In the nearly two years he'd been in the Army, Green had little to do with officers. He'd accepted the caste system of the Army and had lived with it as a part of everyday life. Now it was the same as if a serf had been brought into the presence of a prince, and no matter how common the prince, the serf was ill at ease because he'd been conditioned.

"Now, let me see, where was I? Oh yes. There's going to be an operation. We'll be Task Force Puma. The General has given me its command. It will be made up of elements of the brigade and a few Australians. We'll be used for a backstop for the brigade to drive the NVA into us. Your job is to keep me alive; in case something should go wrong and it appears that capture is imminent, you'll have to kill me. You think you can do that Green?"

Green looked at the floor for a drawn-out minute. "Yes sir, I think I could." Green looked up at the older man across the desk from him as he said it.

"Good. You'll do just fine. You know Green, an old General told me that if I ever needed a guard, to get an enlisted man who wanted to get out of the Army. They're the ones that try to stay alive the hardest." The colonel laughed to himself. Green smiled back.

"Go back to your unit, pack your equipment, and be back tomorrow morning. I'll send my jeep to pick you up."

"Thank you sir." Green got up from the chair, put it back, turned and saluted, and walked back out into the hot afternoon sun.

The jeep driver was asleep, his baseball cap pulled over his eyes. Green walked over, sat down in the front seat and nudged the driver. He raised his head and looked at Green.

"You can take me back to the troop area."

The driver's only response was to lean over, turn on the ignition, start the jeep, throw the gear shift into reverse, and backing out so that the jeep was headed toward the road - all done with a great deal of spinning the tires and spraying gravel. Green smiled to himself at the thought of one SP/4 driving another around, it amused him.

The jeep pulled into the troop area and stopped. Green jumped out, thanked the driver who nodded back. Green walked up the company street, unbuttoning his shirt. He was met halfway by Tango, who had been lying in the cool sand under one of the tents. Green motioned for the dog to come with him; at the door to the tent the dog went ahead, going to his place under Green's cot.

Morning lay asleep on his bunk, Battlford was cleaning his weapon, and Turtle sat waiting as he paged through a men's magazine. Jim walked down the aisle, taking off his shirt and dropping it on his bunk and proceeding down to where Fat Turtle and Battleford sat.

"Where you at, Batman?"

"Nowhere, man, nowhere. Where you at man?"

Green sat down next to him. "What you reading Turtle?" Green reached over and took the magazine from Turtle.

"A cock story. Ain't any good though. Once you've read one, you've read them all. You can have the damn thing."

Green shrugged. "Any pictures?" He paged through the magazine for the pictures of the girls in their underwear or shorty pajamas.

"Naw. There's one where she looks kind of sexy if you turn the picture upside down."

Green stopped at the first of the pictures and turned it sideways, then upside down.

"A real pig."

"Yeah, but better than what you get in Saigon or Bien Hoa," Turtle said, lying back on the bunk.

"What did Winters want you for?" Battleford asked.

"I had to go up and see some colonel what's-his-name."

"What for?" Turtle sat up.

"He's going out into the boonies in a couple of days and he wants me to be his bodyguard."

"Well, kiss my ass." It was Morning from the other side of the tent. He got up and walked down to where they sat, sitting next to Turtle. He took the magazine from Green and started to page through it.

"What's your problem, Morning?" Green said.

"He's going to miss you when you're gone," Battleford said, looking up from his weapon.

"Blow it out your ..." Morning began.

He was interrupted by Battleford. "Morning comes around and the conversation ends up in the gutter."

Morning looked at the picture of a girl with a black bra and panties; he turned it upside down and looked at it.

"This reminds me of your sister, Batman." Morning turned away from the picture to look at Battleford. The other two laughed.

"Yeah, but my sister's better looking than that." Battleford returned to his weapon.

"Boy, I'm glad my mother can't hear the language of the guys that I got to hang around with," Fat Turtle put in.

"What's your mother got to do with it, Fat Turtle," Morning returned.

"I don't know. Just thought I'd say it," Fat Turtle said.

"I just thought I'd ..." Morning was mimicking Turtle.

"At ease, goddamn it. I don't want to hear any of that shit," Green yelled out, imitating Sergeant Winter's voice. They all laughed.

"Hey, Green," Turtle said.

"What?" Green stopped smiling at his own joke.

"Aren't you going out on the mission then?"

"No. I got to report to the colonel tomorrow."

"Does Sergeant Winters know that?"

"I guess so. The colonel said he had already talked to Captain Moes."

"I'm going down and ask Sergeant Winters for the point then." Turtle started to get up.

"Naw, stay on the radio, Turtle. You don't want the point."

"Why not?" Turtle sat back down on the cot, helped by Morning's pulling on his shoulder.

"Cause once you walk point they never let you quit, and sooner than you know you end up dead. That's why. So stay on the radio," Green said very seriously.

"Horse shit. You're not dead and you've been point for a long time."

"Yeah. And besides, you're a good RTO and we got to look out for the taxpayer's interest," Morning put in.

Turtle enjoyed the praise from his friends. It made him feel good. In school he'd been the object of many jokes; he'd always been Fat Turtle who couldn't do anything right, and now he was being praised by other men whom he admired.

"If you guys put it that way, I'd better give the taxpayers a break."

"That's what I like about you, Turtle. You're patriotic," Battleford said, looking up from his rifle.

The others agreed and Turtle sat next to Morning across from Green and Battleford, feeling things that he'd never felt before. The best of this was pride in himself. Fat Turtle had always been just a little too fat, his clothes never looked right. Even for his size the clothes ended up being too big, and he looked sloppy with his stomach sticking out, his hair was too curly and his soft face still didn't need a razor but once a week. His mother had told him not to join the Army because only boys that weren't good were in the Army and the nice boys went to college. But it had been the nice boys who made the jokes about him and meant them. These guys here were really his friends and he was one of them and this feeling of belonging was important to him, the most important thing in the world, more important than living.

"Hey, I got a letter from my mother and she told me that I should talk to my commanding officer about the way the supply sergeant has been treating me." Turtle would read aloud the letters that he wrote to his mother, lying about being a supply clerk. He liked the attention and making the others laugh.

They all laughed.

"Yeah, Turtle, you make sure and see the CO."

Turtle sat laughing on the cot next to Morning.

Later, they went to the mess hall together for supper, sitting at the same table. Morning tried to pick a fight with one of the men in the Cav troop telling him that "Pony soldiers eat shit," but the pony soldier had been backed down by the presence of the three boys. They laughed and joked at the other soldiers around them inside the mess hall. In a way, Fat Turtle was getting back at those high school heroes who had made him the object of their jokes.

Battleford had come from a rough section of New

Orleans, had boxed in the Golden Gloves, and had unloaded banana boats before he'd joined the Army out of boredom. The Army proved not much better until he'd gotten to Vietnam. Now he was looking forward to getting, as he put it, "back on the block." The streets of New Orleans looked better from Vietnam than they ever had when he was there.

Morning's parents were worried about him now, something that he'd never known when he'd been home. There had always been something more important to them than Morning. Now he was getting the attention he wanted from his parents and the rest of the people around him. He also had Green. Without the Army, he and Green would have traveled different circles. But now they were thrown together. It didn't matter that it was just a matter of geography and time. He wanted to be like Green although he knew he never could be. Only now, Green was becoming more like Morning and Morning was becoming more like Green.

Green went along, he wasn't yet aware of how he was changing. He liked Morning but his parents would never have approved of this friendship. Mark Morning wasn't "his kind of people," but actually he was. Who were "his kind of people?" He didn't know. He was at least relating to someone and he'd never done that before. He hated the war, but at the same time it held a fascination for him.

There were personal issues they held in common as they left the mess hall, pushing and shoving, laughing at each other and the people around them. They lived on emotions – even the emotions they fought to suppress. These were inner challenges that each had to deal with.

The others sat around Green as he packed his things in his parachute bag for the next morning's assignment.

Sergeant Winters came into the tent, telling Green that he'd been told about the special duty he was on.

"We'll miss you Green, but the Mission's routine so you won't miss anything. Do a good job and get back."

"Thanks Sarge," Green said. The rest sat quietly, feeling proud because one of them was being singled out. "I'll do my best."

Sergeant Winters left. He'd seen a lot of boys like Green in his sixteen years in the army. He didn't understand them and he didn't try. He wasn't running a day camp, he'd told the First Sergeant once.

After he left, the three made noises and kidded Green.

"You're a god damn war hero," Morning said.

They went down and bought some beer and sat around drinking and then they went to sleep one by one.

The team had left an hour ago. Green sat in the operations hutch waiting for Colonel Woodworth's driver to arrive. He reached for the canteen cup that was full of the mess hall coffee. This would be the first time that he wouldn't be out with Sergeant Winter's team and he felt a sense of guilt.

Green didn't know when Morning, Fat Turtle and Battleford and the rest had left. He could see now he had seen it too many times before; the helicopter hanging two or three feet off the ground, as if suspended by an unseen wire; the tail unsteady as to which way it should go; the air being filled with dirt;

the men on the ground shading their eyes the best they could; the roar from the overhead motor making it impossible to hear; and men making signals to each other because of the roar. The team was running underneath the motor, bent at the waist, the first man out the last one in. The helicopter would hover for a moment with its cargo, then start forward, nose down, then rising very quickly, and then it would be very quiet on the ground again. Each man of the team would be near panic, but would find a way to swallow it, only on the ride he might have to swallow it ten or a hundred times. The men wouldn't look each other in the eye, afraid of what he would see – his own fear. The rhythmic battling of the rotors against the invisible air; the air cool in the early morning.

Below them the quiet of the land; the jungle looking like green mushrooms and quiet. There seemed always to be the high-tension wires that ran the length of the country, man's only hold on the jungle. They would be getting closer; each member would try to get on his feet, still crouching. The men at the doors would peer into the trees for a sign; the rear gunners would make ready. The co-pilot would turn to look at the men and point to the ground; he would have no eyes, they were covered by sunglasses; and no mouth, since the small mike covered it. The chopper would be a few feet from the ground and the first man would be out, causing the chopper to go off balance for a moment; it would right itself, and the men would be off, the tall grass lying flat because of the wind from the rotors. The men would be running, falling, tripping, and running again for the tree line and safety. The chopper lifted off and was out of sight, the sound of its rotors beating the air, leaving them behind. The men crouch and listen.

Green looked up and saw the Colonel's driver standing in the doorway.

"Come in. I'm finishing my coffee." Green waved him in with his hand.

The driver came in, sat down in Sergeant Winters' chair. "I'm supposed to get back right away." The jeep driver took a cigarette from his pocket and lit it.

"Don't worry about it. What's your name? Mine's Green." Jim took another sip of his coffee.

"McCoy, yeah McCoy. You're the old man's bodyguard." McCoy made the words a statement.

"Looks that way," Jim replied. They looked at each other, neither particularly caring for what he saw.

Green saw a tall, thin kid with a sharp nose and curly blond hair. He would have two dimples when he smiled. He wore a clean uniform and polished boots. His blue eyes darted from one object to another. He was twenty-one or twenty-two years old.

McCoy saw what seemed to be an over-confident guy of around maybe twenty-one but not more, close-cropped hair, a deeply tanned face with blue eyes that seemed to sink into his head. The uniform was worn and the boots showed many washings. He wore a shoulder holster, no rank on his sleeves, but a pair of wings and a long blue bar with a rifle in it surrounded by a silver wreath. All in black, McCoy passed him off as too theatrical; he didn't like him.

Green got up, walked to the door, took one last drink from his coffee and threw the remainder on the ground.

"Let's go." Jim turned and picked up his parachute bag, his Thompson submachine gun, and headed for the jeep, followed by McCoy.

As the jeep pulled into its parking space, Colonel Woodworth stood in the doorway watching Green get out of the jeep, pull his bag and Thompson from the back, and walk in his direction.

"Good morning sir." Green stood with the bag on his shoulder, the submachine gun in his other hand.

"Good morning. Come in." The Colonel turned and walked inside. Green followed. They went past the desk into the room in back. "I sleep here." He pointed to a cot in the corner. "You sleep there." He pointed to another cot in the opposite corner. Green walked over, put the bag on the cot, and lay the Thompson over it.

"There's not much for you to do today. I'm driving into Bien Hoa this afternoon around two. You'll go along." The colonel stood with his green T-shirt on, white chest hair curling over the top.

"Fine sir. Bien Hoa is pretty safe these days." Green took off his black baseball cap.

The colonel didn't answer. He walked into the other room, sat down at his desk that was covered by a map. It was a 25,000-meter map of the Ho Bo Woods area. The Ho Bo Woods lay on the tip of what was known at the Iron Triangle. It had been a stronghold of the Vietnamese when they were fighting the French and now the Viet Cong held it. The Ho Bo Woods themselves were a rubber tree plantation where a week before a Vietnamese ranger battalion had been annihilated. The Colonel sat looking at the place marked on the map.

Green sat in the other room, his head against the wall, smoking a cigarette. He got up, found a tin car that was used as a butt can and put the cigarette out. He went back to the cot, took Thompson and leaned it in the corner. He unzipped the bag, spreading it apart, took out his pistol belt with the suspenders attached. On the belt were two WW II Thompson ammunition pouches, one on each side of the buckle. Each one held five magazines; one magazine had a piece of green tape attached so it would be easy to extract the magazine. On the suspender a first-aid pouch was attached with a first aid pocket inside and a cylinder with a hypo of morphine. On the other ring a hand grenade was hung by the spoon, a piece of tape held it in place, with another piece of tape around the ring so it wouldn't pull out by accident. There were two canteens on the back part of the belt. A Marine K-Bar knife was on the right between the ammunition pouch and the canteen. On the left a compass case was attached, the compass taken out and now holding three magazines for the pistol. The heavy webbed material was no longer green, but almost white from being washed. Green hung the harness over the foot of his cot. Next he brought out a helmet, its camouflaged cover worn and white like his pistol belt and suspenders. He put the helmet on the floor by the harness. After this he brought out a soft cloth rucksack, empty, and put it over to one side. He then took out his bedding that consisted of a poncho liner and a soft light nylon blanket, that was also camouflaged in color. Next he brought out an air mattress. He left the poncho in the bottom, replacing the empty rucksack into the parachute bag, putting the bag under the cot. Green sat down, took the air mattress and began to blow it up. After he'd filled the air mattress, he laid it on the cot and put the poncho liner on top. He sat down again to wait for the Colonel.

Green was asleep when the Colonel came into the room. He stopped and looked at Green asleep; sitting up, even in sleep, he looked alert. He noticed and appreciated the neatness of the equipment laid out ready for use.

"Green."

Green awoke, not jumping, just opening his eyes as if he'd never been asleep. "We're going into Bien Hoa now. We'll eat there."

"Okay, sir." Green got up, putting his hat on his head. The Colonel went over to the nail where his shirt and hat hung, and put them on. Green followed him out the door.

McCoy was sitting in the jeep reading a copy of the *Stars and Stripes*.

"McCoy, I won't be needing you anymore. Take the afternoon off." The Colonel got into the passenger side of the jeep.

"Thank you sir." McCoy got out without looking at Green and walked off in the direction of the road.

"Drive, Green."

Green went to the other side of the jeep and got in. He leaned over, turned on the ignition, started the jeep, put it into reverse, backed out of the space and headed for perimeter road. They were waved on by the MP at the checkpoint that led to perimeter road. On perimeter road now, Green speeded up to forty miles an hour. Neither the Colonel nor Green spoke. They drove the two and a half miles of dusty road to the airbase gate that led to the town of Bien Hoa. The A.P. waved them on. Saluting the Colonel. Green turned right at Turkey Road and into the traffic of the little town that had become a city in the past year.

"Go to the Vietnamese motor pool. You know where it is?" The Colonel was looking straight ahead.

"Yes sir." He'd been with Morning enough times when Morning had taken the mess truck and gone into Bien Hoa for a few beers after going to the garbage dump. They passed a laundry shop, tailor shops, bars, sidewalk vendors, three barber shops, dry good stores that offered pans, mirrors, trunks, dolls and other goods that might be sold to American soldier. At the motor pool a Vietnamese soldier stopped them, saw the Colonel, saluted and showed them a place to park the jeep. Green slipped him a hundred pias. The soldier smiled and bobbed his head. Green and the Colonel got out and walked back to the street.

"Thought we'd go to the La Plaza for lunch," the Colonel said, looking at Green.

Green shrugged his shoulders and smiled. "Fine with me. I don't get a chance to get into town much."

"Good." The Colonel seemed pleased with himself. They walked the crowded streets to the La Plaza Restaurant, the best place to eat in Bien Hoa.

As they arrived at the restaurant, they were greeted by little boys, begging, selling shoeshines, some holding their little sisters or brothers. Green motioned them away, yelling, "Dedy mou, dedy mou." They walked into the restaurant with its clean linen tablecloths. One end was open to the Saigon River. The

Vietnamese *maître de* showed them to a table next to the river, gave them a menu written in French, Vietnamese and English.

"Would sir like drink first," the man asked.

"Beer," Green said, without looking at the Colonel.

"Same," the Colonel said.

The *maître de* left them to look at their menus.

"What are you going to have?" the Colonel asked.

Jim looked from his menu to the Colonel. "Don't know." He looked back at the menu. "I guess the shrimp fried rice."

The Colonel was surprised but he smiled. "I'm going to have the filet mignon."

The waiter brought them beer and took their order. "I'm going over to the Advisory Compound to see a friend of mine after this. We were in Ranger school together."

Green didn't quite know how to answer, so he drank some of his beer.

"Where did you get the Thompson submachine gun?" It had been the first thing that he had noticed when Green had arrived that morning.

"I bought it off a Vietnamese about four months ago. Cost me a lot too." Green paused for a minute. He didn't know if he should go on or not. "It is sometimes hard to get ammunition for it. Most of the time I've got to go to a Special Forces camp; they always have 45 caliber ammunition."

"It looks in good shape. Why do you carry it instead of the M15?"

"You mean the M16, Sir." Green stopped; he wished he hadn't corrected the Colonel.

"Yes, the M16, I mean."

"I just like it better. The short barrel is handy in the bush." Green didn't tell him the real reason he carried it. It added something to himself that he liked. When he carried it, it seemed as if he were something more than what he actually was. It separated him from the rest of the GI's. People would remember him as the guy with the Thompson, the one who said very little but was a killer.

They both drank their beer for a short while, not saying anything.

"What do you think of all that's going on over here?"

Green could feel the Colonel looking at him intently. He drank his beer.

"Don't know sir." Green shrugged his shoulders. He didn't look up at the Colonel across the table from him. "Look sir, I have a high school education, that's all. The guys that make the decisions have a lot more than that. I mean, three presidents, Eisenhower, Kennedy and Johnson, and from two different parties, have made basically the same decision." The Colonel nodded; he was somewhat surprised with Green's answer. "So, I keep my mouth shut."

"Then why are you over here at all?"

"I enlisted, so I do what they tell me until the job's done. That's when I get out."

"What about the war protests back home?"

"I don't know them and they don't know me. They think I'm some kind of an asshole that likes all this or I'm a stupid shit that doesn't know any better. I think I know more about Vietnam than they do, at least I'm here, most of them haven't been. What do you think of them sir?"

"I don't really know for sure. They mean well. It's a symptom. If there were no Vietnam, then it would be something else. What makes you carry a Thompson and them carry Viet Cong flags and fight in the streets, I just don't know."

"I don't know either. Do I know what's going to happen when I get back to the States? I've no idea what's going to happen to us when we come home. Hell, I'm just doing my job here, it's just a job."

"Well, you may have a point. What about the reconnaissance work? That's doing just a little more than your job." The Colonel drank some of his beer.

"Well, I do what I can. Take your jeep driver. He does what he can. The guy in supply does what he can. Me, I'm good at my job, at least I'm still around to talk about it..."

"I don't think you believe all that Green," the Colonel said.

Their meals came; they began to eat.

The Colonel liked Jim, this kid sitting across from him eating. He would amount to something someday if he wasn't killed over here. That was the shame of war, so much is lost. This is now my third war and so much has been lost. He wondered if it had been worth the cost. He didn't know about American youth, he had never really known them. But here was an American youth and he had a chance to talk to him and he didn't know how to speak or act with him He ate some of his steak. What do you say? How do I communicate with him?

Green looked up and smiled at the Colonel. "You don't think so, sir. Well then, what would you tell me if I asked you what the hell's really going on over here? Is what I'm doing right or is it wrong? What would be your answer to that, sir?"

"Between you and me... the truth as I see it."

"I'm listening sir."

"Our role here is one of both controlling and stopping Communism. That's what the American people are told; along with side things like self-determination for the Vietnamese people. Myself, I don't agree with that. Somehow we got backed to the wall along the years after World War II and now we're paying for past mistakes. We beat Japan. That left a void in the Far East. Then there was Korea and the rise of China and their brand of communism. Hell, we've lost in the Far East and we've won, if you want to put it in those terms. We lost with Chiang Kai-shek and Nationalist China, we lost in Korea and we won with Japan; but in winning, we lost, because we became the big brother." The Colonel stopped to take a bite of food.

Green had stopped eating now. The Colonel continued.

"We're not losing and we're not winning here. We have three objectives now that our military posture has changed from the enclave theory. We're involved in a land war in Southeast Asia and we're in trouble. In a land war we have three objectives: one to kill the enemy; two, to cut off and destroy his supply and war potential; and three, to take the ground and hold it. We're not doing any of those things. We can kill NVA and Viet Cong 'til hell freezes over and there will still be more. We can't destroy North Vietnam's war potential because they have none. They get everything from the Communist block countries and we can't touch that, and search and destroy doesn't mean hold the ground. We take a piece of land and then we leave and they're right back. We don't have a third of the men committed that we need to hold the ground. No Jim, you got yourself into the wrong war. This is my last one and this is your first and your first is the wrong one. I'm a professional soldier; for better or worse, that's it for me. But I still know enough to say that we're out in left field and there's no bringing back the dead now." The Colonel had finished. He drank the rest of his beer and ordered another.

Green still didn't answer. Morning, in his own stupid way, knew and said it. Green hated it; he hated it all, but there was nothing for him to do about it. He was determined to stay alive. The Colonel even knew and said it, and said it to him right here in this place.

"Why do we keep doing it then?" That was all Green could come up with.

"That's not something I can answer. Maybe someday you'll know. Whether you're right or wrong society takes the blame for you because you're in the Army, unless you go too far and then they're on you like stink on shit. What's going too far?" The Colonel laughed a sad sort of laugh. "You won't know till it's too late, then not even God can help you. Before I came here I taught at a college out East in the ROTC program and because of the uniform, I was a hawk and there was no discussing it."

"Hawk, dove, that's a bunch of shit... I'm no hawk.

Sometimes I don't want to go back to the world, I really don't want to."

"You will, sooner or later you will."

The Colonel went to see his friend at the Advisory Compound, Sergeant Holiday. They had met three years ago. To the Colonel, Holiday was something that only a professional could understand. He was the backbone of the Army, he was the Colonel's friend.

~ ~ ~

At 9:45 Task Form Puma was beginning to materialize on perimeter road. There were three armored personnel carriers from the Australian, Prince of Wales Light Horse Troop, two from the 16th Armored reconnaissance and gun jeeps from the 17th Cavalry and the two infantry battalions. There were several ¾ ton trucks filled with soldiers from the Engineers and other support units. In the settling dust men ran from one vehicle to another. It had all the confusion and yet the sameness, the madness, the sounds of heavy diesel engines, men shouting orders, men shouting at their buddies in other trucks, the smell of fine dust and exhaust fumes from the APC's trucks and jeeps.

Jim Green sat on the spare tire of Colonel Woodworth's jeep, submachine gun across his knees, his helmet lying on the floor of the jeep, a pair of green goggles hanging around his neck. He took no part in the Task Force except for his eyes, which followed Colonel Woodworth as he stood in the middle of the road waiting for the last elements of Task force Puma to arrive. A jeep and a ¾ ton truck, filled to overflowing with infantry men and helmets, with rucksacks hung from the side of the truck, and a 50-caliber machine gun mounted just in back of the driver in the bed, came screeching to a halt; its own dust engulfing it as it stood still, while the Lieutenant reported to the Colonel. They were the last to arrive. They were told to fall in on the end of the column.

Colonel Woodworth walked to the jeep, got in, half kneeling on the seat. He turned and gave the signal to start up the vehicles and follow him. All down the line engines were started and raced with the clutches in. The Colonel's jeep started forward, followed by his Task Force. They were waved through the intersection by MP's that had been positioned there that morning. They drove down the dirt road onto an asphalt highway, reporting in checkpoints to the Colonel as they passed the points. They wouldn't stop until they reached the Ho Bo Woods late that afternoon. The Colonel's jeep would pull over to the road; he'd stand in the seat and watch the assortment of Army ground vehicles pass, then sit down and the jeep would pull out on the left and pass the vehicles again at great speed. Green now wore his helmet and tinted goggles.

The Task Force made its camp with its back against what was known as the Courtney Airfield that had once been a soccer field. The APC and gun jeeps made a line facing the rubber tree plantation, in readiness. Most of the trucks were parked on the edge of the soccer field. Small lean-to tents were set up behind the APC's, and the men were told not to dig in. The reconnaissance jeeps sped down the road in each direction; patrols were sent into the rubber tree plantation, and their reports came back negative to the Colonel who stood next to his jeep. Later that evening choppers came in bringing hot food from base camp at Bien Hoa.

It was morning. Green awoke, sitting up on the ground, his poncho thrown back in the action of getting up. Colonel Woodworth had been up for an hour; he'd been reading reports from patrols from the day before. The reports said that there were Viet Cong in the hamlet two miles down the road. That was where he would go with Task Force Puma.

The hamlet was still a VC stronghold from the reports that he had read a week before. They were a slippery enemy and he wasn't going to give them any advantage. Of course they hadn't fired on any of his patrols with Task Force Puma a few miles away. Neither would he if he were in the same situation. He had to protect his flanks, that was of utmost importance. If he met a force head on later, he had to be sure of what was on the side of the Task Force. The Colonel walked over to the map table and looked at the hamlet. In grease pencil inside of a circle was written "NUMBER ONE TOWN," and an arrow pointing to the dot on the map that had the capability to destroy him at some future point. There was no name to the old road that led to the hamlet.

At the end of the village it looked like there were rice paddies. It would be a stroke of luck if he could drive the Cong out into the open of the rice paddies and destroy them, getting a chance to use his firepower. He would have to keep the APC's on the road or close to it. The ground around wouldn't hold their weight. No, he should go ...neutralize the hamlet, that's what would be the safest thing in the end. The ground around the road and the hamlet was pretty open. That was something on his side but it could work against him; they'd know he was coming and there was nothing he could do about that. If there was going to be a fight, it was up to the enemy.

He would be ready for it, but it was up to the enemy to decide whether to stand and fight or to get the hell out of there. When he left they'd be back, then he'd be in the same situation as before. There wasn't time to keep going back to that goddamn hamlet, this would have to be the time. So he better make it good. That meant only one thing: destroy the hamlet and get the people out of there.

The hamlet was the Cong's only real protection. With that gone they'd be on the defensive, and he'd have the upper hand. He didn't like the idea of leveling the place, but it was the only way to have any confidence in his action. Otherwise, it'd be a waste of time and people, his people, and he had to protect the men as much as he could. War, what insanity, it was the end of the line; it was like an extension of the grave and there was no sense to be made from it. The attraction of what would happen was powerful. How would he react when it came down to the end ... all the preparation, thinking and planning, the mad thought process, the end result, the actual battle. The battle when it was on, would have men throwing themselves into the madness of war. They were paying for the land with blood, the land that wasn't even theirs; it meant nothing except that it would help in protection his flanks when the big fight came, if it did. There was no assurance that they would even drive the enemy to them, yet he had to do it. There was no glory in it, but it had to be done on the off chance that there would be a bigger fight later. Too much thinking. Was this what men and Generals thought about before battle for the last thousand years?

Green stood up, he'd not taken off his clothes or his boots; it was a habit of months in Vietnam. He walked stiffly, slowly, over to the jeep, and took a water can from the back, tipped it over, and splashed water on his face and hair. The Colonel came walking from the APC that he had used as his command post for the night, over to Green and then the jeep.

"We're going to Phong Lock, number one town, that's where the VC are and that's what we're here for." The Colonel stood in front of Green.

Green didn't look at him; he'd heard these words before, he shrugged his shoulders.

The Colonel looked at his watch. "Be ready in five minutes."

"Yes sir."

Green walked back to where his poncho lay on the ground; bent down, took each corner, folded it, and began to roll it. After he'd completed this, he got his equipment on, looked at his Thompson, and was ready.

The Colonel held a short staff meeting with his commanders. He would take three gun jeeps and a platoon of infantry in the APC's. They left at 8:15 with the Colonel's jeep in the lead. They went down the road very slowly, each vehicle staggered to the left and the right of the road. A soldier from the engineers was walking in front of the column with a mine detector. He was flanked on each side by soldiers, the man with the mine detector had no weapon. The column moved slowly, stopping when the man held up his hand. Other men would come up to the front with bayonets and probe the spot indicated by the guy with the mine detector.

Green didn't like sitting in the jeep behind the Colonel, but he could do nothing else. The Colonel sat slumped in the seat watching the men looking for mines. At intervals he would look at his map that lay in his lap. He reached for the hand mike. Pushing the talk button, he told the vehicles to deploy into the rubber tree plantation to the left and to the right. The hamlet was just in front of them. The plantation was still dark, the sun hadn't come in through the trees yet.

It was the APC that was on the left flank that received the first rounds. The infantry was told to dismount and walk behind the vehicles. The Colonel didn't get out of the jeep even though it moved slowly. The village could be seen. The order was given and the APC's and the gun jeeps opened fire on the village. The noise from the 50 caliber machine guns was extremely loud. The vehicles came closer to the hamlet, all of them on line. Most of the line was receiving fire from the hamlet. Green could see no one. He couldn't remain in the jeep any longer. He got off and walked next to Colonel Woodworth who wore only a shoulder holster with a .45 caliber pistol. Three hand grenades were in front of him. He watched both flanks of the line that his vehicles made, looking from left to right. When one vehicle began to fall back, he would radio it. The APC's were breaking down the bamboo wall around the hamlet now. Sergeants were behind the men making them advance under fire.

The Colonel got out of the jeep and walked ahead. The guy with the mine detector had rejoined his squad. Green walked next to the Colonel as both of them went through the gate of the hamlet. The Colonel signaled the jeep to come up. He took the mike and spoke very loudly to be heard over the .50 caliber machine guns.

"Burn it, repeat, burn every god damn thing. I want nothing standing or living." He lifted the three grenades from the dash of the jeep and walked ahead of the jeep again.

A soldier threw a grenade down a bunker and then went on. The Colonel had said nothing to Green. There was a movement from the hut in front of them. Two Vietnamese broke into the street like rabbits flushed from their burrows – they were carrying carbines. Green, without thinking, it was a reaction, in one slow motion move the Thompson level with the ground and began to fire; the Thompson rising from the force of the bullets coming from the barrel. The Colonel watched without moving; one of the Vietnamese was lifted into the air by the force of the bullets hitting him. As Green let the Thompson rise into the air, the pattern of bullets made an almost straight line in the back of the Vietnamese, and as Green stopped shooting, the Vietnamese seemed no longer to be held up in the air and he fell to the ground with the front of his chest gone, leaving his insides open and on the road where he lay. The other Vietnamese disappeared around the corner of the next hut.

"That's it, tiger," the Colonel yelled. It was done and the Colonel moved again. He went for the hut and threw a grenade through the door. After the explosion the Colonel went in. There was a hole in the floor; it was an entrance to a bunker. Before the Colonel could stoop to look, Green filled the hole with bullets. When he was done, he reloaded his Thompson with a new magazine. The Colonel looked at Green and dropped into the hole. He peered into the darkness.

He pulled a boy out by the arm. He was dead. He smelled from his own filth, his hair was filled with lice. The Colonel dropped the boy's arm and climbed out of the hole. They went back into the street. The fire from the Viet Cong was intense, but the Colonel stopped in the middle of the street. Then they moved on. Many of the huts were on fire. They moved on down the street. Green shot another man. The Colonel asked him for another hand grenade; he had used the three he had. The word was hard. Each building was entered, and the men were getting tired; the line moved slower than it had an hour before. It was difficult to see the enemy because the fire was intense. There were wounded and dead now.

The Colonel never stopped; he went into one hut after another. Sometimes Green went in first, but other times he wasn't fast enough and the Colonel went in first. Each time Green waited for that awful minute when the Colonel would be killed by booby trap, sniper or hand grenade. He had to keep the Colonel alive, that was what he was there for, it was the one thing that his mind stuck to that whole morning. He acted on that one train of thought and it almost seemed that if the Colonel died, then he would no longer be able to act and he would be lost, he too would be dead. Green realized that he was using a great deal of ammunition;

his pockets were bulged with empty magazines. He would have been sickened by what he saw, but the thought, the over-riding thought of keeping the Colonel alive blocked out what he saw.

It was like bird hunting when he was home. They would flush the birds and then shoot them. As the Vietnamese were pushed back, they'd be forced to run and then they would shoot them. Some of them didn't run and Green would shoot them were they sat in the hut. With the Colonel next to him he couldn't wait to shoot. They went into one hut and there in the corner two of them sat, not moving, like animals. They weren't animals, but Green didn't wait, he opened up on them and they died fast. It was nothing like he had ever seen before. He'd killed seven men now, close up. No, he had never done this before. The Colonel was always next to him and always saw; they never looked at each other. The dead bodies were very dirty. Many of the men were using ammunition to kill animals. The line was irregular because of stopping to kill both men and animals, then setting buildings on fire.

The Colonel kept them all moving, always to the end of the hamlet. He moved from his jeep to a hut and back to the jeep. Once he stood up on the seat so he could see what the left flank was doing, then he yelled orders into the hand mike. "Too slow, keep moving, too slow."

At the end of the hamlet the Viet Cong had set up machine guns. Most of the line was caught in a crossfire from them. The Colonel and Green had to take shelter from them. Green lay panting, sweat ran down his face and hands; he took his helmet off and put a bandana around his head to keep the sweat out of his eyes. He smelled the burning buildings and the dead. The Colonel lay on his stomach.

"Let's go Green." The Colonel started to rise.

Green prayed for him to be shot. The Colonel fell to the ground. Green hadn't moved. The fire was too intense.

"Jesus, god damn Christ, you trying to get me killed?"

Green looked at the Colonel, his face strained, the main blood vessels at his temple throbbed under the bandana.

The Colonel looked at Green for the first time, both were out of breath, both lay on the ground, their chests heaving up and down.

"You're here to keep me alive." The Colonel tried to get up, he could not. The crossfire was too great.

Yes, keep you alive, that was the justification of all this. To keep you alive so you could go back to the Officers Club and tell war stories about it. Colonel, colonel, colonel shit, all this for nothing, your last war, my first, it was talk. Maybe he was right, maybe now I'm damned and it will always be war for me just like it was for you. It wasn't true the Colonel couldn't be shot, not today anyway. Start thinking about how you're going to stay alive and keep that god damn Colonel alive so he could get us both out of here. That's what you should be thinking about. You're getting yourself into trouble if you start thinking if you're doing right or wrong, if the war is right or wrong, or if there's a God that knows if it's right or wrong. Man, it just doesn't make a difference right now. Only thing that's important is keeping the Colonel alive and that means you'll stay alive.

Green looked at the Colonel lying beside him. He had taken off his helmet and was wiping the sweat from his forehead. "Where's the jeep?" The Colonel put the helmet back on.

Green jerked his head to their rear.

"Well, I got them out into the open."

"What?"

"Nothing."

Green looked down at his Thompson. His knuckles were white from holding it so tightly. He relaxed his grip. His hand ached from the pressure on the Thompson. His jawbone ached from the strain of the morning. He felt very tired.

They were both looking at the jeep and McCoy crouched to one side. McCoy reached up into the jeep, taking the hand mike. He stood up holding the mike in one hand high to signal the Colonel that he was needed. He stood there for a very short time, Green thought, then he fell to the ground face down and didn't move.

The Viet Cong were behind dikes fifty feet away. They couldn't be seen. The Colonel went back to his jeep. Green ran, bent over at the waist, behind him. The drive, McCoy was dead. He lay on the ground. It was afternoon now. The Colonel called for air strikes. The men on each side stayed on the ground, firing as best they could. When the Sky Raiders came, they dropped napalm. After that, Green smelled the burning flesh and heard the cries of the burning Viet Cong. All the men stood up on line and crossed the fifty feet that they couldn't cross before. Most of the Viet Cong had gone into the jungle that edged the hamlet. The ones left had been chained to the 50 caliber machine guns and had been burned alive.

The hamlet was in flames, the burning buildings making noises like rifle shots. The men flinched at the sound. What was left of the men from the morning re-grouped, got into the APC and started back to the airfield. Green drove the Colonel's jeep. The dead were picked up after the wounded; they had not lost many men.

"You were a real tiger today Green," the Colonel said as an approving teacher to a pupil.

"Yeah, that's me, a real tiger." Green fought back the tears that welled up into his eyes. The thickness in his throat made it hard for him to breathe. He sat looking at the ground. "That placed ain't even standing. Oh Christ," Green said, more to himself than to the Colonel. "All those people dead, and I got to get some more ammo." Green got up, his cargo pockets still bulged from the empty magazines.

Was it five or seven or ten that he had killed close up today? He couldn't remember anymore. Close up, that was different than it had been before. There was the kid and the two sitting in the corner of the hut, and the others that he didn't remember anymore. They were all dead and he and the Colonel were alive. Number One Town was gone, it no longer existed. They were dead, he had done it and it was all right that he had done it. Green shook his head. They were dead and that was the end of it and stop thinking about it; there was no use thinking about it.

Green wanted to blame the Colonel, but somehow

he couldn't do that in his mind. There was no one close to him that he could blame and he could no longer think of the system. He could blame no one or nothing and it was left alone for the time being, left to rest in the back of his mind and that was the best he could do with Number One Town. It was put with the rest of the ten months and other horrors that happened during that time.

The Colonel sent out four ambush patrols that night, but they saw nothing. The Viet Cong had disappeared.

Green and the Colonel didn't talk. Green had to be the jeep driver for the rest of the operation.

CHAPTER TEN

BEING PINNED DOWN MEANT THAT THE NVA'S FIRE WAS SO INTENSE THAT IF YOU WERE TO STAND UP YOU WOULD BE DEAD. THE TROOPS HAD LEARNED FROM THE EXPERIENCE. SOMEONE IS GOING TO CALL A FIRE MISSION, WEATHER FAST MOVERS, GUN SHIPS OR ARTILLERY.

ONCE THE NVA GET SMOKED, YOU MOP-UP WHAT IS LEFT OVER OF THE NVA THAT"S HOW IT WORKS.

SOMETIME IT DOESN'T WORK THAT WAY AND GUYS GET **KILLED**.

"**G**REEN?"

"What, Morning?" They were sitting on their bunks in the hutch alone.

"Do you think that because we went through the war and everything together that we'll know each other for the rest of our lives?"

Green rubbed the ears of his dog as he sat in front of him.

"Yeah, we'll be friends for the rest of our lives. When you go through the war with a friend, the war becomes a bond."

"You really think so?"

"Yes, all of us will be friends because we're all part of this and we're to blame, so we'll stick together."

"To blame for what?"

"For what we've done, we're the only ones who really understand."

"I'll buy that. Are we going to join the VFW when we get home?" Green laughed and laughed.

"What's so funny?"

"Nothing." Green said.

The five stood abreast at attention. Captain Moes stopped before each one, asking a question, looking each man over carefully. Each man is of interest to the Captain, he knows what the man has done in the past, if he's married, and how many kids. He knows each man's strong and weak points. Captain Moes is a man to capitalize on the strong points of each, yet never forgetting his weakness. The men are lined up in their patrol order. Green is the first man, he is the point. Next comes Sergeant Winters, the patrol leaders and the compass man. Sergeant Winters' team has never been lost in the jungle. Next is Turtle. He's carrying the radio. Turtle is considered one of the best Radio Telephone Operators in the platoon. Next is Battleford. He's carrying a grenade launcher; he always carries extra ammunition. The last man is Morning. He stands still waiting for the Old Man to get to him. He's impatient to get going. Morning is the rear security of the team.

After the inspection the men get into the truck that will carry them to the heliport up at Brigade; it is still dark. At the helicopter they stand around smoking cigarettes and talking quietly. The chopper crew stands there in their own little group; they refer to themselves as aviators. They are known as the cowboys; they talk and look over at their passengers. They don't understand these men in camouflaged fatigues with the green and black grease paint on their faces and arms. There are other men standing around looking at these men that go into the jungle in small units, existing completely within themselves. The men in the platoon know that they are being scrutinized by their fellow soldiers, so they stand straighter, make jokes among themselves to show that this is an everyday job to them. Each man's equipment is arranged the same on their bodies. The hand grenades are taped for silence, the same green tape is wound around weapons to break the outline, and the muzzle is taped over. Instead of a steel helmet they wear soft-brimmed hats the same camouflaged color as the uniforms. They are tied on with a piece of rope, the brims are sometimes turned up like cowboy hats. The men stand around the chopper waiting for takeoff time.

The time comes and the chopper is warmed up and Captain Moes tells them good hunting and the men get into the chopper. Morning is first in because he will be out last; Green is the last man in the chopper. The men still standing around in the early morning light give thumbs up to the men and hold it while the chopper lifts slowly off the ground. Green smiles and waves back to the men on the ground. The chopper circles the Brigade area and then heads toward the Song Dong Ni River and their landing zone. The ride is short; the pilot gives the signal for the men to get ready. It's not yet full light. The helicopter is high in the air, but now begins to fall with unbelievable speed, stopping its downward and forward motion next to the tree line of the landing zone. Green is the first one out of the chopper, jumping when it is still three feet off the ground. The chopper never gets a chance to touch down. The rest of the men follow Green without hesitation. Turtle lost his balance jumping from the chopper but gets up instantly. Morning is the last man out and he turns to the men in the helicopter and signals that they are clear of the craft and the copter lifts off with great speed. By the time Morning gets to the trees, the noise of the whirling blades is gone and it is quiet.

Morning stays in a position where he can look across the landing zone without being seen. Each man is looking either to the left or to the right, listening and waiting for the sound that will tell them if the Viet Cong are in the area. Green is in front checking to see if the way is clear; he has many things to watch for. In a few minutes he comes back and motions the men to come without a word being spoken. Morning is busy concealing their trail. The team moves farther into the jungle, not making a sound. The team moves slowly, picking its way through the vines and trees. Sergeant Winters keeps his eye on the compass tied to his neck, giving Green directions either to the left or right or straight-ahead.

They'd been moving for maybe fifteen minutes when they stop and form a circle around Turtle and Sergeant Winters, each man taking a point on the compass. They move slowly, almost in slow motion so that no sound is made.

Turtle takes the radio off his back and sits it down very carefully. He takes out the antenna and screws it into place. He then hands the telephone handset to

Sergeant Winters and turns on the radio. The squelch from the radio can be heard but that can't be helped. Sergeant Winters holds the handset to his ear, presses the button to speak in a whisper into the mouthpiece.

"Eagle, Eagle, this is Dove, Dove." He releases the talk button.

The squelch is heard again. The squawk is broken by the CO's voice somewhere in the helicopter above them. "Dove, this is Eagle, send your message."

"Everything Oscar-Kayo, continuing with mission. Over."

"Roger, out." The squawk comes on again. Sergeant Winters nods to Turtle and he turns off the set, then he gives the handset to Turtle. He pulls the map out of his pocket, looks around, then signals to light up a cigarette. The men light up, being watchful. Turtle puts away the radio equipment and places the radio on his back again.

Turtle sat not smoking, he didn't smoke. He sat looking out at nothing, not really thinking about anything, yet he was aware of the sound of insects around him. Where he sat a beam of sunlight came through the overgrowth and fell on his face; it warmed him and it felt good. He would have closed his eyes and leaned back against a tree if he hadn't been on patrol in Vietnam. He was among his friends and if he were killed, he knew they'd bring him out as he would do for one of them. He would have gone to Cambodia with Morning if the others would have gone, he would die for any of them. These thoughts had come into his mind often.

He looked down the trail and he could see quite a

ways till it swung off to the left. He looked in the other direction and he could barely make out Sergeant Winters now in the foliage and he knew that on the other side was Green and Morning and someplace in back of him was Bat...the Batman. Oh boy, would I have things to tell the guys when I got home about these guys, and he was one of them. Turtle, feeling good, really good with himself, leaned back a little. He could smell the chlorophyll in the plants around him. On the trail they would make good time and Sunday would be the party and drinking beer and horsing around and getting drunk and the Trail...Turtle sat up very slowly.

There, coming around the turn, was an NVA, a Viet Cong, the enemy. There he was, just walking down the trail like he was in Saigon or someplace like that. Turtle didn't move, he felt his breath stop in his mouth and not come out. His eyes moved around in his head. Did the others see him? There was no sign, no sound from the other side of the trail, from in back of him. Maybe they didn't see him, and there he was coming, just walking down the trail by themselves, but maybe they were the point for a lot more. God, what were those other guys doing anyway? He had on a big pack, almost bigger than he was. Those guys were sure strong; a pack like the ones he'd seen a lot and made out of a flour sack with rope for the straps. Turtle couldn't keep his eyes off him, he had never been so close to the Viet Cong. He was old, no, young. Hell, he couldn't tell, he never could with them. They either looked like kids or old men. He could see his brown wrinkled face. He was getting very close now; he was talking to himself. He was so close he was mouthing words and talking to himself, just like he did a lot when he was just walking and thinking about stuff. The Viet Cong was almost even with Turtle now. Turtle felt panic sweep through him like a wave of ocean over the shore, and then it was gone, and the Viet Cong had just taken one step past him when Turtle stood up and stepped out into the trail. In one motion he raised his rifle and brought it down on top of the man's head. The Viet Cong's head split open with the force of the blow.

Turtle stood there surprised with his own strength, the force with which he had hit the man, and he sank to the ground under the weight of his own pack. Turtle was aware of motion around him, and he looked at the hump of man before him; the rest of the team was on the trail. Morning moved a little down the trail and Battleford moved up the trail, and Green was standing next to him, then down over the body and going through the pack.

"Christ, did you see that?" he heard Morning ask from up the trail in a hoarse whisper. "I was just going to shoot the son of a bitch and Turtle steps out right in front of my sights and POW on the head. Did he kill him?"

There was no answer.

"He must be a supply messenger; he doesn't even have a gun or anything. Damn, Turtle, you really whacked him."

"Knock off the bullshit and finish going through the stuff."

Sergeant Winters was standing at Turtle's elbow. "Good move, Turtle. I didn't think you had it in you." He looked down the trail in Morning's direction.

"Morning, anything coming?"

"No, Sarge." Morning returned the question in a hoarse whisper.

"Man, he didn't even know what hit him," Turtle said now, under his breathe.

"You can say that again." Green stood up. "He's carrying a bag of rice."

Sergeant Winters looked up the trail at Battleford, but Bat shook his head, no, that no one was coming. "Well, someone's not getting their bowl of rice tonight."

"Turtle, help me pull him off the trail." Turtle reached down and helped with the weight of the dead man and the hundred pounds of rice. After they got him off the trail, Green took out his knife and split open the bag and spread the rice over the ground. "The bugs will get it in an hour."

Turtle followed Green back on to the trail. They moved out right away; Morning stayed behind to clean up the trail a little. He kept saying, "Pow, right in the head. Did you guys see that?" All this had not taken five minutes, Turtle decided, and it was over and they were moving again. He'd held the M16 like a baseball bat and right over the head. Turtle was really surprised with himself. Now he received a certain amount of enjoyment out of it. That was funny, he thought, as he walked behind Sergeant Winters. The picture of himself hitting the Viet Cong over the head kept going through his mind.

It was Sunday morning, and they had gotten off the patrol an hour ago. The chopper picked them up without any trouble; they had been dropped off at the company area and still Green hadn't made a move to get cleaned up. Morning was on his cot asleep, dirty and not giving a damn. Green just didn't feel well and the heat bothered him more than usual. On patrol he'd slowed down, he hadn't cared, he'd just wanted to sleep. He lay down on the bunk and drifted off, the sweat pouring off his forehead, seeping through his shirt and pants.

Morning woke him for the noon formation. Green felt as if he were dragged.

"Man, you don't look good. You feel okay, Jim?" Morning's voice was far away.

"Yeah, I'm okay. He got up and they went to the formation. Sergeant Winters gave them both hell for being in the camouflaged fatigues and not cleaning up. He expected as much from Morning but not from Green. Green didn't care. Halfway through the formation the ground started to spin.

"I don't feel too good Sarge." Sergeant Winters looked at Green.

"You don't look good either, sit down before you fall down," and Green left the formation. The First Sergeant was saying something about no passes because they were going to have a company party that afternoon. Green went back into the hutch and collapsed on his cot.

Later that afternoon Morning woke him. "Hey man, I brought you a beer and something to eat." Morning had a tray from the mess hall with food on it and a cold can of beer.

"Thanks, Morning. I can't eat anything. I got the shits so bad I'll make fifty-nine trips to the shithouse if I eat."

"Well, drink the beer. It's good for you. You won't get beriberi; it's the malt in the beer." Morning gave

Jim the beer and he took a swallow. He put his head back down again and drifted off. Morning sat by the cot drinking the beer that was for Green who slept and sweated. Morning began to worry. He left the tent looking for Sp/4 Washington. He first went to the headquarters section hutch.

"Any you guys seen that damn Washington, never can find his lazy ass when you want him."

The three men in the hutch drinking beer looked up at Morning.

"What's your problem, Morning," one of them said.

"Seen Washington? Christ, you deaf?"

"He's down in the mess hall getting drunk," the same soldier said, pointing towards the mess hall.

Washington was in a corner talking with some other blacks. Morning shoved his way through the soldiers drinking and shouting.

"Hey, Washington, Green's sick, you better come and look at him."

"What's wrong with him?" He didn't move from his place at the table.

"How in the hell am I supposed to know, you're the god damn medic."

"Okay, okay, Morning." Washington got up from the table, drained his beer and they left together.

"You're a good man, Booker T." Morning led the way to Jim's hutch.

"Hey Jim, I brought the Doc to look at you. You're sick."

Jim opened his eyes and saw two Washington's and three Mornings, he closed his eyes again.

"What wrong with you? How long you been like

222

this?" Washington put his hand on Jim's forehead, sat down on the cot. "Hey man, you hear me?"

"Yeah, I hear you Washington. What the hell you want?" Jim kept his eyes closed.

"You got a fever. I'm going to get a thermometer. I'll be right back." Washington left the hutch. He came back with his ammo box that he kept the thermometer and pills and other things he needed to treat the ills of the platoon.

"Morning, get some cold water."

Morning left with his canteen. He was back with unbelievable speed. The thermometer was sticking out of Jim's mouth, his eyes were closed. Washington took the thermometer out of Jim's mouth and read it and put it back in its case carefully.

"Here's three APC's" He took the canteen from Morning and gave it to Jim. Jim took it, put the pills in his mouth and drank. Washington took Jim's towel and soaked it with water and put it on his forehead. "I'll be back." Morning followed Washington out of the tent into the hot sunlight.

"What's wrong with him?" Morning asked. He was afraid it was malaria.

"I don't know for sure, man, I'm a medic, not Ben Casey."

"What you going to do?"

"I'm taking him up to "B" Med. He's got a high temperature."

Washington headed toward the orderly room.

"I'll come with you." Morning followed.

They got the Old Man's jeep, went back to the hutch with it, got Green and took him down to "B" Med.

Morning hung around while the doctor looked at Jim. He didn't know what was wrong either, but as he said he was pretty sick and he'd get him to the 83rd Evac Hospital. So Morning left after telling Jim he'd come over and see him as soon as he could. He promised to take care of his equipment for him. Morning left the hospital tent and walked down the dusty road that led to the company, hands in his pockets, head down. He had forgotten his hat, he was kicking up dust with his already dirty boots. Jim would be all right. He'd steal the mess truck tomorrow and go see him. Morning quickened his step back to the company area.

Green lay on the top bunk of the double decker bed in Ward 1-A 83rd Medical Evacuation Hospital at Bien Hoa, Vietnam. The lights were turned off in the ward. At the other end of the ward the nurse's night-light was on. Green lay listening to the uneasy sounds of the men's sleep. Each man was fighting his own fears in his own particular nightmare. He lit his cigarette, concealing the light as best he could. He didn't want the nurse down there telling him to butt it out. He would have to tell her to go to hell and then there would be trouble.

"Hey Jim baby, you ain't asleep yet?" It was the hoarse whisper voice from the top bunk to Jim's right. Sergeant J.D. Coffie had been occupying that bunk for the last four days. Sergeant Coffie lay on his top bunk, blank hair grown out too long, day after day strumming his guitar, singing his songs, talking about his wife back in the states who was out fooling around on him. As he often said, "When I get home, I'll beat her ass good and then we'll screw." Sergeant Coffie's favorite story one

Jim had heard four times in as many days, was the one where Sergeant Coffie and his wife were in the supermarket and when they were leaving, he was walking out behind her. He noticed another man staring at his wife and he stopped next to the man and stared too. Then he said to the other man, "nice ass," and the other man agreed most fervently and said that he would like to get into that. By this time Sergeant Coffie was in ecstasy with the thought of the story and he said that he then told the man that the woman was his wife. This killed him, the embarrassment of the stranger, but Coffie had told him that it was okay, she did have a beautiful ass. So as Sergeant Coffie lay up on his top bunk thinking of his wife, he thought of new ways to get her back.

"Give me a light of your cigarette."

Jim handed him his cigarette.

"Think that Mexican kid they brought in today is going to live?"

Sergeant Coffie was talking about a boy that had been brought in that afternoon with malaria and pneumonia. He had been out of his head with fever, talking in Mexican in his delirium. Another Mexican said that the guy thought he was home back in California. The Mexican kid kept pulling the intravenous feeding needle out of his arm. They had to tie him down with a restraining strap.

"No, the kid's dead already, he's just waiting for it to happen," Jim said, getting back his cigarette. They both listened for his labored breathing. He was almost crying now in his delirium.

Later that night he became worse and the nurse

switched on a light at the bedside. Both Sergeant Coffie and Green sat up in their top bunks, looking to see what was happening. "It won't be long now," Jim said. The nurse was working over him, but nothing was going to help. She left him and called the doctor. She was gone when he died and when the doctor came, he said that the boy was dead, and two orderlies came and took him to the morgue.

"We're like two vultures, waiting for him to die," Jim said.

"Yeah, that's the way it goes." Sergeant Coffie laughed a little. "They'll tell everybody that they moved him to another ward, they don't want our morale to get low."

They watched the orderlies clean up around the area of the bed and make it up for the next soldier. In thirty minutes it was as if the Mexican kid had never been. Jim almost thought that maybe he'd dreamed it all. The nurse was back by her desk doing some paperwork.

Jim slipped off his bunk onto the floor. He walked towards the light, making no noise in his bare feet. All he had on was pajama bottoms.

"What are you doing up?" she said.

"Can't sleep, thought maybe I'd get a sleeping pill," Jim said.

"No sleeping pills without doctor's permission and he's not given any orders for you to have a sleeping pill," she said, not moving.

"I'll get a drink and go back to bed."

"See that you do," she said.

"Anything that you say ma'am," Jim said, not

moving.

She looked at him coldly. "Just go back to bed. I've got work to do."

"Look, ma'am, don't get shook. I'm just getting a drink of water and I'll go back to bed, so don't jump through your apex." Jim got water from the water cooler next to her desk.

"What'd you say?" she said.

"You heard me the first time, apex." Jim held his hand above his head and made a circle with his finger. "The top of a parachute."

"All right Private Green, what's the problem?" She was exasperated.

"Specialist Green," Green said.

"All right Specialist," she said.

"I've got no problems. I just wanted a glass of water and a sleeping pill and out of this factory. That's not much, is it?" Jim said.

"Specialist, it's been a very trying night." My heart bleeds for you, Jim thought. "So if you'll go back to bed, it will make things much easier."

"Well, we all want things to be easy, yes sir, ma'am, easier." Jim turned around and walked off.

Jim lay on the top bunk, seeing the first light of day come through the window. He lit a cigarette. Sergeant Coffie was asleep. Jim lay in the lower bunk blowing smoke rings to the ceiling. He didn't hear the nurse come up.

"Haven't you gone to sleep yet?" she said.

"No. I don't sleep so good anymore," Jim said.

"I'm sorry."

Yes, I'm sorry too. There is nothing that I can do

about it. I have the same dream and I just can't stand the dream. I'm lying on the ground and a bayonet on the end of a rifle is stuck into my gut and I curl around it like a worm getting stuck with a stick. I can feel the pain, the sweat breaks out on my forehead and I try to scream. I open my mouth and nothing comes out. Yes, I am sorry too.

Jim's buddies came to see him. Morning, Battleford, and Turtle came in that afternoon causing a great deal of commotion. Morning, never changing, looked in need of bath, shave and clean clothes. He had some pink medicine on his jungle rot on his forearms. Turtle was as heavy as ever and Morning was telling him to shut his goddamn mouth. Battleford was wearing a .45 caliber pistol in a shoulder holster. From the minute they came in they caused an uproar in the ward.

"See," Morning pointed at Green. "I told you he wasn't dead. No one gave the order. The trouble with you guys, you forget you're in the god damn Army." Morning looked around; he slipped Jim a pint of peach-flavored brandy. "That's what they should have given you in the first god damn place."

"Thanks," Jim put the bottle under his pillow.

"Where you at man?" Battleford said.

"No where man, where you at man?" Jim answered. Battleford smiled.

"Hi Jim, how you feeling?" Turtle was sticking out his hand.

"Okay. What you say Turtle." They shook hands.

"How you guys get down here?" Jim asked.

"Morning stole the mess truck," Turtle

volunteered.

"Yeah, and I hope that fat mess Sergeant gets pissed too. Maybe he'll fire me." They all laughed.

"Sergeant Coffie, these are some friends of mine. Morning, Fat Turtle and Batlin' Bat Battleford." They said hello and Sergeant Coffie lay on his side watching the four fellows from the same outfit.

"This place any good?" Morning asked.

"No, it's not too cool. Some Mexican died last night. Me and the Sarge watched."

"That's a nice way to spend an evening. Everything back at the platoon okay. Nothing too much going on," Morning said.

They were crowded in between two bunks; Jim was sitting on the edge of his, legs hanging over the side.

"The nurses any good?" Turtle asked.

"No," Jim said.

"I told you before, Turtle, them nurses are just like those do-gooder Red Cross donut dollies. They're here so that the officers can get some drawers. So it don't do any good for a stupid private like you to even think about them. Just remember that the private does the fighting, the officers do the drinking and screwing and the NCO's get what's left over."

"The C.O. says that you'll be getting out of here pretty soon," Battleford said.

"I'm ready to leave this factor. This place gets on my nerves," Jim answered.

Turtle was standing with his hands in his pockets, thinking over the blast from Morning. "Well, at least you can look at them," He said.

"That's about right, too. LOOK," Jim said.

"You're never going to learn a god damn thing, Turtle," Morning said. "You'll be a fish all your life."

"Why don't you guys go to hell?" Turtle said.

"Can't," Battleford said.

"No, can't," Green said.

"That's right, we can't, we're already there." Morning let out a peal o hysterical laughter. "Did you hear? Bat's getting a medal, Silver Star. He's everybody's war hero now. You're getting one too. You guys really impress me. I want you to know that," Morning said.

"For what?" Jim asked.

"For Hill 69," Battleford said.

"No kidding, who put us in, the C.O.?" Jim asked.

"Yeah," Battleford said. Morning had walked into the main aisle, hands in pockets, looking at the different patients.

"Oh, you poor guy," he said to one kid lying in bed. "Can I get you anything? You look bad." Morning was bending over the bed as if he were a doctor.

"Who is this nut?" the kid asked.

Morning walked away, bent over with laughter.

At this point the nurse descended on them, and in particular, on Morning. Morning was still in the aisle doubled up with laughter. He was the cause of the uproar and he would most certainly pay the price.

"What the hell's going on?"

Morning turned around. The nurse was big, bigger than Morning, weighing two hundred pounds at least. She stood there in her jungle fatigues, hands on hips, legs spread apart, her vengeance and wrath coming down on Private Mark Morning.

"She looks like Bango-belly." Turtle got behind Battleford. Bango-belly was the company First Sergeant.

"Yeah man." Battleford was laughing more at the expression on Morning's face.

Morning stood up straight now, his thumbs hanging onto the corners of his pockets, his shoulders moving just a little. He was clearly trying to think of something disrespectful. The size of the woman confronting him had him momentarily at a loss.

"Er-,ah-." He looked at the others; there was no help. They stood in a respectful silence. Morning scratched the top of his head. The big woman kept him the object of her stare. "We-, er- came to visit our buddy that's here in the hospital. To sort of cheer him up so he would know he wasn't missing anything back at the..." Morning was pointing at Green. The woman stopped him before he could even get going on a Morning snow job.

"Private, you're going to find yourself in a great deal of trouble if you don't conduct yourself in a military manner in this ward. Is that clear?" She didn't move. She definitely wanted an answer.

"Yes, ma'am. You see, I've, we, been under a great deal of strain these months and I sometimes forget myself." Morning looked at the floor, he looked at her with his Morning hurt look, eyebrows slightly raised, his gray eyes almost ready to water, then he looked away. He had won, the big woman softened now.

"Just keep it down. This is a hospital ward, not the EM Club."

She turned and walked to her desk. Feeling great

pain for the poor boys away from home in a war unpopular back home, they had little or no thanks for the job they were doing. Yes, she felt a hurt for them.

"I've heard some bullshit in my time, but Morning, you are without a doubt the biggest BS'er in the world." Jim lay back on his top bunk shaking his head.

"It might be the truth. You never know." Morning looked at them.

Turtle looked with great awe at Morning; Battleford stood shaking his head.

"Well, we better get back before they throw us all in jail," Battleford said. "Take it easy, Jim." He turned to go.

"Yeah, we'll see you Jim." Turtle followed.

"Hey, wait for me, damn it. We'll be back, James." Morning walked away in his Groucho Marx walk, knees bent, head turning from the left to the right.

"See you guys. Thanks for the pint." Jim watched them walk out of the ward. They were a trio.

CHAPTER 11

HOW SHORT ARE YOU, MAN?

- 250 DAYS AND A WAKE UP. LAUGHTER
- I'M SO SHORT I CAN SLEEP IN A MATCH BOX
- I'M SO SHORT I'M GOING HOME ON A POSTAGE STAMP, FIRST CLASS
- TWO DAYS AND A WAKE UP. COLOR ME GONE, MY MAN.

JIM GREEN sat up on his cot. It was dark in the hutch and he heard the radio playing. He shook his head to make sure he was awake. He felt he had to wake up so that there'd be no doubt in his mind that he was awake. The hutch smelled of sweat and mildew. The radio was playing "Hang On, Snoopy Hang On." No one was awake. When he looked at his watch, he saw it was four o'clock in the morning, but he wasn't sure of the day or month. That persistent dream came as it did every night; it woke him up tonight. Jim reached over and found his cigarettes on the night stand, they were damp and difficult to light. It occurred to him that he hadn't yet said anything, but there was no one to talk with. That didn't matter but it seemed important to speak aloud – say anything – just so he could hear his own voice.

"Hello," he said out loud. His voice trembled, but he said it again. "Hello." It comforted him and he relaxed a bit. "Hello," he repeated, taking a long drag from his cigarette.

Now I can think about the dream, he thought. I can remember it now that I'm really awake. He sat slumped over; the radio was playing "When Smoke Gets In Your Eyes" by the Platters. He listened to it until the dream came back. Tonight he knew that he'd be able to remember it and then maybe it would be all right. The song brought back thoughts that weren't really true about high school and the summer after high school. It hadn't been great, but that summer, in the remembering, it was great, and it was all right to make them good now. Remembering didn't matter anymore; the dream slowly returned.

He was lying on the ground in the jungle. He felt the dampness as if he was really there, and he was frightened. Then he knew why, because he was shot; although he desperately wanted to move, he couldn't. Meanwhile, it was getting darker, light was fading and he lay helpless on the ground. Then he could see feet in sandals made from tires and inner tubes, and then, two skinny brown legs. He didn't look up any farther, so he never saw who it was. Then he saw the old rifle and it looked like a Springfield, with a long World War I bayonet attached to it or was...no that was what it was and the feet stood there for a long time not moving, and time passed so slowly.

He wasn't sure if that were true or if his mind had slowed down. Then the bayonet came closer and closer and he couldn't move. He felt the tip on the soft part of his stomach, and he couldn't move. Sweat covered his body and with sure, steady pressure, the bayonet was pushed further and further into his gut; and he didn't make a sound, but curled around it like a worm curls around a stick if it is poked; and he started to scream, and then he woke up like he did tonight. But tonight he stayed awake to remember it. Jim got up and walked outside in his bare feet and urinated on one of the sandbags. He walked back inside, lay down and smoked and listened to the radio. I should have looked at the face of the man, Green thought.

The team rode the chopper from Song Bien south to Long Tuck where there was a muddy airstrip and a mountain of supplies. This was where the 25th Infantry Division was currently holding operations. The job for the team was to find where the Viet Cong wounded were being kept and how they were getting out of the area. Somebody up top had decided that the wounded and supplies were getting in and out by the river in sampans, and that there was a central depot that was high and dry along the river. This was the delta area and high ground was hard to come by, so it seemed an easy matter to locate this staging area, but it had been almost two months now and nothing had been found. As it was explained to Green and the rest of the team, all this theory wasn't enough to commit a Brigade. The command had one area in particular where they wanted to go; however, if they were to keep to the time table, they had less than thirty-six hours before they were to move to another operation farther north. The only way they could extend the present operation was to find something big. That's what the long-range reconnaissance team number two was going to find, something big.

They were going in from the south; another team

was going along the river, and the third team was coming down from the north area. The plan was simple. The team along the river would recon for hidden bridges and port area and the two teams coming from the north and the south would cut straight across the area in question, being picked up on the opposite side from where they went in. In this way, one of the three teams would find something if there was anything to find. They had thirty hours to do the job. On their say so, the Brigade and part of the Twenty-fifth Division were going to be committed.

Team Two stood around the airstrip waiting for the time to move out. A convoy of three trucks, and a squad from the 25th would move them as close to the area as possible without being seen. The trucks that were going to carry the team were covered; the drop-off point was just outside two villages. Green, Battleford, Fat Turtle, Morning and Sergeant Stocky, the new team leader, were there. Sergeant Winters was acting as the overall operations NCO for this operation and would not go, so the team was starting out one man short from the beginning. Green had been made the assistant team leader and would take over in case something happened to Sergeant Stocky.

This was Sergeant Stocky's first mission and he was scared. Not so much of what was out there waiting for him, but that he was in command of the team when he should really be the assistant team leader and work his way into the job slowly. There had been nothing that could be done about the situation. So now Sergeant Stocky was stuck with it and he was going to make the best of it. He looked at the men on the team. Morning was crazy, but he did his job; the kid called Turtle was a question mark. He looked too young, too plump to be any good. Battleford was a good man, one to be depended on, and Green was to be second in command but he was too damn friendly with Private Morning and it made Sergeant Stocky uneasy. Sergeant Winters had said that Green was okay, a good man, but still Stocky didn't trust him. Besides this, he understood that he was an outsider to the team. He was new to the outfield and to the relationships that had been formed. Sergeant Stocky told himself he was in command and what he said was law, and the orders he gave were to be followed to the letter.

To the rest of the men this was just another patrol with a little more theatrics involved. They weren't worried about Sergeant Stocky; all he had to do was follow the plan and nothing would go too wrong, and they had to do what they always did out on a mission. Green had checked the men himself and he had made sure nothing had been forgotten. Sergeant Winters had taken him aside and told him to do the job the way it was supposed to be done, the way they had always done it, and he would be waiting for them at the pickup point. "You know what has to be done, so do it." Green had said that he would do his best. Sergeant Winters had said, "I just got you bums doing things the right way. I would hate to have to start all over again."

They had a half hour left before the trucks were to show up. There wasn't much to say now; the men just sat around looking straight ahead. As usual, Morning was goofing off, telling some kid in his second week in Vietnam a wild story that was so erroneous it brought smiles to the faces of the rest of the men. The kid would surely repeat this story, and that's how most lies were started about the teams and the Brigade; Morning finding some new guy and really giving him the business.

The team was sitting down, Green stood off to one side. He had to show that he was the assistant team leader; that's what the Army called for. He felt a sense of pride and admiration for the team, almost as if he wasn't one of them, but an outsider. Sometimes he couldn't believe he was in this country or in this war, even though he'd been here over ten months now. He'd seen the rainy season come and go. Jim thought again, had he been here ten months or was it almost twelve? He realized he didn't know what month it was or the day of the week. What day had they gotten their malaria pill? That was no good; he never took the damn pill anyway. No, he couldn't figure out the date that way. He thought about the stupid orange pill. Maybe he inwardly hoped to get malaria so he'd have an honorable way out of the war. No, he didn't like that thought. He wasn't chicken. There were a lot of other guys that were, maybe, but he wasn't one of them.

SP/4 Green stood on the muddy airstrip in Vietnam looking at the heavy gray, white, black cloud, not knowing the day of the week because it just didn't matter; he was more worried about being afraid. "Chicken." This was his fear on the surface, the one he had to fight every day, ever hour. He couldn't show it. Green was a tall boy, not yet twenty in tailored camouflaged, tiger-striped fatigues. His hair was close-clipped under a round and floppy hat, his skin darkened by the sun, now covered by green and black camouflaged grease paint; his eyes were sinking further into his head, the whites becoming even more white by the contrast.

Two three-quarter ton trucks came lumbering down the muddy road. They tipped first to the right and to the left, their canvas tops flapping in an unmilitary manner. The men in the back of the uncovered truck sat slumped over moving with the jolting motion of the truck. There were eight men, four on each side. The squad leader sat in front of the truck with the driver. The squad was dirty, eyes red-rimmed, hollow-cheeked men waiting to see the reason for their discomfort this time. Their interest picked up when they say the team.

The truck came to a stop in front of the team. "Where you guys going?"

"We're going to Hanoi," Morning called back to no one in particular. He might have been talking to the truck for all he cared.

"Maybe you're going, man, but I'm not." This was the cause for laughter in the back of the truck.

Morning's interest in the truck became more acute. He studied the men in the truck and, in particular, the one who was doing the talking. Sitting in the truck he was neither tall nor short, he was neither dirtier nor cleaner than any of the other squad members, he wore no rank or unit insignia, and his dirty clothes and unshaven face took their place. He and Morning could be much alike, or they could be very different, but this month and this year they were the same.

"The trouble with you legs is you got no class." Morning waited.

"The trouble with the airborne is you got no

brains." The soldier mimicked Morning very well. Again, he was supported by his squad with laughter.

Morning walked closer to the truck, shaking his head. He acted as if he was going to do something that he was going to be sorry for; do something he didn't want to do, but he had no choice. "If I don't have any brains, and of course you have, how come you're in the same place I am?" Morning nodded his head to punctuate the question. He didn't give his adversary a chance to answer. "You're so smart, boy, that they made you a god damn private in the Army, and you like it too." Morning was laughing. Morning really appreciated his own humor. The team stood around enjoying it too, and it would have gone on for a long time but the time had come to get into the truck. The Sergeants took command and they got down to the business of war.

"Knock off the bullshit you guys," shouted the Sergeant of the squad who was already in the truck.

Green walked over to Morning, stood in front of him. "Let's go into the other truck, Morning." Morning looked at Green with a hurt expression and walked over to the covered truck and got in with the rest of the team. Green and Sergeant Stocky were last.

It was dark and hot inside the truck. The only lights were the pinholes of light coming through the canvas. It reminded Green of the last two lines from a poem he'd read in high school. "And of course there must be a reason, because there's something wrong in wanting to silence any song."

He hadn't particularly cared about the poem in high school, even if Robert Frost was a giant in

American Literature. Yes, that was the way the teacher had put it, a giant in American Literature. He wondered why he remembered it now. Green was aware of Morning's squirming around. If Morning ever sat still for ten minutes, it would kill him. Green didn't like telling Morning what to do, it didn't seem right somehow.

The truck rolled along, its motion pushing each man into the other; the intense heat and the crowding caused sweat broke out on each man's face, breathing became labored, and the truck was becoming unbearable. Morning lit a cigarette. Battleford told Morning to put it out and Morning told Battleford to go to hell, and Green said, "Put the damn cigarette out," and Morning did with a great deal of putting and snorting. Green liked himself even less now than he had before. He thought that Sergeant Stocky should have told him, but he hadn't and most likely he wouldn't have. He seemed to be almost afraid of Morning. But then Sergeant Stocky didn't say much to the men. It seemed he always had someone else around to do that, and Green realized that he disliked Sergeant Stocky.

The truck stopped and the other Sergeant came around to the back of the truck and told them they were at their destination. The men got out of the truck, melting into a bush or a tree, becoming a part of the landscape. That was their protection. The other squad had made a circle around the truck for security. They were ordered back to the truck. They were too close to a village, and the sound of voices could be heard. Green sat in the tall grass; Sergeant Stocky checked and rechecked his map. The two trucks turned around in the small clearing and after they were pointing in the direction from which they had come, the squad piled in and with a great deal of planned noise and motion they left, leaving the team to do the job they were there for.

"We better get away from this village, Sarge." Green moved closer to Sergeant Stocky.

"No, let's wait a minute. I'm not sure. I don't think we got off at the right place." Sergeant Stocky looked despondent.

"Wait, hell, Sarge. Someone from that village will stumble on us and the mission is aborted. At least let's get away from the village."

"Yeah, okay, Battleford take the point." Stocky pointed in the direction he wanted to go.

Battleford got up and moved out slowly, picking his way around trees and through trees. The rest of the team got up and moved out in their turn, as they had always done. Moving slowly and quietly, Green was in front of Morning. Morning, as usual, moved at his own pace, covered up the terrain and sometimes going out of sight of the others. Always in a few minutes he would be up again with the team, being too close to Green. Green waited impatiently for Morning when he fell back and was glad to see him when he was back with the team again.

As they moved ahead, the ground turned into a swamp. They started following the stream that had been on the map as a blue wavy line. There were large trees on each side. Green didn't know their names, moss hung from their limbs. The light was dim. A number of insects, other than mosquitoes, swarmed up from the water as they made their way ahead. It was quiet, but far off they could hear the shouts of children playing in the water by the village. It was difficult moving in the knee-high water. Each man moved his feet very slowly so there would be no splashing, just ripples moving outward.

Morning, behind Green, puffed hard with the work of walking in the water and the mud.

"Hey man, does that Sergeant Stocky know where the hell he's going?" Morning was right behind Green, no more than six inches away, puffing the words out in Green's ears in a whisper.

"Don't worry about it, Morning. You want his job?" Green returned. He didn't like Morning's question. He knew Morning. This was his way of causing trouble for the sake of trouble, just to make things more interesting. The trouble with Morning was he got bored too easily and he was a born instigator.

"Yeah man, I'm working my way up to be President of the United States." Morning dropped back and was soon out of sight of the others.

The team moved on until they came to a small dry piece of ground. Sergeant Stocky got out of the water with Turtle. He wanted to make a radio check with Captain Moes. Turtle sat squatting Vietnamese style, putting more oil on his weapon. Battleford found a place up ahead. Green stood at the edge of the dry ground in ankle deep water. Morning came up to the dry ground, looked at the Sergeant and Turtle, then at Green. Morning spit in the water and walked over to a tree with a low hanging branch, pulling himself up onto it; he sat on it, out of the water, got his cigarettes that were wrapped very carefully in plastic so that they wouldn't get wet. No one spoke. Each movement of the body seemed exaggerated in the stillness. Morning took out his cigarette, lit it, and then very carefully wrapped them back up, putting them into the pocket sewed into the upper part of his right sleeve. Morning made Sergeant Stocky uncomfortable, and he wasn't good at hiding his discomfort so Morning was enjoying himself. The rest of the team was used to Morning and his actions, and in a strange way he relaxed them and lessened the tension. Only Morning would crawl up onto a tree limb for the hell of it and they liked that. Now the rest of them lit their cigarettes too.

Sergeant Stocky looked around. He was unhappy with what was going on. If he told the men to put out the cigarettes, he'd have to get up and go back into the water and he didn't want to do that. He looked at Green. He saw only a pleased face looking at him behind smoke from a cigarette hanging out of the corner of his mouth. He went back to the radio and the maps that he felt were so important. These were the tools to get back to safety.

They stayed there fifteen minutes and then continued on their way. The water became deeper, it didn't show this deep on the map, but it was up to the waist now. According to the map they had to pass between two small hamlets and then they would be almost to the area they were to reconnoiter. They could never be seen passing the villages, even if they were friendly; if they were seen, their only real protection was gone. Without this protection they would become six vulnerable men and they would most likely die for it. The team could hear the people in the hamlet now. Battleford dropped back closer to the team; Morning was walking backward almost all the time now. It was his responsibility that the rear was protected, and this was important to Morning. They moved very slowly now, they didn't seem to breathe. They were so close to the people in the hamlet where women were washing clothes in the stream and children were swimming. There was maybe ten feet of this growth between them and the Vietnamese who could not be seen, only heard.

The team was out of danger now, the hamlet was passed; Battleford rounded a bend and froze where he stood. Standing in knee deep water was a man in black pajamas. He had been setting out fish lines; he hadn't heard them coming. Now Sergeant Stocky and Battleford stood frozen looking at each other. Battleford raised his rifle and the man didn't move. He smiled and bobbed his head up and down. Battleford moved up to him and felt him up and down for a weapon; there was none. Sergeant Stocky and Turtle stood looking at him. Green and Morning looked around the area and found nothing.

"We got to kill him," Morning said, smiling and bobbing his head up and down at the old man. The old man returned his smile. He started to speak but Morning put his finger up to his mouth. The man with white wispy hair didn't speak. Battleford moved up the stream a few yards, it was clear.

At Morning's words, Green looked at Morning and they knew that it had to be done. Sergeant Stocky turned to speak to Green but Green had already moved around in back of the old man and stabbed him in the right side of the back about where the kidney would be. Morning moved up keeping the old man from falling and at the same time putting his hand over the old man's mouth. It was not needed; no sound came from the old man. His face twisted in pain, his body went into convulsions for a moment and he was dead. Morning bent over the old man and cut off the old man's left ear.

Sergeant Stocky looked at Green unbelievingly, his eyes didn't believe what he saw; it happened in a matter of seconds.

"Wars are a pain in the ass, Sarge," Green said. He didn't move. There must be something wrong, in wanting to silence a song, Green thought.

"But you didn't know who he is," Sergeant Stocky said, looking at Green with hate and disgust.

Green turned back to look at the Sergeant. His face set hard at the accusing look of the Sergeant. "You never know who the enemy is Sergeant. You don't know if he is Viet Cong or not."

"It doesn't make any difference. The only thing we got out here is the fact that they don't know we're here. When they do, it's a matter of time and we're all dead." Green started to turn away, but thought better of it.

"If he was, he'd tell. If he wasn't, he might say something innocently and before you know it the Cong know and we're dead. If you don't have the stomach for it, get out of the platoon..."

The Sergeant turned and moved down the stream again, motioned to Battleford to move out.

"Morning, you shouldn't have taken the old man's ear." The two of them stood in the water facing each other.

"Well, you want me to put it back?"

Green gave Morning a dirty look. "Get rid of it, that's all."

Morning shrugged his shoulders.

The team moved slowly; it was starting to get dark now. Green didn't bother to look back at Morning or the old man again. It didn't matter about the old man, it was him or us. It was the fact that you didn't know who was going to kill you. No, you never knew so you had to be a son of a bitch, there was no other way to stay alive.

As it got darker, the team moved closer together.

Just after sunset the team left the stream that could have been classified as a river now. In the darkness they struck out for their objective. In leaving the stream they didn't leave the water; the open area was flooded with water no more than a foot deep. The bottom was mud where the men sank down two or three inches. The going was slow and tiring and they felt it. Their feet became tender as the water softened them up. The mud, adding weight, made each step an effort; each step became a heavy one.

Morning and Green both took Benzedrine tablets to stay alert and to fight fatigue. There would be no sleep that night or the next day. On the next break the rest of the team followed suit. Sergeant Stocky didn't like the idea of the pills, but it was standard operating procedures.

During the night Battleford stopped the team and pointed to a house that wasn't there. Green kept seeing a hand holding a compass; each time it would go up in smoke.

Three times that night they tried to cross that same stream that had turned into a river. Each time they would approach the river and the water would slowly become deeper until it was past the shoulders. They stood looking out into the darkness. Across the river they could barely see the shore or what looked like the bank.

"We can't make it over there," Sergeant Stocky said. They had bent over the tall grass and were sitting on it. Battleford was at the river on guard. They were at the place on the map that showed two possible outposts; two knolls of high ground in the middle of the swamp. Morning sat with Green.

"We can get across, I know we can." Green was exhausted from the long walk and from carrying Morning on his back due to the deep water. "We have to, we've gone too far to stop now."

"I don't know, it doesn't seem like a big deal to me," Morning said.

Stocky was on the radio trying to get Captain Moes.

"I have a message for Eagle, over," Stocky said.

Turtle sat eating his rice that he had prepared that afternoon. He smacked his lips eating, snorting through his nose. Every few bites of rice would call for a few dried fish about the size of guppies.

"That damn Turtle would eat anything, you know that," Morning said.

"Yeah, I'm going down to the river. Maybe I'll find a place to cross."

"Or be killed." Morning put his hand on Green's shoulder to keep him where he was.

"Let Sergeant Stocky do it. That's what he's here

for." Green sat where he was.

Sergeant Stocky was off the radio now. He gave the receiver back to Turtle. "Green, come over here." Green got up and made his way over to Stocky. "The Captain said we should keep trying to get across. If we can't, he'll pick us up tomorrow morning."

"You mean that you aborted the mission?" Green said accusingly.

"Not really. What could I do? We don't know how wide that river is and we might lose people going across. We'll stay here and get some sleep and tomorrow morning we'll try again in daylight."

"No, Sergeant that's not good enough." Green got up and walked back over to where Morning was sitting. However, Morning had taken advantage of the long break and had gone to sleep rolled up in his poncho.

"Hey Morning, get up. We're going down to the river." Green shook Morning under the poncho.

"Get the hell out of here and go play down at the river. I ain't getting killed tonight." Morning didn't even uncover his head.

"Thanks pal." Green stood up.

"Don't mention it." Morning played like he was asleep.

Green walked down to the river. Sergeant Stocky and Turtle were lying down to sleep. Green was in knee-deep water now. He looked off across the water, straining his eyes, but could see nothing that would be any help in getting across. If there were Viet Cong outpost on the other side, they would be hurt crossing the water. He walked out until the water was up to his neck and came back because he couldn't go any further.

He returned to the bank and the knee-deep water.

"Where you at Bat?" Green could see no one but Bat way down here somewhere.

"Over here man. What's going on?" Private First Class Battleford was sitting on a tuft of grass. His M-60 across his knees.

Green walked over to Battleford, bent over a tuft of grass and sat down.

"He says we can't make it, so we're gonna sit here all night, he says." Green rubbed his eyes with his hands.

"Stocky isn't too swift. What you going to do?"

Green wanted to be in charge. He wanted to do something to show up Sergeant Stocky. He'd get them across the river and do what was necessary to make this mission worth the trip.

"Let's go look for a place to cross." They heard someone coming down, it was Morning. "Over here, Morning." Morning turned in their direction. "Thought you were sleeping?"

"How in the hell can you sleep with them stupid Bennies keeping you awake."

"So what you want here, Morning?" Green asked.

"I just came down to see what you're doing," Morning returned.

"How you gonna get across the river?" Green asked.

"How in the hell do I know. I'm still a Private," Morning said in a whisper.

"I'm going to swim across and see what's on the other side. If something happens to me, write home." Green took off his pistol belt and the rest of his equipment, leaving on his .32 caliber pistol that he carried in a shoulder holster under his shirt. He swam to the other side and found that it was much drier. A few yards to his left there was a tree with a limb sticking out maybe eight feet over the water, cutting the width of the river in half. The night was warm, even though he was wet he didn't feel cold. It seemed quiet. There was no sign of the Viet Cong, but then that didn't mean anything. Green ventured twenty feet from the river going up the tributary that was next to the tree. He came back to the river and swam to where Battleford and Morning crouched in the high grass.

"We can get over. We'll tie all our utilities ropes together, they'll make it across easy." Green stood in the water.

"I'll go and get Stocky's and Turtle's ropes," Morning said and left the other two.

The utility ropes were seven feet long and were used in repelling. Green got his and tied it to Battleford's with a square knot. They waited for Morning. It took Morning twenty minutes before he got back. He brought the ropes.

"I stole them. They don't even know they're gone," Morning said, very much satisfied. Green tied the ropes together; then he took a piece of nylon parachute cord and tied that to the end. He would tie this to himself while he swam. He walked back into the water that seemed very warm. He swam very quietly; he found that he was really enjoying himself. He reached the other side, found the tree limb and tied the rope securely to the limb. He then swam back to the other side. Battleford had gone to get the Sergeant and

Turtle.

They soon came down and were standing looking at the far side of the riverbank that they couldn't see in the darkness. Green stood holding the rope.

"All you got to do is go hand over hand on the rope. Morning, you hold it on this side. I'll go first and take your equipment and then I'll pull you across." He gave Morning the rope. Morning pulled it tight and Green, after putting on his equipment and patting Morning on one shoulder, waded back into the water, holding onto the rope. After he reached the point where he could no longer touch the bottom, he pulled himself across the rope sagging under his weight. He got to the other side, putting his equipment on the dry ground. He stopped and listened and there was no sound of danger. Turning, he waded back to where the rope was and tied and jerked on it. The next man came across, the rope bending under the strain; it was Turtle.

"Doing okay Turtle, go until you see the equipment and then pull some security." Green was holding the rope out of the water as best he could. Turtle moved past him, nodding that he understood what he had been told. Green jerked the rope again, someone on the other side started across. It was Sergeant Stocky pulling himself.

"Turtle's up there a few feet pulling security." Sergeant Stocky was holding onto Green's shoulders trying to get past him.

"You're doing a fine job, Green." Green didn't say anything. He just helped the Sergeant to get behind him. Battleford came next in the same manner. Green stared pulling on the rope and brought Morning over.

"That's fun. Let's do it again."

Green smiled and shook his head while he untied the knot on the tree. The two of them waded up to the bank and put on the equipment.

Sergeant Stocky told them to move out and they did as before. They checked out the two knolls and found nothing. They had one long open space to cover and the sun was just coming up. They moved fast. They didn't want to get caught out in the open in the daylight. The water was still ankle deep and it made the going tough. They hit the trees just when the day came to full light through a waist high stream and they were in the trees. Sergeant Stocky called a halt and got on the radio and told his position. He was told to keep on with the mission. They ate some of their rice, but no one was hungry; they sat smoking. Morning found a leech on him; it was four inches long, he used his bug repellent and his favorite curse word and the leech let go and fell to the ground, leaving a trail of Morning's blood.

"Everything in the god damn country is out to get you." He stepped on the leech for good measure.

The rest of the team watched and then, as a unit, became crawly. They dropped their pants, one man checking the other around the ankles and the backs and the buttocks. Sergeant Stocky stood alone and he dropped his pants to check himself over. They all heard the almost whispered scream. Stocky stood, his legs spread apart. He was holding his penis in his hand, looking down at it, slapping it with his right hand. There was a large leech on the head; it was almost six inches long, big and fat on Sergeant Stocky's blood.

There were three others on his inner thigh. He stood slapping and screaming. "Get it off, get it off." The tears began to run down his cheeks, his face was twisted in tears. Green was the first over to him. Morning and Battleford grabbed the man.

"Get it off, please get..." Sergeant Stocky was crying.

"No sweat, Sarge. I'll have it off in a second." Green took his mosquito repellent and squirted it on the leech. It fell and Sergeant Stocky pounded his heel into it.

"Relax Sarge, they won't hurt you. I've had them on me lots of times. Morning's voice was kind and soothing. Green got the other leeches off and checked Sergeant Stocky over carefully. Blood dripped down Stocky's leg from where the leeches had been. His sobbing had stopped, and he started to pull up his pants; he was very quiet.

"Sergeant Stocky, wash the blood off." Green handed him his canteen, a roll of C-ration toilet paper that somehow he had kept dry. Stocky took it and started to wash himself off. Green went to his pack and dug around until he found a tube of grease for burns that was part of the first aid kid he always carried extra. He put some on a piece of gauze and, after carefully putting away the kit in the waterproof bag; he gave it to the Sergeant and told him that it would stop infection.

Sergeant Stocky seemed to have drawn into himself. He said nothing; he very carefully cleaned himself off and put on the gauze, pulled up his pants that were around his ankles.

Almost as a machine, they knew that it was time to

move out and without a word from Sergeant Stocky, they let the Sergeant point out the direction he wanted Battleford to go.

They found signs of the Viet Cong: two campsites, and once they heard a shot fired and some voices yelling excitedly. It was eleven o'clock and time that they should be picked up. They had not really found anything of importance. There were Viet Cong in the area, they were sure. They came to the edge of the trees and the stream was in front of them. The open area where the helicopter was to land was just on the other side. They sat on the ground looking out at the open area; it was always hard to go out into the open. Sergeant Stocky was on the radio and he was told the chopper would be there at 11:30. They should move right now to get across the stream and into the tall grass. But they did not. Green looked at Sergeant Stocky, he was beginning to worry.

"We better get going, Sarge." Green was sitting next to the sergeant.

"Not yet Green. Wait." Sergeant Stocky didn't look at Green. He looked out at the stream.

"Sarge, now. We're running out of time." Green looked at his watch. There were twenty minutes left before the chopper came. What's wrong Sarge?

"Nothing, nothing. Not a god damn thing." Sergeant Stocky was almost hypnotized by the water in front of him.

"Let's go then," Green persisted

"No. I'm going to get another pick-up point." The Sergeant didn't take his eyes off the water in the stream.

"We can't cross that water."

Green looked at the Sergeant, he didn't believe his ears. "What?" he said.

"You heard me. The water, the god damn water." Sergeant Stock said this very loud. "We can't cross it."

"That's crazy. There's nothing wrong with the water. The water isn't going to hurt you. We can't get out of here if we don't cross the water."

There was a rifle shot; the team was on guard. "Where did it come from?" Nobody knew.

Green knew that they had to leave now and get to the chopper, it was almost time. He told Battleford to go across with the panel marker and signal the chopper when it came. Turtle was on the radio. Battleford got up and went across the water and ran a few feet, hitting the ground to lie in wait for the chopper. "Morning, go across with Bat." This was cause for more shots to be fired at them. It must be a sniper, Green thought. He asked Turtle if he was ready to go and Turtle nodded and Green told him to go. Again the sniper shot, but Turtle made it to the other side and into the high grass with the others.

"Let's go Sarge. Time to go." Green turned to the Sergeant.

"I'm not crossing the water." He said nothing else.

The sound of the chopper could be heard but it couldn't be seen yet. Then it came from around the trees to the left, traveling low to the ground. The side gunner had seen the last shots fired and was shooting into the trees. Green grabbed the Sergeant by the arm and went into the water. The Sergeant yelled, "no, no," and thrashed about. The shot came again and the

Sergeant fell dead in the water. Green pulled him to the other shore. The chopper landed and Green ran to the others. Morning and Battleford were in. Turtle was on the runner waiting for Green and Sergeant Stocky. Green came up to the chopper, motioned that Stocky was dead and that his body lay by the water. Morning, Battleford and Turtle got off the chopper and the four of them ran back to where Stocky lay. The sniper was shooting again now. Morning and Battleford and Green picked up the dead man and carried him back to the chopper and piled on behind the body. The chopper rose into the air and was gone from the clearing in a matter of seconds.

Back down on the ground in the base camp Green told everyone that the Sergeant had been covering for him; and that he was hit by the sniper that way. Morning said that he would have been an okay team leader if he'd lasted. The Brigade moved out of the area; there hadn't been enough evidence of Viet Cong to warrant an air assault by the Brigade of the 25th Division.

CHAPTER TWELVE

"BE NOT AFRAID OF SUDDEN FEAR, NEITHER OF THE DESOLATION OF
THE WICKED, WHEN IT COMES." *Proverbs: 25*

THE **WOMAN STOOD THERE**; she wore black pajamas. Morning and Green didn't see her right away. Morning was the one that shot her; he did it with four shots. It all happened quickly. Morning looked at Green. Green shrugged his shoulders and walked over to the dead woman. There was a hand grenade in her right hand. They set fire to the house and while they were walking away the fire sounded like rifle shots. The house didn't burn long.

"There was an old lady who lived in a shoe,
She was a Viet Cog and we knew what we had to do;
We shot her dead.
The moral of the story is: don't be a Red."
Private Mark Morning laughing and singing his fool head off.

Nine o'clock in the morning and it was already steaming hot. In another half hour heat waves would start to rise from the ground. To the left stood the abandoned rubber tree plantation; it was cool, dark and green. The creek on the right had almost dried up and the water didn't run anymore. Jim Green and Mark Morning stood in the field that had been cleared four months before by the engineers. Under the jungle that had been there the soil was white sand and was very good for filling sandbags. Most of the units in the brigade came here for the white sand.

"All I do is fill sandbags." Mark Morning threw the bundle of empty sandbags on the ground. "Sandbags! Sandbags! I can't take it anymore." Morning threw himself on the empty sandbags with force, beating them with his fist while Green watched with amusement, holding a shovel in his hand.

"You want to dig or hold?"

"Neither, God Damn it." Morning sat up. "What am I going to tell the guys back home? Fight? No, not really. I filled sandbags for a year. Shit." Morning put his head in his hands, resting his elbows on his knees.

Green sat down next to Morning to ponder the question and to waste time. He hated the sandbags as much as Morning. "Sergeant Winters said we had to fill all of them today."

"I should have gone on sick call. I'm losing my touch, maybe I got battle fatigue."

Green gave a grunt in reply and started to unbutton his shirt.

The two of them sat in the hot sun; Green with his shirt off, both looking out at the rubber tree plantation. Green still held the shovel; now he was resting his head on the handle. Slowly, he got up. Standing with his feet spread apart, he tested the ground for softness with the blade of the shovel, poking here, jabbing there. He found what seemed to be the best place. In slow motion he put his foot on the shovel and forced it into the ground, resting on the handle when it was up to the hilt in the sand.

"Come on, Morning, let's get a couple done anyway."

Morning lifted his head from between his hands and looked at the shovel sticking out of the ground. Slowly he got off the sandbags, without standing up, and broke the string that held them together. He took one sandbag, opened it up so that Green could shovel the sand in. "Maybe if we just buried the sandbags, Winters would forget them."

Green's answer was to pick up the shovel and unload the sand in the bag, filling it halfway. They both looked at the half full sandbag. Green shoved the shovel into the ground and repeated the process, filling the bag. Morning tied the top and let the sandbag fall over on its side. He moved over a foot and sat down on it, taking another sandbag and opening it.

The process was repeated and repeated again. The sun rose higher in the sky. The heat waves rose from the ground, disappearing into the sun. Sweat dripped from Green. Morning dropped the sandbag that was in his hand and looked down the path at a figure running. Green sat down next to Morning, waiting for the figure coming towards them.

"Looks like Fat Turtle," Green said, taking a cigarette from his shirt.

Morning growled an answer.

"What you think he wants?"

"I don't know. Maybe the war's over."

"Yeah, maybe," Green replied.

Turtle was standing in front of them now, sweating and breathing hard. He was wearing his web gear and held a rifle in his hand.

"Don't think the war's over," Green said, looking at Turtle.

"What?" Turtle puffed out.

"Nothing. Wasn't talking to you."

"Yeah, he was talking to me. What you want out here in the sandpit anyway?" They both sat looking up at Turtle who was still breathing hard.

"Sergeant Winters said for me to tell you guys that if you had enough of filling sandbags, you can go on a patrol to Bein Cat. I heard the CO saying there was a tax collection point and we're going to go

"Hey, Jim." Morning was looking at Green now. "A VC collection point. It beats filling sandbags. Come on, let's go." Morning was smiling for the first time since he'd been told to fill the sandbags, his face was filling with that crazy joy.

To Jim it sounded as if Morning was saying, "Here's some guys playing basketball, let's play."

"Oh man, wow, I'm not going nowhere."

"You chicken, Green? Keep talking like that and you'll be Sergeant Green before you know it." Morning was standing next to Turtle now.

"No." Green stood up, putting his hands in his pockets.

"Come on, man, we'll screw all over Charlie. You don't want to make Sergeant, do you?"

"Shut up." Green looked down at the empty sandbags and the shovel. "What the hell, might as well." Green looked at Morning again letting out a long breath. Maybe it was just a wild good chase after all. "Got nothing better to do anyway."

They both left, walking away from the sandbags, shovel and the white sand. Fat Turtle led the way. "Bat's coming too," he said, over his shoulder.

They stopped at their tent to get their equipment and Fat Turtle had to get his flak jacket.

"What are you taking that for?" Turtle was lifting the heavy flak jacket off the cross bar that held up his mosquito netting.

"Cause we're supposed to," Turtle returned.

"Well, if you're cold or something, they're fine." Morning pointed at the flak jacket in Turtle's hands. "They're no damn good, just something extra to carry." Turtle looked at the heavy sleeveless jacket in his hands.

"Come on Morning, get your shit together and lay off Fat Turtle. Green already had his equipment and was reaching for his rifle hanging over his coat. He stuck the butt under his armpit like a hunter and took the .32 caliber pistol from its holster to make sure of the magazine.

"You don't have your flak jacket," Morning said, getting on his equipment and taking the rifle down from its place by his cot.

"So what." Green headed for the doorway of the tent, followed by Morning.

Turtle looked at the flak jacket, then threw the jacket down on his cot and followed Morning and Green out of the tent.

Down the road sat four gun jeeps. Each one had an M60 machine gun mounted on back. Battleford was on the lead jeep, standing behind the machine gun. Turtle went over and sat in the driver's seat. The windshield was folded down and the glass covered with sandbags. There were sandbags on the floor in front and back. Morning sat on the wheel well behind the car commander's seat. Green hopped onto the gas can that was strapped onto the rear of the jeep. Each jeep had the same number of men. They were waiting for the car commander of the first jeep. The car commander was a new man that Green hadn't seen before. Green nodded to the new Sergeant when he got into the jeep.

Morning looked at Green with a smile. "Just like old times, huh."

Green shuddered at the thought of Morning sitting there on the lead jeep. Leave it to Morning to get on that jeep.

Turtle started the jeep and it lurched forward down the road toward the rubber tree plantation.

No matter how many times Green went out on patrol, he got a funny feeling in the pit of his stomach and he'd wish that time would stand still. It wouldn't go forward or backward, but at some point he would find himself back home. He and Morning would be lying on the beach with a couple of girls or on a cold night sitting in some bar having a few drinks and shooting the bull with a couple of guys about the war. But first he had to get through it all so that it would be all right. The last time he'd been home on leave he'd had a good time. There were a lot of places to go and he hadn't cared that all the people he'd known weren't around anymore. A lot of his buddies that he'd gone to school with had married and couldn't go out. He'd tried going over to their places but he stopped. They had nothing in common anymore. So he'd stopped that and had just gone around by himself. That hadn't been too bad.

The jeep lurched along and turned right at an intersection and headed north on the asphalt road toward Bien Cat. They went past some Vietnamese soldiers and they waved at each other. They saw women with heavy loads on their backs and men on bicycles and motor scooters. They rode for almost an hour. The car commander said that they were getting closer. There were no Vietnamese along the road. The countryside had changed. It had been open almost as far as the eye could see, now the road moved through open large rice paddies. The rice paddies began to get smaller and were hemmed in by the jungle. Turtle slowed down the lead scout jeep now; it slowly poked its way along the asphalt road. The jeep was coming to a bend in the road. Jim was getting nervous; if they were that close, they should be walking.

At that moment the explosion came. The sound came before the shockwave, before the screaming metal came through the air. There was shouting and another explosion. More shrapnel came whining through the air. Jim was lying face down on the road. He felt frozen. Then slowly life seemed to come back into his brain. He moved his leg. There was shooting now, the high crack of carbines being fired. There was another explosion near the jeep, or at least in front of him. There was the dull pounding of a 50-caliber machine gun firing. He didn't know where the bullets were going. Jim raised his head, the jeep was about a yard in front of him. No one stood at the gun. The jeep that was behind the first jeep before the explosion was pulled off the road. There was shooting from it. Someone was shouting an order. Jim crawled toward the jeep. There was a steady throbbing of the Viet Cong 50-caliber machine gun now, as he made his way to the car commander. Jim couldn't see Morning anywhere. The car commander was still in his seat. Jim reached up and pulled him down on top of himself. The man was dead. Shrapnel had taken most of his face away.

There was another explosion, only off in the trees this time. The enemy fire was heavy now. There seemed to be return fire from the other jeeps. The driver, Fat Turtle, was dead. Jim could see him lying on his back on the asphalt road. There seemed to be a great deal of blood. The lead jeep had taken the brunt of the claymore mines when they exploded. Where was Morning? Jim reached up and grabbed the M-16 rifle that had belonged to the car commander. He took it off safety and fired into the jungle on the side of the road at nothing in particular. He just fired twenty rounds and reloaded another magazine. Where were Morning and Battleford? Why weren't they firing? Jim looked around. Nothing. He crawled to the other side of the jeep. There was Morning and Battleford. Neither one moved. It had only been about five minutes since the first explosion.

Jim lay on the road listening to the shooting that was going on above him. He watched the two bodies for movement. There was none. Jim crawled to Battleford; he was the closest. He had been hit in the face, throat and chest. He was in the process of dying. Soon his bowels would let loose and he would be dead. Jim crawled to Morning, going over the dead Battleford.

Morning was still alive. Green lay next to Morning now on the asphalt road. Morning was all messed up. He'd been hit with a lot of shrapnel. He was bleeding from the neck, arm and chest. Jim tried to stop the bleeding by holding the severed jugular vein. He tried to stop the bleeding but he couldn't, he felt the blood pump through his fingers. The blood was very sticky and warm in his hand and on his forearm. It changed from red to brown, the blood beginning to smell in the afternoon heat. The enemy fire never stopped. Morning began to stink even before he died and still the firing never stopped. Jim lay there holding onto Morning.

It seemed a long time to Jim as he lay on the asphalt road. He didn't try to move anymore. The other jeep called for air support and the gun ships came firing rockets along the road, and Jim didn't move.

It was late afternoon now and the enemy fire stopped. The medic came, but nothing could be done. Jim got up, the smell of blood was in his nose and mouth. He went with the rest of the men into the trees. There were two dead Viet Cong, the rest were gone. Jim looked down at one of them before he was dragged out onto the road. He kicked the one in the head, he was dead. Green went back to where Morning, Fat Turtle and Battleford and the new car commander were lying together on the asphalt road, waiting for the evacuation chopper to come.

Green looked at Fat Turtle and Battleford. The medic asked him if he was all right, he said he was. Green then looked at Morning for the last time. Tears filled his eyes and fell next to Morning on the asphalt road.

"That's the trouble with being with the Cav. They always get the shit knocked out of them," the medic was saying. But Jim turned away from Morning and walked toward the other three jeeps.

After the chopper picked up the dead, the jeeps were turned around. The last jeep took Green's jeep in tow and made their way back to the company area. When they pulled in, it was almost dark. Jim smelled from the blood on his clothes. He took his equipment and rifle and started across the road up the company street. The hutch was empty; the rest of the platoon was down at the mess hall eating. Jim mechanically took off his clothes, grabbed his towel and went out back to the homemade shower bucket. When he came back, he looked at the empty cots and began to clean his equipment.

Green looked up from his equipment at the empty cots of Morning, Battleford and Fat Turtle. He realized that they would be replaced in a few days by three new guys and they would be the same. Then what was different? He'd...they'd seen a lot of new guys come in the last eleven or so months and they'd not been different from the ones that they'd replaced. But the last eleven months with the three of them, it was the war that he hated, not them. No, he couldn't confuse the war with them, they were separate, they were dead, they were no longer here, but the war was.

Green looked back down at the Thompson he was cleaning with an old toothbrush getting the dust out of the seams. Where was the importance? The question tore at Green as he sat there cleaning each little seam for the Thompson submachine gun. His friends were gone and yet they were still with him as if they were alive. All of them had fought, all carried the great weight of their action but they hadn't needed the weight of war. They had fought authority, they fought responsibility, they fought themselves, and they had fought each other. The war was bad, but were they any better? Green looked down at the Thompson, he raised it and sighted in on nothing in particular. He held the Thompson, then began to move it from object to object. THEY! It was him too, he was part of them. Green let the Thompson drop back down to his lap.

Sitting there remembering, he had to get it straight in his mind and yet he couldn't. Then it hit him, hit him hard. The dream, the men in the sandals with the bayonets, the face he had seen. The face was always the same face, and there was no mistake. The face belonged to Morning, Private Mark Morning; that was what he had never been able to remember. It was in the instant of curling around the bayonet that he would look up, and it was Morning dressed in black pajamas and with the body of a Vietnamese, but the head belonged to Morning. Panic swept over Green now, and he looked around and then down at the Thompson. His knuckles were white from the tight grasp he had on the weapon. It had been Morning all the time.

Now, to sit there, it took everything that Green had inside of him to remain in the hutch, on the bunk, and not to move. Because if he moved, he didn't know if he could stop, and slowly he began to relax, very slowly, only he still kept a tight grasp on the Thompson submachine gun.

Yes, he was sure it had been Morning in the dream.

There was no mistake. He got up from the bunk and laid the Thompson down on his bunk and walked out of the hutch. Down the company street he walked to the orderly room, and the first Sergeant sat at his desk. He looked up when Green walked in the door.

"What's wrong with you Green, you think you're on the Riviera that you walk around in a bath towel and shower shoes?"

Green looked down at himself. He saw the shower shoes and the towel and his body. Green looked up at the First Sergeant and smiled. "Sorry First Sergeant."

The First Sergeant grunted.

"Look, First Sergeant." Green hated the man; he symbolized the whole thing sitting there. "Me and Morning filled out those extension papers a while ago."

"I heard about Morning, damn," the First Sergeant stopped.

"I want to sign mine now. I'm going to stay a while longer."

"You crazy Green, look what happened to Morning today. You crazy bastard."

"I just want to sign the papers, I saw them the other day all typed up."

"It's your ass, not mine." The First Sergeant got the papers and threw them down on his desk. "Sign, you crazy..."

Green looked at the papers and signed them, turned and walked out back toward the hutch. The hutch was hot and dark when he walked back to his bunk and sat down. He sat there very still, then began to dress in clean jungle fatigues. He hated the Army, he hated Vietnam and Morning had been the one in his dream, and now look at what he had done. It had all been bad, and what could he say if he went back to the States. He had been as bad as any of them or worse. No, it was better now that he stay where he was; it was all so confusing now. If Morning was his enemy and the NVA were his enemy, what he had done no longer made him good. Morning had been his friend and they had come from the world together; now he saw that Morning was also his enemy. Then he would stay, there was no place else to go. No, he had to stay right where he was; it was the best place.

Green put on the clean fatigue shirt, buttoned it very carefully. He was very neat about the uniform. He was sweating freely, but that didn't matter, it was a way of life here and one got used to it. He still felt clean. Then he remembered Morning's stupid poem.

"Our father who art in Washington, Johnson be thy name. Give us this day our daily pay and forgive us our AWOL's while we forgive those who mark them against us. Lead us not into the Brigade. Give our rank, glory and honors to the National Guard, Draft Dodgers, and the panty raiders who stayed behind to entertain our wives and sweethearts, while we are overseas. May God have mercy on them when we return."

Green smiled now, "when we return." No one ever returns because it's not there when you get back, because it's not real and this is real for what it's worth, and he looked around the hutch.

"Green, there's a formation." It was a new guy from the third platoon.

Jim got up, there were too many new guys, he thought. He followed the new guy from the hutch into the company street. Men were coming from all the hutches now, going down to the formation in front of the orderly room. As they passed, some nodded hello. Others that didn't know him walked on by. Green put on his baseball hat, the visor down low over his eyes. He was an old timer now, been around a long time. Two soldiers walked past.

"That's Green," one of them said to the other, "If you can believe what you hear, he's a wild son of a bitch."

"Is he the one that was with the guys that were zapped today?"

"Yeah, right. I was just talking to this guy today down at the orderly room. He said that the guys that got killed were the wild bunch; he said they were really crazy, he said that they didn't give a shit for nothing."

"You mean that his buddies got it and he's standing out there like nothing's happened. Man!"

Green watched them walk down together; he couldn't hear them anymore. "The Wild Bunch," Green couldn't help but smile now. He was the last one left from the Wild Bunch. He turned and started walking along the company street. His street, he'd laid a lot of the sandbags that the new guys didn't even notice. He guessed that Sergeant Winters' team would go into training for a while now that he was the only one left, he and Sergeant Winters. After dinner he'd go down to the beer hall and get some beer and go back and pack their things so that they could be sent back tomorrow. Green felt sad, alone, a separation, but it was not the deaths that were a part of it. He felt he had no future; there was no future. He looked back down at the ground again. It came back, all the time it had been Morning, but he shut off that thought.

At the formation he went to his place in Recon Platoon. It was smaller now, he nodded to Washington, the medic.

"Sorry about the wild bunch," Washington looked back down at the ground.

Green nodded. The formation was called to attention by the First Sergeant. Green automatically went through the motions. Sergeant Winters walked out in front of the platoon. He stopped in front of Green and looked at him for a long minute. Green looked back but didn't say anything. Sergeant Winters put his hand on his shoulder, then took it away and took his place in front of the platoon. Green was going through the motions of standing in ranks. The First Sergeant turned the Troop over to the Commander.

"Men, we suffered four casualties today on a combat patrol to Bien Cat. They were: Private Mark Morning, Recon Platoon; Private First Class Battleford, Recon Platoon..." The names went on but Green didn't hear them. "They died in the performances of their duties. God rest their souls." There was a pause; the formation was silent. Green looked straight ahead, souls nothing, he thought, they died for nothing. No, they died for themselves; no, they died for...no, they're just dead, just dead. Jim now looked at the four pair of boots that sat in front of the formation. One of the pair stood for Morning, Mark Morning. He hadn't noticed them before.

"Present Arms!" Each man saluted and held the salute.

"Order Arms!" The hands fell in union to their

sides.

Sergeant Winters turned and looked again at Green. Green looked back and he saw the Colonel, then Sergeant Winters, then Morning and then Sergeant Stocky and he closed his eyes very tightly. When he opened them again, Sergeant Winters had turned around again and it was Sergeant Winters.

"First Sergeant!"

The First Sergeant came forward and saluted the Troop Commander. The First Sergeant turned to face the Company. He read from a sheet of white paper. "For wounds suffered in action against a hostile force, April 7, 1967, PFC Randolph Peterson, PFC Peterson front and center."

Peterson came forward. Green had seen him around, he was a grunt in the cav and he remembered when he had come to the Troop. The Company Commander pinned the Purple Heart onto Peterson's short. They shook hands, saluted and PFC Peterson returned to the ranks of the formation.

"That's one I don't want," a voice from behind Green said.

Green turned and looked at the soldier. It was one of the two who had been talking about the Wild Bunch. "Shut your face, if you know what's good for you." He then turned around.

The soldier behind him looked at Green's back with amazement, and then he shrugged his shoulders.

The First Sergeant raised the white sheet of paper again. "Effective this date, Specialist 4 James Green to be promoted to grade of Sergeant E-5."

Green heard his name, fell out of formation and

walked to the First Sergeant. He stopped for a moment at the boots, then continued on till he was standing in front of the First Sergeant. He handed Green a copy of the orders and a set of stripes.

"Sew these on and be down at the NCO Club tonight."

Green turned and walked back to the formation.

EPILOGUE

There is no closure. It's not an option.

Warriors sit together singing the song of the wind, the clouds sweeping the pain and sadness away ... away from our hearts.

The songs of peace, these are the songs of the wind and clouds that take the weight of war away.

The weight we no longer carry. Singing our song will release us and will let us walk softly through this world. Our song will go on forever to our children and grandchildren.

The Warriors Song
- Robert Stave

SERGEANT JAMES GREEN, RA 17648050, had somehow navigated his way through his second tour in Vietnam. He thought it was his duty for accepting the third stripe on his sleeve. He had kept most of his guys alive. At the end of his eighteen months, Greene DEROS'ed back to the world. He arrived without fanfare to the Oakland Army Terminal where he and Morning had started a year and a half earlier. The homecoming was disappointing: the barracks were more dingy and definitely raggedy around the edges. The barracks were filled with soldiers coming and going to Vietnam, a sea of green and olive drab. There was the mandatory steak dinner, cold beer and the re-enlistment pitch. A Captain sat down next to him. He offered Green a place in the next OCS class at Fort Benning after his thirty-day leave and a bonus of ten thousand dollars.

"Would that be in small or large bills?" Jim asked with a half-smile. Before the Captain could respond he added, "I really don't think so sir. I've had enough war to last a lifetime." The Captain said nothing. In his heart, he easily accepted Green's response judging by the rows of multi-colored ribbons, CIB, Silver Star and Purple Heart on his tunic.

Green's time at the Oakland Army Terminal was bittersweet. There were long lines, bored clerks and the continuous reading of the list of names and service numbers RA, US or NG being informed that they are shipping out. Speakers were even in the latrines.

In the end, Jim Green couldn't leave the war behind, no matter how he tried. Counseling at four Vet Centers around the country, VA Medical Centers and Jim Beam didn't release him from the war; Morning, Fat Turtle, Battleford and all the rest ... they remained ghosts in his house.

Jim went through professions, jobs, wives, and geography always moving on over the years. At some point he realized that every move he made or personal relationship he left behind occurred about every eighteen months to two years. He was DEROS-ing and ending his tour. Even after years, his sleep was fitful at best. Feelings of joy or happiness were hard to come by.

Eventually, Jim became a facilitator for other Vets and a Veteran Service Officer to the VA. When a Vet got better or when a claim to the VA was awarded, the vet would DEROS back into the world. It had taken many years but Jim finally found his place and some peace. Erasing some of the anger and guilt he had carried for so long.

Jim went on to represent his Vets or to the VA Regional Office and to Washington, to the Board of Veterans Appeals, the Supreme Court of the Veterans Administration and won cases on behalf of his Vet clients.

Glossary

AK-47 The AK-47 or AK (also known as the KALASHNIKOV) is a selective fire (semi-automatic and automatic) gas operated 7.62x39 mm assault rifle, developed in the Soviet Union by Mikhail Kalashnikov after WWII. Officially known in the Soviet Union as the AVTOMAT KALASHNIKOV (AK-47). The AK-47 remains the most popular and widely used assault rifles in the world, because of their substantial reliability under harsh conditions with low production costs and simple to operate.

AO Area of Operation

APC Armored Personal Carrier

C & C Command and Control

CAV 1st Calvary Division (Airmobile)

CIB Combat Infantrymen's Badge is an award that is only given to individuals who have taken part in direct battles with the enemy.

CMH Congressional Medal of Honor, the highest award given to a soldier

CO Company Commander

COMMO Communication

CP Command Post

DEROS Date of estimated return from overseas

FAC Forward Air Control

G I'd Washing and/or cleaning ones area, a fellow soldier that does not bathe or clean his pots and pans

G P Tent A large olive drab tent used for general purposes or a mess hall, platoon barracks or temporary First Station. A bitch to put up or take down.

HU-1b Basic Helicopter or sometimes called a "Slick."

KIA Killed in Action

LRRP Long Range Reconnaissance Platoon

LT A second lieutenant platoon leader. Life expectancy about three weeks in country.

LZ Landing Zone for Helicopters

LZ Bulldog Most LZ's were given names such as LZ English

M-16 Basic Infantry Rifle. Troops would refer to the rifle as Made by Matel the toy company.

M-60 A belt fed machine gun. Individual or crew served.

MP Military Police, sometimes called F Troop in Fun.

NCO Non Commissioned Officers from E-5 to E-9

NVA North Vietnamese Army

PFC Private First Class, can't get much lower than PFC in the enlisted ranks

PLF Parachute Landing Fall, performed when a paratrooper hits the ground after jumping out of a perfectly good plane

Pony Soldier A derogatory name for a member of E Troop, 17th Cavalry.

Prick-25 A portable radio used by the Americans combat troops in the field.

RTO Radio Telephone Operator

Sit-rep A report on the current situation.

SP/4 Specialist E-4 also called a Speedy Four.

TOC Tactical Operation Center, different than a CP the TOC is way behind the lines in a safe area.

TO&E The equipment a platoon or company have allotted to them.

WIA Wounded in Action

Thank you for reading.

Please review this book. Reviews help others find Absolutely Amazing eBooks and inspire us to keep providing these marvelous tales.

If you would like to be put on our email list to receive updates on new releases, contests, and promotions, please go to AbsolutelyAmazingEbooks.com and sign up.

About the Author

Robert Stave is a former Airborne Ranger and currently retired at one hundred percent disability due to his combat experiences. He served with the 173rd Airborne Brigade (Sep), E Troop, 17th Cavalry, LRRP and the 101st Airborne Division, Recondo School. After separation from the Army, he went on to teach at the University of Minnesota and Shattuck School. He was also an outfitter/guide, rancher and cowboy in the western eleven for over thirty years. He now lives with his wife Pam in Delray Beach, Florida.

ABSOLUTELY AMAZING eBOOKS

AbsolutelyAmazingEbooks.com
or AA-eBooks.com